Acclaim for
THE APARTMENT
by Greg Baxter

"Baxter has written a novel of subtle beauty and quiet grace; I found myself hanging on every simple word, as tense about the consequences of a man finding an apartment as if I were reading about a man defusing a bomb...It is one of the best novels I have read in a long time."
— Stacey D'Erasmo, *New York Times Sunday Book Review*

"Absorbing, atmospheric and enigmatic...With its disorienting juxtaposition of the absolutely ordinary and the strange and vaguely threatening, the novel evokes the work of Franz Kafka and Haruki Murakami, while its oblique explorations of memory suggest a debt to W. G. Sebald...Baxter's provocative, unsettling novel is, among other things, about the inexorability of identity and 'the immortality of violence.'" — *Los Angeles Times*

"Despite the lack of incident, the novel exerts a hypnotic force...It is precisely this sort of subversion, along with the author's shimmering prose, that makes THE APARTMENT such a surprisingly compelling read and so apropos; it captures the mood of the current moment and what seems to be a new 'lost generation,' one formed not so much by exposure to violence as immunity to and alienation from it. Once upon a time, there was no place like home; in Mr. Baxter's world, home, it seems, is no place." — Adam Langer, *New York Times*

"In this bleak but affecting novel, an unnamed American expat spends a day walking through a frigid, unidentified European city in search of an apartment. The narrator is a veteran who subsequently amassed a small fortune working as a civilian contractor in Iraq; he calls America 'the kingdom of ambitious stupidity' and has chosen his new home at random, wanting to live 'in a cold city,' where extremes of emotion are 'extinct.' What he really wants, though, is to rub away all traces of personality—to 'anonymize' himself and live purely in the present tense. The details of his day are rendered with anaesthetized precision and achieve a cumulative force of grief, equanimity, and resolve."

—*New Yorker*

"A true gem…Lucid, often hypnotic and, at times, even transporting. [Baxter] keeps his sentences short, his adjectives limited, his pacing leisurely. The paragraphs are long and there are no chapter breaks, yet his acute observation means this is no mere minimalist undertaking…The Iraq sections are astonishingly well done, and the man's history as a Naval officer feels almost exactly right to the former Naval officer who happens to be writing this review."

—*Los Angeles Review of Books*

"The shadows of James Joyce and *Ulysses* loom over THE APARTMENT as Baxter takes us on an elaborate and riveting one-day ride down our hero's rapids-racked stream of consciousness. He pounds the icy pavement of the city with a young woman named Saskia. Memories—some sanguine, others violent—spiral through the un-chaptered (and nearly dialogue-free) text. Baxter's ear for detailed, unpredictable inner dialogue is keen. He guides us with precision and nuance through this man's mind, a prickled fog where anxiety and resentment and optimism and guilt swirl together in a solo conversation that builds carefully and deliberately... Violence, lurking offstage through-out the story, makes a shocking entrance near the end, setting in place everything that's come before. The effect is devastating, in the most satisfying way." —*Denver Post*

"In a year marked by epics, it's a relief to delve into this quiet, sur-prisingly tense debut novel—small enough to fit into a stocking but packing a huge emotional punch." —*Entertainment Weekly*

"In just over 200 pages, THE APARTMENT impressively and tactfully covers everything from the effects of American inter-ventionism on its relationship with Europe to questions of per-sonal identity." —*Esquire*

"'I was born to hate the place I came from.' Greg Baxter's first novel THE APARTMENT is a short but powerful exploration of that sentiment, uttered halfway through the novel by its narrator, a 41-year-old American ex-Navy officer and Iraq War veteran." —*Chicago Tribune*

"A beautiful meditation on brutality and culture, which are some-times one and the same." —*Minneapolis Star Tribune*

"An elegant portrait of a man half-fractured, half-intact—a post-war somebody caught between repair and capitulation, control-ling his own fate and imprisoned by regret." —*Texas Observer*

Munich Airport

Munich Airport

A Novel

GREG BAXTER

TWELVE

NEW YORK   BOSTON

Grand Central Publishing Edition

Originally published in the UK by Penguin Group, July 2014. This Grand Central Publishing edition is published by arrangement with Penguin Books Ltd, 80 Strand, London WC2R ORL, United Kingdom.

Twelve
Hachette Book Group
1290 Avenue of the Americas
New York, NY 10104

HachetteBookGroup.com

Printed in the United States of America

RRD-C

First U.S. Edition: January 2015
10 9 8 7 6 5 4 3 2 1

Twelve is an imprint of Grand Central Publishing.
The Twelve name and logo are trademarks of Hachette Book Group, Inc.

The Hachette Speakers Bureau provides a wide range of authors for speaking events. To find out more, go to www.hachettespeakersbureau.com or call (866) 376-6591.

The publisher is not responsible for websites (or their content) that are not owned by the publisher.

Library of Congress Cataloging-in-Publication Data
Baxter, Greg.
   Munich Airport : a novel / Greg Baxter.
      pages cm
   ISBN 978-1-4555-5795-0 (hardback) — ISBN 978-1-4555-5794-3 (ebook) — ISBN 978-1-4789-8319-4 (audio download) 1. Brothers and sisters—Fiction. 2. Families—Fiction. I. Title.
   PS3602.A977M86 2015
   813'.6—dc23
                            2014008011

For James and Andreea Monnat

Munich Airport

WE'VE BEEN SITTING for an hour or more here, up high, in the airport's main food hall, which overlooks the duty-free, clothes, electronics, accessories, and souvenir stores below. The airy, immense space is gleaming artificially because beyond the tall glass walls, where the tarmac, runways, and mountains ought to be, there's just fog, a soupy black fog that has covered the airport and delayed everything. The inbound jet got diverted, and will not even depart from its current location until the fog starts to burn off. Our layover in Atlanta was going to be more than six hours—we booked the flights just two days ago, so we took what we could get—but now it's going to be tight. It's possible we could miss it, but we haven't yet begun to worry about that. We—my father, me, and Trish, a US consular officer who was assigned to our case, my sister's case—have been quietly monitoring the departures board near our table.

My poor father, my poor sister. I push my seat back, stand, and excuse myself. Because of the delays, the terminal is badly overcrowded, and I have to step over lots of feet and suitcases. But everybody is calm and polite. There was madness at check-in, but here there is serenity—the anxiety just dissolves into the air and light of the terminal. I excuse myself as I walk, and the people I step over, or whose bags I step upon, beg my pardon for being in the way.

At the restroom, I have to wait in a line of men leaning against the wall of a long, plain, windowless, glossy-blue corridor. A line of women wait on the other side, too. We let people with children go ahead. They don't ask to go ahead, we urge them ahead, we wave them forward. The line for the men's room moves swiftly. We apologetically pass the women in their line, who do not move. I walk into an empty stall even though I do not need to use the bathroom. I just stand there and rest—and realize that I cannot rest, I don't have the energy to rest, and the first chance I will have to rest is when I am crammed into my seat on the airplane. I think I might start to weep, but I do not weep, I just open the door, walk to the sinks, and wash my hands for a long time. Then I dry them under the hand dryer for a long time.

My father and I have been here since early morning, since darkness. We overnighted in the Airport Mercure Hotel, which is in fact five miles from the airport. We could have stayed in the city, in a nice hotel, but it seemed right to stay somewhere that made our last night in Germany feel less pleasurable and more businesslike. I was awake until three or four. I watched television until midnight, then I opened a book. I haven't been eating, and I find it hard to get regular sleep. I took notes from the book, because it's my habit to take notes when I read. The room was hot, and I couldn't find the thermostat, so I opened the window. I drew back the curtains and saw fog rolling in. It came swiftly, and in patches, and it created the sensation of flying, of the hotel flying through clouds. The fog thickened in a hurry. I put my book and my notebook on the little round table by the window and leaned my arms on the windowsill, and I felt as though I was piloting the hotel. I stood there for a long time. It was freezing outside, but the air refreshed and calmed me. The hotel was a lot like an American motel—low and sprawling, with a big parking lot. Streetlamps shined copper-colored light brightly on a handful of cars. After a while I couldn't see the cars. There was just a fast-moving fog that had copper-colored lights distantly within it. I left the windowsill. I closed the curtains but not the window—I left it slightly cracked. I took my shirt off. I took my socks off. I'd been wearing those socks forever, and taking them off made me drowsy. I fell asleep on the end of my bed, with my pants still on, legs off the bed, feet on the ground, like I'd been drinking. Around five, there was a knock on my door. It was my father. He couldn't sleep, he said, and was thinking about heading to the airport. He was distressed. There wasn't any point trying to convince him he needed the sleep.

The shuttle-bus driver was asleep on the couch in the hotel lobby. He was a little man in a big black jacket, a jacket with a furry hood, and I felt bad about waking him. My father and I stood over him for about a minute, watching him sleep. I could see that he was dreaming about his wife, or someone he loved, and that it was a good dream, and I could also see that he had good dreams very rarely, that normally he had nightmares, normally he could not sleep. I knew that when we woke him, he would hate us. So I did nothing, and my father did nothing, but our proximity to him must have made its way into his dream as a dark force. Perhaps suddenly his wife was drowning. He opened his eyes in a panic but did not move. There we were, standing in front of him, over him. The lobby was dark and empty, though there were a few people making noise in the restaurant, where

3

breakfast was. The driver was small, slight, younger than me, but not by much. He was Turkish, for sure. He had black hair and dark-brown eyes, he had a very subtle mustache. We told him we needed to get to the airport. We had our bags, we had checked out of the hotel, and we were ready to go. For a little while he didn't understand that we were reality, that his dream had ended. When he did, he sat up straight, coughed, and shook his head, and swallowed the cobwebs in his mouth. He suggested we wait. The conditions were treacherous, he said. I explained to him that it was urgent, and he didn't argue. We walked outside into the freezing and fogged-over morning. I told him his jacket looked warm and he said it was, yes, warm. I couldn't see the shuttle. I couldn't see anything in the parking lot. I could barely see, behind us, the glass doors we had walked out of. The driver went ahead. We heard a door open and the engine start, then the headlights came on, as though from far away, but they were right beside us. The driver jumped out and grabbed our bags and threw them in the back. My father's was an old, heavy, burgundy suitcase, one of a set of bespoke cases he'd received half a century ago as a wedding present. It was in pretty dire shape, but that seemed to be what he liked so much about it, and why he refused to consider, on more than one occasion over the past three weeks, my suggestion that he upgrade to something that I didn't have to carry for him. He also had a brown leather satchel as a carry-on. My big case was black, rectangular, tall, extra-thin, and could roll on four or two wheels. I had a carry-on that was the same case in miniature. The driver closed the back door and opened the sliding door on the side. My father got in first. I helped him. He held my arm and I told him to watch his head. I got in after him and the driver closed the door behind me. The seats in the shuttle were ice-cold. The driver took a rag out of his coat pocket and wiped the fogginess from the inside of the windshield, then he blasted the defroster, which filled the shuttle with a cold breeze. My father pulled the hood of his coat over his head and stuffed his hands in his pockets. I pulled out some gloves and a hat and put them on, and I pulled the collar of my wool coat up, and held it tight around my neck. The driver obviously knew the route, and he must have sensed that there was nobody else on the roads, because he drove as he liked. We hit a few curbs and drove over an island at a roundabout. I saw the man's eyes in the rearview mirror. He was sleepy. My father said, Sir, would you please drive a little slower? The driver said, I can see fine. My father said, But we can't.

About three weeks ago, my sister, Miriam, was found dead in her modest, cheerless apartment in Berlin, and my father and I went there to make arrangements. It had been four or five years since I last saw her. My father flew from home, and I flew from London, where I've lived for twenty-five years. And for three weeks we've been in Germany—mostly in Germany—waiting for her body to be released. We couldn't decide what we'd do with her body—bury it here or fly it home and bury it there. A cremation would have been cheapest and simplest, and probably what Miriam would have wanted, but my father, after a lot of contemplation, couldn't do it. So we flipped a coin—heads, burial in Germany, tails, burial at home. The difference was twenty thousand dollars, for starters. We were sitting on a park bench, and my father said, after a deep breath, Forgive us, Miriam, and I flipped a coin. Now her body is somewhere in a cargo hangar, having been signed off by a German undertaker, and is waiting for departure on our flight.

I come back to our table to find my father once again thanking Trish for being here, for waiting with us. She works at the US embassy in Berlin, but her husband recently moved to Munich, and she spends most weekends with him. Her flight back to Berlin isn't until later in the evening.

Everything okay? asks my father. Everything's okay, I say. You were gone for a while, he says. Trish gives our untouched plates commiserative glances. She ordered omelettes for us when she arrived. We needed food, she said. My father and I agreed, but then we didn't eat. My father cut his omelette in half and the cheese and ingredients spilled out, and, as inconspicuously as possible, without trying to appear ungrateful, he pushed himself half an inch back from the table. I said mine was too hot, I'd let it cool off, and I never touched it.

The first week in Germany was a surreal and solemn week, an ordinary week, emotionally, under the circumstances. We kept ourselves busy, we saw many things, but we were, essentially, waiting. We were waiting with the expectation that something might happen at any moment. We assumed the coroner would release Miriam's body quickly. I have no idea why we assumed this. We didn't know that, in Germany, people are not buried in a hurry. We also didn't understand how dispassionate German bureaucracy could be. Trish telephoned the coroner's office every day to check on the status of Miriam's case, and every day, during that first week, she was given no information. There was no point complaining. We had the freedom to feel wronged, but that freedom was meaningless. Finally, at the end of that first week, Trish spoke with the coroner. It would be another week at least. So we took a vacation. My father rented a car and we treated ourselves to a road trip. My father was born in Germany, but at the age of nine he emigrated to the US with his mother. We drove around some places he wanted to see, since it was likely he would never get here again. During our road trip, we ate too much, drank too much, and stayed in expensive hotels and B&Bs. I guess we were temporarily deranged. The night after we came back to Berlin, back from our travels in the rental car, we went out and had some drinks, and on the way home we actually sang Happy Birthday to a man who said it was his birthday. He was sitting on the curb and looked a bit lost, so we started up a conversation. And before we left him, we sang Happy Birthday to him. The next morning, a third and final phase of our stay in Berlin began, a phase in which my father and I, until Miriam's body was released, spent very little time together.

This is the airport from which my father decided he wanted to fly—he didn't want Miriam's body on a plane out of any other airport. He said he knew it sounded strange but he wanted her on one flight out of Europe, not two connecting flights, and he wanted her flying out of an airport that was—he searched awhile for the word—classy. There are two Berlin airports, both grim and claustrophobic, and neither operates direct flights to Atlanta, which is the airport my father wanted us to land at. I arrived, three weeks ago, at Schönefeld Airport—that was the day I identified Miriam's body. My father, the next morning, first thing, arrived at Tegel, on a one-way ticket—I went to pick him up in a taxi. They are not airports to be stuck in, and I am sure I couldn't bear an eight-hour wait in either one.

We've been in the food hall since Trish arrived. Time has oozed by, it is seeping. The mezzanine level is very large, but narrow relative to the great pentagonal breadth of the level below. The food hall stretches almost all the way around, in a sort of horseshoe, and we are sitting close enough to the edge to see much of the level below. In the center of everything—a typical if slightly larger-than-normal airport bazaar—there's a race car, an actual Formula One race car, which, I presume, you can win in a raffle. Spreading outward from the center are hundreds and hundreds of seats, seats in irregular rows, all of them swamped by bags and bodies, and the spaces between the seats are swamped with bags and bodies. And from there, in two directions, the terminal stretches outward toward a circulatory system of long corridors to the gates.

Trish is, I would say, in her mid to late twenties. Or possibly she is just a very young-looking thirtysomething. She served in Afghanistan, with the army. She did ROTC at Vanderbilt before that. She's black and has a mild and appealing Southern accent. She is wearing brown pants, a white blouse, and a dark-brown suit jacket. She is heavy, but her clothes make her look athletic. A wool coat hangs on the back of her chair. In our time here, I have seen her wear it on a number of occasions, and it makes her extremely handsome. Would you like, she asks my father, anything else, some coffee, a cup of tea? My father contemplates the question by moving his plate around in small circles, and then he says, I haven't slept, not a wink, maybe there's a lounge somewhere I could lie down in, is that possible?

Trish says, You'd like to sleep?

Just rest my eyes, he says.

My father is in his mid-seventies. He retired about seven years ago. He taught European history in California, but he was always taking leave to teach, for short stints, at universities closer to home—by which I mean the South. He edited an academic journal—which was small but respected—for three decades. He published a lot of articles, and he wrote two books.

The first was a highly specialized study of law codes in the time of Charlemagne. It was published by an academic press and went straight to libraries as a reference document. His second book was a generalist history of the Middle Ages. It had been written for bookstores, not libraries. He had a New York publisher, and he received a healthy advance. But it took him forever to write. He started it six or seven years before my mother's death, and when she died he set it aside for a while. He finally returned to it and delivered it to his publishers, who had grown totally disenchanted with him, and who took a long time to get it to print. They also didn't put a whole lot of publicity behind it, because in the intervening period between my father's advance and the delivery of the book, another history of the Middle Ages had appeared, one with the title my father was originally going to use—*The Middle Ages*. Before my mother's death, I think the failure of that book would have been devastating for him. When she was alive, I'm sure, success was something he would have welcomed—it might have allowed him to cut back on teaching and editing and spend more time at home, where he hunted, fished, bird-watched, attended small-town college football games, and used his study to smoke pipes and read and think. But after she died, his attitude changed, and he took the book's failure with a cheerful fatalism. And he never started anything ambitious, at least on that scale, again—or if he did, he did so secretly, and it never came to anything, not even a mention, in all the conversations we have had since his book came out, and all the times we have seen each other, as a joke or an aside, or an earnest admission of a small disappointment. When I call him from London, these days, and he's at home, he's watching golf. He watches golf from all over the world, at all hours of the day—golf in Japan, in South Africa, in Sweden. I don't know if days and nights mean much to him now. The only regularity imposed upon his life is the upkeep of the house. He has a man come by once a week to clean the swimming pool. Another man comes once a week—or twice in spring and summer—to look after the garden. And a woman comes once a week to clean the house. There isn't much for her to do, because he disturbs only a fraction of it. He tells me, when we talk on the phone, about the wonder and frustrations of getting things done with the Yellow Pages. He can't look at a computer screen for more than half an hour without fainting, he says. So the Yellow Pages are his Internet. He says things like, I found some guys who can build me a deck really cheap, or, I'm probably going to get solar panels on the roof. But he has not yet built the deck or got solar panels.

Trish says, answering my father, Of course we can get you a spot to lie down.

My father says, Maybe there's nothing of the sort.

Trish says, They must have something.

Why not try the airline's executive lounge? I say.

That's a great idea, says Trish. I'll go.

No, let me go, I say.

Trish thinks this is a bad idea. She is certain she is more likely to succeed. I am just an ordinary traveler, and she is from the Embassy of the United States of America. I know that she is right, and ought to be the one to go, but if she leaves, I will be stuck here, in this chair. My father will fall asleep and I will be alone to stare at the mess we've made on the table, the large plates of food we haven't eaten, the napkins we have blown our noses with, and too tired to distract myself with something constructive, such as reading or working.

Go together, says my father. I'm fine, I'll just sit here, shut my eyes, rather do that on my own.

Trish and I glance at my father to see if he is serious. His eyes are already closed. I say, Someone should stay with you.

I'm fine, just tired. If one of you stays I'll feel obliged to stay awake and keep you company.

He opens his eyes. He digs in his bag for his sound-canceling headphones and puts them around his neck. Then he says, I've run out of Tylenol. Do you have some? I've got a headache.

I'm out, I say, but I'll get some more. I push his glass of water toward him and tell him to have a drink. He takes a sip—perhaps to prove he's rational, that he really wants to be on his own—then closes his eyes again and says, If they say I can lie down in the lounge, one of you can come back and get me.

My father is dressed in a flannel blue plaid shirt with various shades of brown in it, and a white undershirt that is tight around his neck. The flannel shirt is tucked into a pair of blue jeans hiked up very high, and he's got on a very flash pair of fluorescent yellow running shoes. This is his travel gear. He likes to be comfortable when he travels—he also has the sound-canceling headphones and a neck pillow. In Berlin, however, and even during much of our trip to the Rhine, to the Ardennes, to Luxembourg, and to Brussels, he wore old suits, the suits he wore as a professor—suits that are now oversized on him. I don't know what my father looks like when, back at home, he's out and about. If I call him and he is not at home watching golf, he is usually down some megastore aisle of tools or groceries stacked thirty feet high on either side of him, looking for screws, or comparing prices of pasta, or considering a new weedeater that he will use once, maybe twice, then give to the gardener. Other than these places, I don't think he goes anywhere. I don't think he goes to the movies, I don't think he goes for walks, I don't think he drives to the coast—the Gulf—as he used to do, when we were young and he was home from teaching. So far as I know, he has no friends. We talk about once a month. When I catch him at home, we hang up the phone and go on our laptops, so we can see each other, and usually he's in a white sleeveless muscle shirt, though his arms are just his bones, and he's unshaven. About twenty minutes into any conversation, he says, I'm about to faint, gotta go. Sometimes, if it's hot, he doesn't wear a shirt at all. His skin is pretty loose, and you can see his ribs.

Trish and I stand at the same time. We leave my father alone at the table. He slumps in his chair. He seems instantly asleep. Just looking at him, I yawn. I hope this works, says Trish. Me too, I say. We go down the escalator, through the wide and weightless slow space of the terminal. I cannot think of anything to say. Trish and my father have spent a lot of time alone, but Trish and I have never been alone, or only so rarely and briefly that it doesn't really count. I decide not to say anything. This is a solemn occasion, after all, and speaking isn't necessary. Trish's phone beeps. Throughout our hour together in the food hall, her phone has beeped several times. It's her personal phone—she also has a clunky old Nokia for work. I know, from my father, that she and her husband are going through a difficult period. I don't know Trish well enough to ask about it, or even to offer sympathy. But my father told me it seems destined to end, and it would not surprise me if it has just ended. She reads her phone. When she's done, she looks up at me and I realize I'm staring at her. She gives me a funny smile. Sorry, I say, I was just lost in thought there.

How long will you stay at home? she asks.

For me, by now, home is London, I say.

Of course, she says—when will you go back?

Soon, I say. I can't afford to stay away much longer. I'm supposed to be starting something new.

Surely they'll wait, under the circumstances.

Maybe, but not too much longer.

What do you do?

I'm a marketing consultant.

I know, I was just wondering what you did as a marketing consultant.

I devise marketing strategies for clients.

She gives me a look that says, I know that, I meant *what kind of strategies do you devise*. But instead of pressing any further, she says, Your dad says you're quite successful.

Does he?

She nods.

I say nothing. It doesn't sound like something my father would say. For a moment I'm not sure I ought to believe her—maybe she's trying to mend a rift she's perceived between my father and me, a rift for which she may feel some responsibility. But she isn't responsible. And I am not really successful—by which I mean not as successful as I once believed I should be. I did International Business in college—at Princeton, which was where my father went—and I did all right. I decided not to do an MBA. I wanted to work. I didn't want to waste any time. But I also wanted to travel. I passed up some good job offers in the States. An internship in London came up—unpaid—and I took it. I never planned to stay a long time in London, but over the years I became increasingly convinced that I could not return home, that I could not leave London and somehow find contentment in a place like

Tampa or Dallas. I'd grown accustomed to, and much preferred, the way people lived on top of one another in London. And I suppose I very much liked the fact that I was a boy from a place where we all drove big trucks on big roads and where space and solitude were easily attainable, and now I was living in a place where nobody I knew had a car and where space and solitude were not features of the landscape but conditions one had to manufacture in the mind. There was, yes, always New York, but I had been to New York several times while at college. There was something in the distance of London, something about a body of water between me and where I came from, and something in particular about being a foreigner. I have a nice, if very small, flat in Spitalfields, which I sublet from an architect. I run my own one-man consultancy now, and I keep busy. I've just left a client I'd been with for many years—a supermarket chain. It was a nice situation. I worked three days a week at the client's main London office. I had a badge. The other two days of the week, I worked for other clients. Just before the news of Miriam's death, however, I left the supermarket chain. I found something new—not necessarily better, but different.

We're here, I say.

The door to the lounge is translucent. There isn't a handle. Trish puts her palm flatly on the glass and pushes. The door opens and we are met, unexpectedly, by another corridor, which is narrow, and which leads to another door, also of translucent glass. It is like an airlock, in which the wealthy or well traveled can spend a moment decontaminating their thoughts, preparing themselves to switch from chaos to luxury. Behind that door, the coffee-brown lounge is making noise. It seems like such a far-away place, something like—at least from our side of the door—a memory. We approach, open the door, enter, and a woman meets us. She is handsome, tanned, and she wears a gray suit, not a uniform but a suit. Past her, there are large leather chairs and recliners. Most are occupied by businessmen—some look European, they wear nice suits with slim legs, and some are American, they wear slacks and button-down shirts, they have gadgets attached to their belts—but there are families there as well, families traveling business class, kids playing with tablet computers or listening to music with headphones. It is quiet. It is a perfect place to snooze. The seats are deep and obviously soft. It's very full, Trish tells the woman. The woman says, with an English accent, even though she is clearly German, Normally it's less crowded. Everyone looks satisfied—what better way to take advantage of executive lounge privileges than to use it on a day when all the flights are delayed. Everyone looks at home here. The only thing that seems to have disturbed the equilibrium is our presence. Some of them are waiting to see if we'll be allowed to enter. Beyond the leather chairs and coffee tables is a dark bar with bottles glowing blue and gold and green on glass shelves, and there are huge red lampshades that hang from the ceiling. The lampshades, which are wide and round, remind me of a place, but I cannot remember where. The woman in the gray suit asks us for our boarding cards or our membership cards. I think of how I might begin to propose what we're proposing. I had a script in my head a few moments ago, but now that I see the lounge, now that I am standing in it, I realize that script has no value. What is to stop hundreds of people—economy passengers like us—from coming here, complaining of extreme fatigue, and begging for a seat to sleep on? If extreme fatigue were all one needed to get a seat in the executive lounge, everybody would be here. I can't speak. I'm overwhelmed, I suppose, by how obvi-ous it is that we are not going to get my father a place to sleep, or by my embarrassment for having had the naivety to believe it was possible. I should return to him immediately—go get his headache pills and admit that this was a foolish attempt. But I don't move. I look up and remember why it is that those lamp-shades, which hang very low, seem so familiar. Then Trish begins to speak. I don't really listen to her, because I know it is point-less. The lampshades remind me of a lodge in Scotland, a little mansion on a lake in the Highlands. It was where my mother and father honeymooned, where they visited a few times thereaf-ter, and it was where, after my mother's death, my father visited twice. The lampshades here remind me of the lampshades in the lodge restaurant. The restaurant has great big booth tables in the center of the dining room, all situated so that they face the lake, more or less, and all underneath a large red lampshade, which dimly illuminates the tabletop. It calls to mind Mafia or Rat Pack dinners in Vegas. My father always reserved the same booth. He and my mother sat there. He and my wife and I sat there once. Then he and I sat there, on our own, another time. I went there, not too long ago, by myself, but the booths were booked out. Miriam never came. She was invited, and my father and I both offered to pay for her, or help her afford the trip, but she always said money wasn't the problem—she was too busy. I know my father offered Miriam money a few times, but I don't think she ever took it. My father and Miriam didn't speak often, and he never saw her after she left home, twenty years ago. The time that had passed was how I argued to Trish, and to myself, against al-lowing my father to see or identify Miriam's body. He would not have known what he was looking at.

Trish says, I understand, of course. She's speaking to the woman in the gray suit. She turns to me and says, Let's try something else. I thank the woman for her time, even though I've missed the exchange. She tells me she's sorry they cannot accommodate my father. I hang on to the end of her sentence for a moment, because I am certain she's going to add something—an alternative solution. But she doesn't. She just smiles. I'm leaning a little forward now, so I straighten up. Of course, I say, it's no problem.

We decide to get my father's painkillers next. Trish rubs her temples and casually says that she needs something for a headache, too. I've been so fixated on my own lack of sleep that I've failed to notice hers. But she doesn't complain, or at least she doesn't complain to me. I still find it quite strange to look at Trish and think of her in the army, in places where real conflict was ongoing. I haven't asked her about it. I wouldn't know what to ask. I've always had a low opinion of people in the military. I've always had a low opinion of patriotism. My father finds Trish's background fascinating. I'm more interested in her work for the State Department. For the rest of her life, every four or five years she'll move to a new city. She'll learn a few more languages. She'll meet people from all over. She doesn't know where she'll go next. After Berlin, she'll go back to the States, probably for a year, then get posted somewhere else. It sounds like the perfect life, I said to her during our first week in Berlin, and it even felt true to say. If it suits you, it suits you, she said.

Trish points to a drugstore ahead of us. It's crowded. Like every shop, and every square inch of the terminal, it's crowded. Though it is a sick time of year, and there are many people who badly need cough syrup, cold and flu relief, or something to stop runny noses, the drugstore—I no longer call them drugstores, but Trish and my father call them drugstores—is mostly full of people who do not actually intend to buy anything. It reminds me of the way tourists walk through chapels and churches—they process very slowly, head vaguely for the altar, then circle back out, pretending to feel neither underwhelmed nor foolish. I can't really tell where the line begins. I just squirm through some people, then stand around and try to make eye contact with one of the people at the cash registers, which is, I've learned, how Germans queue. When I finally get eye contact, I tell the woman, in my rudimentary German, that I am looking for acetaminophen. She warns me that acetaminophen is actually a toxic substance that causes organ damage, and an overdose can lead to death. Trish, who is staring at her phone as we wait, briefly looks up to check that she heard the woman correctly. Ask for ibuprofen, she says. Do you have ibuprofen? I ask. She says she has ibuprofen. The woman is wearing a white lab coat and is very suntanned and wears tortoiseshell glasses that make her seem kinder than she actually is. Ibuprofen can change the structure of your kidneys, she says, after three or four years of continual use. Then she says, Your condition will improve tomorrow anyway, without medicine, but you can never repair the damage you might do to an organ. I look at Trish. I don't really understand what is happening, or what I should do next. Trish says, Germans don't take medication, they just suffer. I tell the woman I want the ibuprofen. I ask Trish if she wants her own box or if she just wants to have some of ours. She says she'll just take one from ours.

I'm going to take four of these pills when we board, I say, and get some sleep. I'd like to sit down, fasten my seat belt, close my eyes as we taxi away from the gate, and wake as the wheels hit the runway in Atlanta.

When was the last time you were in the States? asks Trish.

About a year after my dad's retirement, about six years ago.

And that was the last time you saw him?

That's right, but before that I saw him much more often.

There are, here and there, gray doors in the tall gray walls—we pass half a dozen as we make our way back to the food court. The doors are almost invisible in the walls, and beside each is a key-pad for airport personnel. The doors are numbered but otherwise unmarked. Trish says, I bet they have a break room somewhere, or a first-aid room, I bet they have a room with a cot or a couch in it.

The first man she flags down tells us to try the Airport Clinic, which is an actual hospital attached to the airport, but my father isn't sick, he's tired. And it's a very long way, a different terminal. The next person we find, a woman, gives us no help at all. This is impossible, utterly impossible, it's preposterous and self-evidently illogical—that's the gist of her response. Trish storms back to security, pulls out her diplomatic passport and protocol ID, and declares that she is a US consular officer and she's in need of assistance. We are taken to a small white room. It's a room that seems designed to make people feel uneasy, and the moment I step inside I feel guilty of something. I start to sweat and feel nauseous—now the hunger is coming, and the fatigue. It is an office with no windows, no telephone, no clutter, nothing on the walls, just a desk and some chairs. There are three doors in and out of it. There is the door we have entered, and two others, one on the right wall and one on the left, and when a woman finally does appear, she treats our sorrows with an equanimity that suggests she could, at any moment, walk out either of those doors without an explanation. She carries nothing with her. She looks at us like a doctor might look at two hypochondriacs. She sits down opposite us and asks for our flight details. She speaks to us in English. Trish refuses to use English. I hand over our boarding cards. She asks for my father's passport, and Trish says, This is unnecessary, this is utterly unnecessary. I say, I don't have my father's passport. The woman looks up very slowly from our boarding cards, as if to say, What can I possibly do for you if you do not have your father's passport?

Do you know why we are here? Trish asks.

The woman does not answer that question, either. Instead she says that she is here to take our information. And that is when I realize—and Trish must realize it at the same moment, because she puts her head very softly in her hands—that this is a room where requests are slowly, agonizingly declined, that nothing is possible in this room. Let's go, says Trish. I ask for the boarding cards. The woman doesn't want to give them back, and for a tenth of a second I consider the possibility that we have actually gotten ourselves detained, which is of course absurd, but it is how the room makes you feel. The woman hands the boarding cards back. She smiles as though she has done us a favor, and then disappears out one of the side doors—not the one she used to enter. This makes me think that she is moving through a row of rooms, and meeting people like us, people with hysterical requests, rejecting them one after the other. When we leave the room, I ask, When did you learn German? When I arrived two years ago, she says. Do you take lessons? I ask. I take lessons in Arabic and Chinese, she says, twice a week in each. But you're done studying German, I say. I speak German, she says.

We return to my father. He is upright in his chair with his eyes open, but his gaze is absent and he seems unconscious. For a moment I think that I will have to shake him, and then I think that he is possibly dead. I am inclined to try to lift his hands and see if they drop. I am inclined to shout, Wake up! Instead, I stand and wait, and I observe him. If he really is dead, I think—and then a sharp and undesirable thrill bolts through me—I shall have to bury them both, he and Miriam, and I must permanently move into his house. I will get to wear his skin, inherit the pace of his life. I see myself—I am a little bit older and a little bit fatter—in my father's pool, my skin is bright red, I am drunk. I float in a pool chair with cup holders. From time to time, I splash water on myself to cool down. I take long floating naps. In the background, the television plays golf or financial news shows. Nobody is there but me, except for the pool guy on Mondays and the gardener on Tuesdays and the maid on Fridays. I refuse to answer the phone. Every once in a while I get in the truck and head to the hardware store, or the gardening supercenter, or shop for groceries at the slowest pace imaginable, using coupons. Then my father blinks, consciousness strikes like a bell in his head, and he turns to us and says, Any luck? Trish says, None, I'm really sorry.

We tried everything, I say, apart from admitting you to the hospital.

My father says, You know, I feel quite a bit better. I feel like I've slept. How long were you gone?

I say, It's been about half an hour, at least.

Yes, he says, I must have slept, a good half hour has done the trick. But my back is killing me. Let's go for a walk anyway. Did you get anything for a headache? Some ibuprofen, I say. I pop two tablets out of the foil and hand them to him. He swallows them without water. I take two myself. I hand two to Trish and she puts them in her bag—a small side pocket—for later. Trish looks at our trays of food despondently. They are untouched. Are you absolutely certain you won't eat something else? she says. My father says, I can't, sorry. Maybe later, I say. Trish softly shakes her head. My father stands. He is a bit wobbly. He has been sitting a long time and nearly has to sit again. I've had to help him stand or walk or sit a few times this trip, and it never gets less strange. The last time I saw him, six years ago, just a year after his retirement, he was fit, stable, and he still had enough strength to lift heavy things from his truck. But now, just six years later, he's an old man. He's frail. He can't lift anything heavy. He gets tired easily. It's perfectly normal for his age. What's more surprising, perhaps, is how fit he was at the age of seventy. Here, I have walked him up hills. I have walked him down steps. I have helped him cross very busy roads. I have had him put his arms around my neck and lifted him out of a taxi. I tucked him into bed one night, because he'd become light-headed and a little breathless, but refused to go to the hospital. When I turned the light off, he said, Goodnight, son. I said, Goodnight, Dad. Now, as he wobbles, nearly falling back into his seat, I take his arm. Now I guide him from around the table. His balance returns—it comes slowly, arising in his eyes—and he seems steady, so he draws his arm away from mine. You okay? I ask. I'm okay, he says. Without fuss the four chairs around the table are taken by others.

When my father and I arrived at the airport this morning, we said good-bye to our driver, the Turkish man with the huge, furry-hooded jacket, and had a brief argument over whether or not to tip. We didn't tip. We simply said thank you, and he told us to have a safe flight. It was still dark. But the bright white lamplight along the entrance to departures, in the fog, made the darkness glow. We watched the shuttle drive away. Part of me had wished to say to the driver, Listen, we've made a mistake, any chance we could go back to the hotel? Maybe they would be merciful and let us check back in to one of the rooms, just for two or three hours. If not, then at the very least we could find some couches in the lobby and close our eyes for a while. I really don't know how I am still awake, and I don't know how my father is still awake. I have slept four, maybe five hours in the last two days, and my father has probably slept less. We arrived in Munich yesterday, very early, off an overnight train, and we paid a visit to the undertaker to make sure Miriam's body had arrived without any problems, and that all was set for the journey today. On the train we had a compartment to ourselves. When we realized that we were on our own, and we closed the door for the night, we figured we would sleep for sure. We stretched the seats out into beds across the whole cabin. The beds were wide. Though the seats we'd reserved were beside each other, because we had the whole compartment we chose to leave the space of one bed between us. We lay down, propped up on some pillows, but fixed cushions that ran vertically between the seats meant we couldn't see each other, only our bodies and legs and feet. We pulled white bedsheets over ourselves. They were coarse and smelled like soap. My father had no book with him, so I gave him a music magazine I'd brought with me. My father gave the magazine a perfunctory flip-through and sighed and asked if he could switch off the light. Of course, I said, and I turned on a little penlight that arched down from the console behind my bed. I had a book about Europe during the Thirty Years War—more than any other type of book, I read history books, and I had picked it up at an English-language bookstore not far from Miriam's apartment in Berlin. I read and took notes for an hour before finally turning off my light and closing my eyes. My father said, I can't sleep, it's no good, you can turn your light back on if you like. I said, This is a fascinating book. He said, You've always taken notes, but what for? I haven't *always* taken notes, I said.

You sure have, obviously before you can remember, you were taking notes.

Was I?

You were taking notes since your mother was pregnant with Miriam. She was monitoring her progress—because she'd had the problematic pregnancy with you—and you monitored her progress with her. Then you didn't stop. When Miriam was four or five, you taught her to take notes.

Otherwise I can't focus, that's why I take them, I said.

I'm the same, or at least I was, he said. But where do they go, once you've got them down?

I thought for a bit. I said, Nowhere, my memory, I suspect.

We spoke for a while longer, and when it was obvious that we weren't going to fall asleep soon, I drew the curtains wide so we could watch outside. We propped ourselves up on the pillows again and watched the dark countryside go by. The train was smooth, but we were really flying. We shot through isolated clouds of fog. We saw some snow. Mostly it was sleeting. Every once in a while, something bright went by—a bridge, a fortress in the distance. From time to time the train slowed down at a fogged-over station, or in fogged-over towns. Sometimes it stopped, and the hydraulics whined and exhaled. My father tried to convince me that once we got to the States, I ought to stay for a while. It was obvious, to him, that I needed to get out of London, even if it wasn't obvious to me, even if it hadn't occurred to me. I told him I was doing fine, and anyway it wasn't possible. I needed to get back to work. After that, we started to doze off, but by then there wasn't a whole lot of night left. When we got to Munich and met the undertaker, he asked if we'd like to see the coffin, which was closed, and my father, surprisingly, said it wasn't necessary, that we'd wait until we arrived in the States.

When the hotel shuttle was out of sight, I said, I could use a coffee. I could use some coffee myself, said my father, what time is it? It's six, I said. When are we meeting Trish again? he asked. Ten-ish, I said. My father said, Oh. But he knew what time it was, and he knew we had to wait until ten to meet Trish. I was worried he was going to start complaining that I should not have let him leave the hotel, I should have forced him to try and sleep, but he just yawned. He looked behind him, through the entrance, and up—the structure on that side, the check-in side, is a great glass box, and there are four levels in it, arranged like steps—wondering if he would finally run out of space to outpace his worry and his sorrow. Yesterday, when we arrived in Munich, we left our bags at the train station because check-in at the hotel wasn't until the afternoon. The visit to the undertaker's upset him, and it really hadn't been necessary, everything could have been confirmed with a phone call. He asked if the coffin would be loaded discreetly and humanely into the airplane. The undertaker assured us that it would be, and moreover, it would be situated separately from ordinary luggage. The coffin would rest in a dedicated section of the cargo hold, and be placed there in a dignified manner by the undertakers, working with the baggage handlers. The undertakers themselves would ensure that the coffin was safely in place and secure. But what about our connection in Atlanta? he asked. The undertaker, who was of medium height, bald, with a thick mustache, and who wore the customary black suit with a white shirt and black tie, said that the American undertaker, who would receive the body under the terms of agreement, would make sure everything was handled appropriately in Atlanta. When we were finished, we still had a couple of hours before check-in at the airport hotel. Before we left Berlin, Trish had offered to come meet us while we were in Munich, treat us to a coffee or a drink, but my father told her it wasn't right or necessary, that her coming to the airport on Sunday was enough. But as soon as we left the undertaker's, I could see he regretted her absence. He wished to see her. His nerves were destroyed, and he was pale, and his eyes were red and melancholic, and I figured it was because he'd run out of things that had to be done before our departure. I said I was going to the museum where they had some Klimt paintings. A painting I had loved all my adult life was here—though I had only seen it in books and on computer screens—*Music I.* My father was disappointed in me. I told him to go for a walk and meet me later.

He turned back around to me. He was still yawning, so I had to yawn. It was cold. It was windy and damp, and there was no visibility. Instead of rushing inside, we waited in the fog. We'd be indoors for a long time, breathing indoor air. I was trying not to let myself think of the journey itself. I was trying to think only of our destination, of landing and getting our bags. It's hot at home, so once we step into the night air our clothes will feel heavy. The funeral will take place two days from now, on Tuesday. I advised my father to keep it small, but he's invited all my mother's old friends, so it won't be small. He gave Trish the numbers of my mother's closest friends—women to whom he has probably not properly spoken since my mother's death, since her funeral—and they took over. My father's car is parked at the airport. He says he's certain he's parked in the long-term lot, but I'm worried it's the short-term lot, and we'll have to pay a couple hundred dollars. We will drive home from the airport with the windows down. I will drive. The journey from the airport to my father's house takes about forty-five minutes. On that drive you find long stretches of pine forests and swampland, and refineries loom and blink beside the interstate. It is very close to the Gulf. The air smells like sewage, petroleum, and salt. When we get home, my father will turn the lights on in the kitchen and the living room, but not any other lights, go to the bathroom, take his various pills. He'll look through his mail without opening any envelopes. We might take a walk in darkness around the backyard. I might dip my feet in the pool. We will sit in front of the television, try to find a movie or some golf, or check the weather. He will fall asleep a few times finally and declare that it's bedtime. He will get up from the sofa, stretch and yawn away the stiffness that's accumulated in his arms and neck and back, walk sleepily to the doorway to his bedroom. He will turn around and salute me and say See you in the morning.

When my mother died, twenty years ago, I expected that my father, Miriam, and I would go through a brief period of centripetal anguish. I expected I would come home from London to bury her, see my father and sister mourning, and closeness would develop, a strengthened sense of being responsible for each other's well-being. I expected we'd all spend a few days together in the house, having dinners, doing housework, discussing whether to sell the house or refurbish it—my mother left instructions to sell and move away, but if we did not sell, she wanted us to renovate, tear down a couple of walls, make the place more modern, and put in skylights. Miriam had said to me, on the telephone, when my mother got sick, that she was going to quit college and travel. She had taken a while to get through three years' worth of credits at college—more than three years, anyway. She did extremely well, but lacked motivation, and in her opinion, the time she'd spent going to classes, taking exams, studying and writing about subjects that didn't excite her, was too long already. I knew how eager she was to leave the country—I had been just as eager, and the longer I lived in London the happier I was that I'd left home. Now she could finally go. I had a few hundred pounds saved and exchanged them for American Express travelers cheques, and had planned to give them to Miriam.

My mother died at the age of fifty-three. She and my father first met in New York. He was studying history at Princeton. She was at Vassar, studying anthropology. My mother came from a semi-prominent and highly conservative Southern family, and she used to say it was embarrassing for all of them that she went to college in the northeast, spent all her time in New York City, and met a German-born academic who was neither handsome nor dashing nor rugged, just quiet and polite and modestly intelligent, and who seemed to come from no family at all—his mother was in California, alone, and he never saw her. My parents married after my mother graduated. My father completed his doctoral studies and started teaching in California. My mother moved there with him. I used to look occasionally through an album that contained photographs of a small green wooden house on a small patch of dead grass. In one, my mother and father are standing in front of the house on a sunny day. My father's arm is around my mother. My mother is smiling but my father is not—he smiles all the time, but never for photographs. I don't know if my parents had few or many friends, but I like to think they went to parties and felt like part of a community. They looked like a couple that people would want to meet and know. When I was a teenager, that photo gave me the idea that living in a little green shack on a dead California lawn, with a German husband who taught history at a liberal university—on top of four successful years at Vassar—had given my mother a sense of having achieved a small victory over the people she had grown up among.

But I was not to be a Californian. Shortly after I was born, my mother's mother became ill, with the same disease my mother would die of, and my mother moved with me back to her hometown. It was, I believe, understood that my father would follow. He liked the idea of his children growing up in a place where their mother had deep roots, and he intended to take a comparable position in a comparable university in the region. They would have more children, possibly many more. But then, when my mother was pregnant with Miriam, he got that editorship, which was something, my mother told me, that he did not feel able to pass up—it was, professionally, a major achievement for him. The natural thing to do next would have been, I'm sure, to pack up his wife and children and move us back to California, but that is not what he did. My father came home in the summers and between terms, and a number of times he got visiting professorships that moved him closer to us. But he remained, until he retired, a full-time professor in California. I had no sense, in my childhood, that this arrangement was a cause of unhappiness for either or both of my parents, and I suppose it suited them both to some degree. But it must have been difficult for my mother, and

I think over time my father, who perhaps never stopped viewing the arrangement as provisional, came to feel a sense of shame about it—made worse, perhaps, because his wife and children never blamed him for it.

My father had months to prepare for my mother's death. But when she finally died, he told us that he didn't have time to think about the house, whether to sell or renovate—it was a very busy time for him. Then he promptly returned to California and went back to work, though not on his book. My mother left behind an inheritance. Rather than leave everything to my father, she divided it equally among the three of us. The travelers cheques I had been planning to give to Miriam felt like unnecessary charity.

I went back to London. I met a woman, a lawyer. We got engaged very quickly. We were engaged before we'd even told my father and her parents about each other. My father found this highly irregular and responded by saying he was too busy to come to the wedding, even though we hadn't set a date. Her parents were unhappy as well. So we got married quietly and invited almost nobody. Her parents responded by giving her a huge amount of money. We combined that money with my inheritance and we bought a nice flat in Fulham Broadway.

I got the news about Miriam's death first, before my father. The Berlin police telephoned me. I was walking into a meeting with the firm—an aerospace firm—that has taken me on to run a project for them. Though I was still officially a consultant, I'd be working on-site five days a week, and the contract was for two years. The meeting was a kind of induction. Some people from the Paris office were over—the firm was headquartered in Paris—so there'd be lunch afterward. This was over three weeks ago. It was a cold morning in London. Just as I was about to walk into the meeting, my phone rang. I was going to ignore it, but the number was not a UK number, it was a German number, and I thought it might possibly be Miriam—and since she never telephoned, it had to be an emergency. I excused myself and took the call. It obviously wasn't Miriam, and at first I couldn't make out who it was or what it was about. I walked toward a window—I had a view of a little lane. On the line was a very sympathetic-sounding policewoman. She asked if it was me. I said it was. I had never gotten a phone call from the police in my life. The woman explained that Miriam had died. I do not remember how I responded. I do remember asking, at some point, Has my father been told? She didn't say anything right away, and I realized that if he had been told first, it would have been him on the phone, not the Berlin police, so I changed my question to a statement, which was just me thinking out loud. I said, I guess I will have to inform my dad now. Again, she waited, she said nothing. The meeting room was filling up. I could sense, without even seeing it—I had walked a long way to find the window I was looking out—that everybody was seated around the table already, trying to look prepared or eager by flipping through papers. I could hear some chatter, low, subdued, but it was coming from everywhere. The way an office sounds. Finally I asked the policewoman, How did you locate me? She answered, and she spoke of death notification procedures in general, and I listened very carefully. I decided I would like to know these things in order to explain them to my father. I thought my father might become emotional and I wouldn't have the slightest idea how to deal with it, except to offer, as a pill for any pain he might feel, a diversion into the eccentricities of death notifications in Germany. I have such a vivid memory of staring at that little lane while the policewoman spoke. She was patient and polite, and at some point during her explanation I realized that I would have to travel to Berlin, and so would my father. I would be seeing my father for the first time in six years, and this time Miriam would be there, in a manner of speaking.

During the policewoman's explanation, a man crept up behind me, stopped a bit short, and whispered, loud enough to make it impossible to ignore him, Everything okay? I turned around and straightened up, and I was going to give him a thumbs-up and a smile, but then I saw he was pointing at his wrist, at the watch on his wrist, and he was irritated. Everything okay? he said again, but louder. I did not smile, but I held up two fingers and silently said, Two minutes. When the policewoman finished her explanation of death notifications, she turned her attention to our case, to Miriam. She had been discovered in her apartment. They had gone through her personal effects and found my contact details. A coroner's inquest would follow as a matter of procedure, and then the body, Miriam's body, would be released. How long? I asked. Not long, she said. Even though it did turn out to be long, I don't think the policewoman was lying. It was just that *not long* meant something different to her than it meant to me. I asked what would happen once the body was released, and she gave me the contact details of somebody in the American embassy who had already been fully briefed, and who had asked that I call as soon as possible. That turned out to be Trish. I hung up. I went into the meeting room and told everybody I was sorry for the delay. There were no questions about the call, but there was a woman in the room who looked like she was going to ask, politely, if I needed to go home. In the room sat the director of marketing, the senior marketing manager, two senior sales managers—one of whom was the man who came out to the corridor to hasten me—and this woman, the one who seemed a little bit different from the rest, possibly from human resources, I can't remember. The meeting room was in a refurbished part of a grand old building, and the walls of the room were glass, and we could see, and be seen by, several people working in other glass enclosures around us. I had been briefed about the project I'd been hired to work on, but now they gave me a more specific briefing. I offered some ideas I'd been developing. The director of marketing was a woman with a French name but a London accent. She had short gray hair. She was reassuringly intelligent. The senior marketing manager was younger than me, probably in her late twenties. The two sales managers—both men, one was short with red hair and one was tall with black hair—wore identical suits, and were either terrified of the director of marketing or hated her, but it was easy to see that without her leadership they'd have been lost. With every sentence I spoke, the woman who might have been in human resources seemed more and more disappointed in me. As a result, I became more and more disappointed in myself. The meeting ended, and everyone seemed satisfied, and I was surprised to find myself thinking that the presentation had been more convincing for the numbed manner with which I had delivered it. So I was weirdly excited to have passed the first hurdle so successfully and also, simultaneously, experiencing acute and brief paroxysms of devastation and anxiety. The lunch was to take place at a French restaurant I didn't know. Presumably the folks from the Paris office knew it and liked it. Presumably it would be outrageously expensive. We would eat and eat and eat. The wine we would order would be unaffordable without business expensing, and even though it would be magnificent, we would all pretend it was merely adequate, and that we were accustomed to wine of that standard. I thought these things when they told me the name of the place—which I have forgotten—and they all turned out to be true. We ate so much we all felt sick. We had several courses and desserts, and we got drunk, especially the London team. The men and women from the Paris team were incredibly handsome, and they made the London team seem physically repellent—they would have done so to almost any nationality. They really were some of the most beautiful people I'd ever seen. The English, said one of the French guys in the bathroom—he was standing by the urinal, unzipping his pants, and I was washing my hands, looking up at him through the mirror—are a deformed and revolting race. I smiled. I have no idea if he knew I was American, and thought it might be funny to insult the English, or if he thought I was English, and wanted to let me know, in private, how much my face disgusted him. In any case, I told him I couldn't argue, not if he were comparing the English to the French. My mother was beautiful—of Scottish descent, way back. It was too bad Miriam and I didn't look more like her.

Between my induction meeting and the lunch, I took a walk. The director of marketing wanted me to tour around the place and meet some of the staff, find out what they did and why they did it, but I wanted to call my father and the embassy in Berlin. I apologized and assured her it was quite important that I make a telephone call to the US, and promised to meet everyone at the restaurant. Outside, the day was still cold, still windy, still overcast. I thought it might rain, but I don't believe—when I try to remember—that it did. Or if it did, it must have been very light rain. I walked much farther than I expected to walk. I walked out the doors of the building where the aerospace firm was and pulled my phone out, but I didn't make the call. I put the phone back in my pocket and walked up toward Covent Garden, then a little bit farther, winding around, looking in shop windows, looking into cafés and businesses. I hadn't consciously intended to walk to Bedford Square when I started out. I just kept making turns that led me in its direction. I just kept considering and rejecting, for no real reason, all the quiet spots I came across, all the spots from which I could have made a phone call. Bedford Square is a place I've always had a strange attraction to, and I'm sure that at some point during my walk a voice inside my head said, Well, I guess we're heading to Bedford Square again. I hadn't been there for a year or so, ever since the last time I met a woman I was seeing.

The park in Bedford Square is off-limits to nonresidents, but there are a few benches just outside the black wrought-iron fence that surrounds the park. The woman I had an affair with mysteriously had a key—I think it was because she worked for the British Museum. I sat for a moment on one of those benches, but it was so cold that I got up and began to pace around the park very slowly. The square was, as it always is, exceptionally quiet. The trees are immense, and even though the park was wintery and the trees had no leaves, the branches scattered way up high and dominated the view of the sky. I stared for a while, right up at them. It's still strange, to me, after all the times I've visited, to find such a pleasant and untrampled section of London less than a few blocks from Oxford Street and Tottenham Court Road, which can feel, at certain times of day, like hell on earth. You can find quiet squares all over Bloomsbury. Places nobody knows about, or places too dull to visit. Bedford Square was one of the first places where I sat down and thought, I'm in London, and for that reason it acquired a sacred status in my thoughts. As I paced, slowly, around the outside of the park, I took the phone out, went over what I might say to my father, then called. It rang about five times. My father usually picks up immediately. Suddenly I remembered the time difference. It was six in the morning there. I hung up. A moment later my phone was ringing. It was my father calling me back. I didn't answer. I could not think of a way to tell him. I'd need another couple of hours. I stopped pacing, because now I felt really foolish for not having stayed with the marketing director and toured the office with her. I stood very still and thought about hurrying back. But I had been walking for a while, and it actually wasn't long until lunch began. I could head to the restaurant, get there a few minutes early, have a drink. I watched a gray Mercedes take a very, very long time to park in a space that was probably too small for it. A man stepped out. I could not see his face, but he had silver hair. He examined his parking job, decided he did not approve, and got back in to do it again. I walked to a different corner of the park, so I would not have to watch. I called the number I'd been given for the woman in the US embassy in Berlin. Trish answered. She was professional but warm, and asked how I was coping. Well, I said, it's a shock, though I haven't seen her in years, we spoke less than I'd have liked. Trish said, It's difficult to keep in touch when you live in different countries. I said, I never went to Berlin to see her, I should have. Trish didn't respond, and I said, Listen, sorry, in the shock of everything I forgot to ask the policewoman how Miriam died. Trish said, Are you asking me to tell you now?

I suppose, I said, if you know.

Trish told me what the police had told her, that she died of malnourishment, that she had starved. Trish said this matter-of-factly, without any weakness in her voice. Oh, I said. Trish said, Did you know she was having difficulties? No, I said, I didn't. But that was not the truth.

On my father's first day in Berlin—which was my second day—we hung around near our hotel. Miriam had lived in a cheap little apartment in a Turkish neighborhood, overrun, nowadays, by non-Turks. We stayed in a different part of town, which was thoroughly gentrified and full of boutique clothes and coffee shops. We got a feel for our surroundings. My father was jetlagged, so he took an hour-long nap. I sent the marketing director at the aerospace firm an e-mail saying a family member had died and I would be out of contact for a day or two—I was not to begin work until the beginning of the next week anyway. I sent a few more e-mails to other people saying I'd be out of touch, but I gave no explanation. I set up an auto-reply on my e-mail. My father and I walked around and looked at stores, we even went to see a part of the Berlin Wall. It was cold, and my father was freezing. I let him wear my coat and we bought him a funny, colorful, striped winter hat and some big black ski gloves. Trish met us for a late lunch. I asked her not to say anything to my father about identifying the body—and I asked her to trust that I knew what was best for him. I assumed this would be their only meeting. I had no idea how important Trish would become to my father during the trip. They made a deep and instantaneous connection. She told him he was good to come all this way. He confessed his dream to have a family that belonged somewhere. That dream was ruined now, he said. I could see what my father was doing. I should have never let Trish meet him. My father became a little bit emotional, and Trish put her hand on his arm, and he put his other hand on her hand. I said, Dad, you're exhausted.

On the second day, my father and I decided to go to Miriam's apartment—we would meet the landlady to see about her things, and it was agreed that Trish would come along. I woke around ten. Though I didn't know it, my father had been up since six, and he had walked to a department store in Alexanderplatz and got himself a proper winter coat. I woke, showered, came downstairs, and had my breakfast at a nice café right next door to our hotel. It was an ice-cold, sunny morning. I was just about to get up and go check on him when he arrived, at the window, looking like a man lost in the Arctic. Because we suspected we'd be leaving in a day or two, my father laughed about how much he had spent on something he would never ever wear again. I should have bought it in a bigger size, he said, so you could take it back to London. I said, You can't wear a coat like that in London.

An hour after that, having met up with Trish, we walked over the threshold of Miriam's apartment, one by one, gravely, with our hats in our hands, into the cramped, cluttered, and distressing space where she died. My father was the first to go in, then me, then Trish, then the landlady. The landlady, who was from Denmark, stood just inside the door, observing us. The walls were faintly yellow. The windows were cloudy. They were so cloudy that they were just overbright images of glare. There were two rooms connected through an open archway, a small kitchen, and a bathroom. The main room contained a dining table, a couch, and a couple of pieces of furniture. The bathroom was cluttered and neglected. It had been examined by the health authorities. My father stopped and stood still. He crossed his arms. Trish came and stood beside him. I kept going, toward the archway to the second room, which contained books and boxes and clutter. There was a space where, obviously, a small bed had been. There was also a large wardrobe full of clothes. The whole apartment, weirdly, smelled of rust. And also quite sour. The heat was on, and the place was warm. I said, There's a lot of stuff here. My father was sitting at the kitchen table. He didn't look up. I guess he didn't care about the stuff, or what we were going to do with the things she left behind, and I felt a little embarrassment for having spoken the first sentence in Miriam's apartment, a sentence that nobody cared about. The landlady moved from the doorway, and, perhaps because she felt the need to do something useful, turned the taps on, as though she was checking them. I felt like sitting, too, but I didn't want to sit at the table, because my father seemed to command all the grief in that part of the room, and I didn't dare sit on the couch, because I did not know where she had died, and, just in case she had not died in bed, I did not want to sit where she had died. After a few minutes of complete silence, my father looked up at the land-lady—having arisen out of the depths of the memory of his life, and his memories of Miriam as a girl, out of his wishes that she were not dead, and out of the commonplace shame of not knowing her well enough as an adult—and said, Who found her?

The landlady said, I did, and some repairmen, we found her in the bed.

How long had she been dead? he asked.

Not long, she said.

My father leaned back and looked at the table. I sat down on the couch. It was an old green couch that was very soft, and if it had been a little less dusty and if it had smelled a little cleaner, it would have been a fine piece of furniture. It could easily be fine again, with a little attention. In fact, a lot of her stuff seemed quite nice. It took a couple of visits to realize just how nice and how valuable some of the furniture might be, but even then, on that first visit, I was struck by the fact that although the apartment was cramped and cluttered and dusty and foul-smelling, Miriam had, at one time, taken care to live among objects that were worth something. Perhaps the apartment became, in the end—I remind myself that speculation doesn't help, but I can never stop myself—a forgery, perhaps she gradually awoke, or even suddenly awoke, to the realization that happiness was permanently out of reach, that her suffering—or whatever constituted her suffering—was permanently coiled around the roots of her determination to reject suffering.

After my marriage ended, I moved out of the flat in Fulham Broadway. I didn't want to live in a nice flat. I didn't want to have nice things. My wife bought me out. She made me an insulting offer, or at least an offer that suitably reflected just how hateful we had become to each other, and I accepted, because she threatened me with a legal battle if I didn't. I found a room in a house in Peckham Rye. The house had mildewed walls, single-glazed windows that went cloudy with condensation on cold days, rickety furniture, and a bathroom that turned to ice in winter because it had no radiator. It was just the kind of house I wanted to live in. It seemed that I had been steadily moving upward since I arrived in London, surrounding myself with ever-increasing comfort, convenience, and abundance, and when the marriage ended and I had an opportunity to observe how far up I'd come—how inflated my expectations of luxury had become, how hedonistic my perspective—I threw myself off that great height. It was actually Nunhead, not Peckham Rye, but nobody knows where Nunhead is. I had a housemate, an arts student who was always sick, and he had nothing to his name but his clothes, a TV, and a nice camera, with which he took pictures of himself, what he called studies of his illness. He showed me his photographs. He had protruding ribs. He had bony hips. And he had a large and slightly blue penis. I had to live in our kitchen, because he had turned the couch in our living room into his own personal deathbed. He was twenty-four or twenty-five. Our kitchen was nothing but a freezing and breezy little hallway with a door to some steps that led to a stinking narrow alleyway full of cats and garbage, and it never saw sunlight in winter. Meanwhile, in the living room, tissues piled up on the floor as he—I am unable to remember his name—voyaged through the depths of television. Often he lay beneath his duvet, in which he entombed himself, and, when he decided to change the channel, which was very rare, a hand with a remote control would emerge, extend, strike, and disappear. I remember long runs I used to take when I lived there. My runs began at five in the morning. I came home late in the evenings and set my clothes out in the order I would put them on. Each night I set out my running shorts and shirt and windbreaker and socks and shoes and a little winter cap that, when I ran the next morning, invariably I pulled off after one minute, no matter how cold it was. I set them on a rickety wooden chair beside my bed. My alarm went off and I sat up. I always, at this moment, felt sick and unutterably tired, but I told myself, Run, get up and run. I was seeing somebody at the time—an old friend of my ex-wife's—and if she came over to sleep, which was rare, because she hated the place, she would groan when my alarm rang and cover her head in pillows while I tried to dress in the darkness. I was drinking. I wasn't sleeping. It seemed to me that I was all alone, that nobody could live like I was living. I derived great energy from that, and I presume that's how I was capable of waking myself up to run. I got dressed, brushed my teeth, stretched for five minutes, and left the house. I ran the same route every morning, to Battersea Park and back. While I ran, I could think of how alone I had made myself. I felt wondrously distant from people, even though I was living in one of the world's great cities. I ran very fast, the fastest pace I could maintain. There were days I got home and threw up. Then I showered, dressed, typically had a bowl of cereal, and left for work.

I lived in Nunhead for one year. During that year, I underperformed at work. The people I worked with knew my marriage had ended, so they allowed me to underperform for a while without complaint. But after five or six months I started getting hauled in to discuss mistakes, missed deadlines, poor organization, and even, on a few occasions, my physical state. I had never really made mistakes before, I'd always done good work, I had always worked hard, I had always arrived early and stayed late, I wasn't particularly friendly with any of my colleagues but I got along with them, and I wore nice suits and nice ties and had my shirts dry-cleaned, and I shaved, and so on. So I had become unrecognizable to them. I managed a few people, and they were constantly going to my boss to complain that I'd become unpredictable and unkind. Finally, they told me I had to attend a management re-training retreat in Sutton for a week. I could picture it—bullies, sexual harassers and aggressors, alcoholics, morons, sitting around listening to a man and a woman go through slide presentations and lead role-playing games and administer personality tests. I asked them to reconsider. I explained that I was nearly done. With what? they said. But I couldn't explain. I left early that day. I guess I actually walked out without any explanation. I walked around London and realized that I would never be done with whatever was happening to me so long as I worked for those people, or for anybody. So I decided—probably unnecessarily, since surely they had made up their minds, when they saw me storm out, to fire me—to quit. I found myself excited and eager to go tell somebody about my decision. But after the marriage ended, my wife took all her friends back, and I didn't want to talk to anybody from work, so I went home and woke my artist housemate. I told him to get up, put some clothes on, and come out for a drink. To my surprise, he came with me. That night it rained heavily, and we had to take umbrellas with us. We walked about twenty minutes to a pub that had blacked-out windows and no women. The artist and I got drunk, and I talked about my plans to start a business, to work for myself, and to work from home if I wanted—this would require me moving out. The artist took the news indifferently. We grabbed a burger and chips up the road, and ate them under umbrellas in a parking lot. I had all the buy-out money left. I hadn't spent a penny of it. I could use it to live on while I got my business started. That's what I did. I stopped drinking, got regular sleep, found a new flat, and prepared myself, after more than a decade and a half in London, to become a new kind of success.

I stopped running in the mornings, in darkness, in the rain and wind, and switched to a treadmill. I became a member of a gym on the fourteenth story of a central-London highrise. It's not easy to get a membership. It's full of executives and start-up guys and investment bankers. It's also full of people in entertainment. I pushed very hard to get membership, because this was a place where you could meet people. I joined a lot of other clubs, too. I got involved in the chamber of commerce. I went to a lot of lunches and dinners, a lot of conferences. I got myself on every mailing list I could think of. For about six months, all I did was meet people, make pitches, exchange business cards, talk about the future of marketing. I didn't buy nice furniture or a television for my flat, or gadgets and appliances. I'd achieved, at the very least, a healthy separation between my desire to run a successful business and the temptation to surround myself with the objects that successful people feel the need to own. At executive functions, chamber of commerce lunches, and conferences, people asked about my clients, and I explained that I was just starting, and I wanted to be selective. But the truth was that after six months of getting no work, I was asked by my old employer to come back in and do some of the same work I'd done as an employee, and I ended up back in the same office I stormed out of, except in a different corner of the room, and without health benefits or paid holidays. I started and finished a distance-learning MBA at Duke, and when I had the MBA I left that firm for a slightly more independent role at the supermarket chain. I still have my membership at the gym. Though I run far less often, and with far less determination, than I did twelve or ten or eight years ago, I attend the gym when I can—or when the journey doesn't seem too far—and I hop on a treadmill after half an hour of weights or whatever. The treadmills are all in a line, facing the same direction, putting all the runners at the front of a curiously graceful and unwinnable race. We can choose to look through blue-tinted glass windows over the Thames and toward south London or watch financial news on huge televisions. Muscular young men in tight white shirts, and beautiful young women in white tracksuits—the gym staff and the trainers—come by and check on us. The guys nod. The girls smile. I don't go for the networking anymore, though sometimes it happens. I go because I like the treadmills. I like the view. I listen to classical music, mostly, because I don't have any other type of music on my phone. More than anything else, I listen to Gould playing Bach. One of the reasons—and I cannot explain this properly—that it makes such good running music is Gould's humming. Gould hums while he plays, but sometimes I think that I myself create the humming, that it comes from my own body. Also, if the music is the right tempo, and the pace of the treadmill is the right speed, and I am feeling fit enough to run fluidly, to take long strides and hold my shoulders still, I can attain a style of motion that seems to require no exertion at all, and in which the world slows down so profoundly that everything I sense and experience detaches from the fluidity and connectedness of reality into discrete components that my thoughts can rearrange in space, so that Gould's humming can be placed within the blue glass of the window, or in the clouds, and the piano music can be placed in the streets of London below, as though the notes that Gould plays are the cars and buses and bicycles penetrating all the distant silences.

In the airport, now, my father is re-energized by his brief sleep. He stops and enters every store, even stores for handbags and women's clothes, to browse. My fatigue is getting worse, and so is the nausea from hunger. My legs are heavy. Trish walks beside my father and they talk. I am five or six steps behind them. We go very slowly. We spend ten minutes in a souvenir shop. Another ten or fifteen in a place where authentic Bavarian sausages and meats are sold. My father picks nothing up. It is not a forensic exploration. It is just a philosophic stroll, something I imagine he might do around the grounds of a university, accompanied by one of his students. I happen to be the kind of person who picks things up. Whatever momentarily distracts my father—the objects he points out to Trish, or that Trish points out to him—I have to handle in order to examine. Even dresses. Even clothes for toddlers. He used to say, when I was a boy, that I was going to become an archaeologist.

Outside the shops, the terminal has got busier. The fog is beginning to evaporate—At last! says my father—and the departures boards have crowds in front of them. A freestanding advertisement in the middle of everything—a tall, backlit obelisk—contains, on both sides, an advertisement for *The Economist*. The ad includes a reproduction of an article. I stop and read. My father stops, puts his glasses on, and reads it with me. Trish stops, too. The story is about two companies vying to send the first commercial passenger flight to the moon. It's an effective, clean bit of advertising. Just the article—black text on a white background, with *The Economist* in red at the bottom. The two companies are Space Adventures and Excalibur Almaz. Once they sell all the tickets for the flight, they'll build the spaceship. It—whether Space Adventures or Excalibur Almaz builds it first—will be made using old Soviet parts. Excalibur Almaz will use an experimental electromagnetic propulsion system that will keep the mission in space for six weeks, and take humans farther than they've ever been from Earth. Space Adventures, I guess, will just use old-fashioned solid fuel. A ticket on either will cost one hundred and sixty million dollars. Already, one ticket has been sold. Trish reads the advertisement, too, and is the first to comment. Somebody has paid a hundred and sixty million dollars to fly to the moon, she says. My father, who finishes the article last, because of his eyesight, and because he is a more careful reader, says, suspiciously, and slowly, Interesting.

Munich Airport is a blue airport, there is blue everywhere. The blue is a serious and efficient blue but also an ebullient blue, full of promise and optimism and reassurance, a blue that says, Everything will be on time, society is safe, planes become faster and faster and also burn cleaner and cleaner, our floors are bacteria-free, the sandwiches are fresh, only beautiful people fly, all destinations are beautiful, everybody is getting wealthier and taller, we are conquering our weaknesses, soon we will all travel to space together. The blue is numinous, full of depth, somehow both spiritual and electromagnetic. And it is contained by a sober gray that you almost do not notice, a gray that says, The blue is where you want to go, but I am how you will get there. It is a gray that does not change shades and that has no depth. I begin to see, through the dissipating thickness of fog and haze outside the window, that it is going to be a clear and marvelous, if frigid, day. It's a shame there isn't a way to get outside for a few minutes. It's a shame there isn't something like a prison yard, surrounded by high fences and barbed wire, guard towers, whatever it takes, in which travelers could be free to walk in circles, breathe the air, and get sun on their faces.

The nausea from hunger finally becomes acute pain in my stomach. I feel dulled and dizzy and sick. I stop and bend over, with my hands on my hips, and Trish and my father stop and wait. I must be sweating. I sense that I've begun to stink a little. You look green, says Trish. It'll pass, I say. I mean really green, she says.

I realize that this is my opportunity to get away from them. I am not annoyed with them, I am merely exhausted, and want some solitude. I've got to go to the bathroom, I say.

We'll wait here for you, she says.

No, go and try to find some seats, I'll text you and find you when I'm out.

My father says nothing, but he takes his saggy leather carry-on from me. Trish immediately takes it from him and throws it over her shoulder.

Okay, says Trish to me, we'll see if we can find something.

They are a hard-to-miss pair in a German airport, but in no time they are swallowed up by the crowds, and I lose them. I've grown so accustomed to the nausea caused by hunger that I no longer instinctively want to eat, or feel I should eat. I have learned, over the last few days, that if you can withstand the wave of pain that hunger causes, the nausea itself becomes a sort of nourishment, and the longer I can withstand the wave—especially if I can keep from getting sick—the more enriched I feel. During our second week here, we fattened ourselves like swine. We ate pork sausages and *Bratkartoffeln* and drank wheat beer for breakfast. In our car, as we drove around from old towns to forts to old cathedrals, we ate cakes and Danishes and ice cream, and played silly songs on the radio and talked with our mouths full. I bopped the steering wheel along to the music. My father splurged on a comfortable midsize Toyota Camry with automatic transmission. It was black. I kept saying, apropos of nothing, This is one *sweet* ride, or, I *love* to drive. Once I threw the keys at a hotel bellhop, then shot him with my finger, like a cowboy. We ate pizza slices and cheeseburgers along the motorway. But now, here, in the airport, I realize that I am not going to be able to withstand the nausea and I need to throw up. I am perspiring now, all over, and I have stomach cramps, and I've gone very weak and hollow. I get my carry-on and roll it toward the bathroom. My father, smartly, packed his gigantic coat into his check-in luggage, but I didn't notice this at the time or perhaps I thought my coat might come in useful, or maybe I was still just really cold, but now I have to wear it or carry it. I'm wearing a suit jacket, sweater, and a shirt already. The men's room has a short line for the stalls, and also a long but swiftly moving line for the urinals. The two lines separate at the door, and every once in a while somebody comes in, bypasses both lines, realizes his mistake, and leaves. The floor of the place is a little wet and the trash of toilet paper and paper toilet-seat covers is strewn around a bit. It isn't hideous or unexpected, but my nausea makes it difficult to bear. There is also the quake, the trembling hands and chattering teeth that flow out of a disagreeable emptiness that is nearly, I don't know, not quite in your gut, but in your hips, and also your teeth and ears and feet. And the headache that stabs at the eyes and makes the top of your head tingle and prick, and that ibuprofen can do nothing about. I close my eyes. I try to concentrate on something that pleases me. A single memory of comfort and pacification.

The line for the urinals moves swiftly, but the line for the stalls is stagnant. There is a bushy-haired man in a pin-striped suit who has just filled a newly empty spot at the urinal. I look at him for a long time, and I do not know why I look at him, until I realize that I recognize him, I know him. His name is Richard and he is, or was, the VP of marketing at one of the big banks. I know him because his wife was a friend of my ex-wife's. He's a tall, handsome man whom I remember always smiling and always a little tipsy. Though we always got along fine, I don't think we ever liked each other enough to be friends independent of everybody else. His suit is tailored. I have a suit a lot like his suit, a similar shade of blue. And I wear it with shoes that are nearly the same as his shoes, a light saddle-brown. I recognize him because of his hair and because of his height and the fact that one of his shoulders is slightly sloped. I am standing by the sinks. He finishes, zips up, turns around, and sees me. I smile and he gives me an uncomfortable smile back. He doesn't recognize me. The men along the wall of urinals, all of them, finish all at once, and everybody, including Richard, walks to the sinks, which sends them right through us, the line for the stalls, osmotically. As Richard washes his hands, I sense that he's looking at me through the mirrors. He dries his hands. He takes a while, and I know now that he has, at last, recognized me, and has to decide whether he will stop and say hello. Perhaps I don't look well enough. He passes. He goes right by, and he does not slow down or lift his head. The time that elapses after that, between his departure and my turn in one of the stalls, is a kind of infinity, and when I shut the door behind me and am finally ready to throw up, I feel, surprisingly, fine. The nausea is gone. I do not sit. I just stand and close my eyes and put my forehead against the door. I cannot imagine the fatigue Miriam must have experienced, without any bodyweight to burn. It makes, of course, perfect sense that her apartment was, by the end, such a mess, so untidy. Over the past few days, I have thought often of the stillness that must have inhabited that apartment at times, when she was very tired and lying in bed. I presume, or at least I hope, that the nausea and the headaches and everything else are something your body absorbs after weeks or months or years of malnutrition, and that the hunger, especially at the very end, the last days, didn't cause her a huge amount of pain, and didn't add any more madness to the madness that allowed her to decide to die from this.

The place where we stayed during our first week in Berlin—the week before we briefly upgraded to a private apartment, then got

a rental car and drove to the Rhineland—was a grubby little hotel that had, in each room, a tiny single bed pressed up against
one corner. I didn't fit on mine, and so my father, who is the same
height as me, could not have fit on his. On each bed was a thin
duvet that was half as narrow as the mattress, and made you sleep
completely straight, like a plank, as well as a thin pillow that I
had to fold up many times. Sleep was stressful and unrefreshing.
There was an orange chair in my room and a yellow chair in my
father's room. They were tulip chairs. Beside the chairs were little round tables. The bathrooms were green, entirely green, from
the sinks to the tubs to the toilets to the towels to the toilet paper. The walls of the room were brown, the brown of fresh, strong
coffee. The rooms had light, white, cloth curtains for privacy during the day, and at night, to shut out light, you pulled down metal
shutters. I did this the first night without thinking and had an
anxiety attack when I woke in the middle of the night in pure
darkness. I rolled around the room like a lunatic for a while, giving off silent screams, grabbing the walls, knocking everything
over, crawling around the floor, until I found the door, opened it,
and threw half my body into the dimly illuminated corridor, and
lay there until my breathing went back to normal. I have a real
sense that this darkness, and this panic, is what my death will be
like, except I will never reach the door and find the corridor. I'd
forgotten all about these attacks. I used to have them often, at
night, in hotel rooms at conferences, when I'd drink a little bit
too much, close the curtains out of habit, and pass out instead of
properly falling asleep. I can easily fall asleep in darkness, but I always wake, always from recurring nightmares, and if I wake and
find myself in total darkness, if my eyes cannot adjust to explain
why I am not in my bed—always, for a moment, I forget where

I am—I suffer an acute anxiety attack and usually end up falling over furniture in an attempt to escape wherever it is I think I am, or simply to agonize over my blindness. The rooms didn't have key cards. We had keys that were attached to metal blocks inscribed with our room numbers, and we left them at reception if we went out. Two people rotated at reception—a woman, probably in her fifties, orange hair, very tanned, voluptuous, freckled cleavage, with a stern and humorless gaze, who manned the desk in a mean and unforgiving way during the day, and an Arab man with thick eyebrows, small shoulders, and powerful but dwarfish arms who answered the hotel door if we happened to come home after eleven p.m., when it was locked. We spoke to him on a few occasions, because we feared him less than we feared the woman, and he said he drove a taxi during the day. When do you sleep? my father asked him. When I'm here, he said. It was never a relief to enter my room. I couldn't sleep well, because of the small duvet, because the mattress was too soft in the middle, and because I had to leave the shutters open, so the bright lamplight outside poured in all night. My father, that first week, couldn't sleep either, and I heard him every morning, around three-thirty or four, showering and getting dressed, pointlessly flipping through channels on the television.

My father left Miriam's apartment, after our first visit, in a total fog, an incoherence that was massive and still. He never returned, though I would, three times, with the key that the landlady handed me out of a hope that I would clear up the mess. We walked slowly from Miriam's apartment toward the square. My father walked alone, ahead of us. Trish walked behind him, right behind him, waiting, I presumed, for an opportunity to console him. The immediacy and magnitude of her affection for my

52

father was a mystery. It seemed that her affection and his woe were symbiotic. They walked so slowly that I had time to stop and stare into the windows of stores and offices, a café, a dive bar, and through the open archways of apartment blocks. I was thirsty, I wanted some water, so I went inside a place that served takeout coffees and had a fridge full of drinks—it was not quite a café, not quite a convenience store, just an unadorned room for people to sit in and smoke cigarettes. There was one table, a counter, and four Turkish men who were smoking at the table. None of them wanted me there. Even after I had picked the water from the fridge and placed it on the counter, and taken out my change to count it, it took one of the four men an eternity to get up from his seat at the table and ask me if the water was all I wanted. His tone of voice suggested that if water was all I wanted, I should go somewhere else. So I got a coffee. By the time I ordered it, I actually wanted a coffee. But the coffee he served me came out of one of those machines where you put a cup in a grungy and stinking slot and push a button, and I did not feel like drinking it.

Once I got outside, I poured the coffee out and threw the cup in a trash can. I looked up and saw my father and Trish not too far ahead, approaching the main street, across which was the square. They stopped and waited for me. I didn't rush. I drank my water. I thought, This is the street Miriam lived on, and every day she walked down from her apartment to the square, just as I do now. I almost took some photos with my phone, but after turning this way and that I realized I'd be better off misremembering it. The street was narrow. Some of the buildings, like Miriam's, seemed derelict, even though they were not. There were trees, and I could imagine that in spring and summer, it would be pleasant. The road at the end was busy, and the square on the other side was crowded, there was a market full of junk. I caught up to them. Trish said, I think we should sit down. Let's find a place to catch our breath, get coffee or a snack.

Let's get away from this square, I said.

I agree, said Trish. I know a nice street a few stops up on the U-Bahn.

I'd rather walk, said my father.

I said, Trish has to get back to work, Dad.

My father looked at the sky, then back at me. Of course, he said.

We settled for a place along a bright, treeless street that was full of interesting cafés, bicycle shops, and places selling old cheap furniture. From the outside, it looked like a restaurant, but inside it was clearly something else. It had the dimensions of a railroad car, and it served kebabs and falafels and baked potatoes and slices of pizza and cheeseburgers. We should have turned around and picked another place along the street. We all seemed to be thinking the place was wrong, but nobody said it. My father put on his glasses to read the menu above the man behind the counter, and the man, as my father perused the items on the menu, seemed to grow impatient. All I really want is a coffee, I said. Trish got a slice of pizza. The man asked what she wanted on top, and she said, Oh, you know...He made a suggestion, and she said, That's fine, some of that. My father got a baked potato. It came out so overcooked and soggy, however, and the toppings seemed so lifeless, that he set it aside. Trish nibbled at her pizza, but only after removing the toppings. Tomorrow, said my father, speaking to his set-aside potato, we should go see the Bundestag or something. Trish said, Oh, definitely, you should book at the café and you can skip the lines. My father said, It's been such a long time since I've been in Berlin. Yes, such a long time, I was a student. I came to Europe quite often for a while, when I started teaching. When I started editing the journal I found I didn't really have the time to travel, I don't know, maybe I did, I could have come to Berlin to see Miriam, I never did.

I said, You came to Scotland, she didn't make it.

My father looked distantly at his potato. I could see that he really did not like the potato, and wished it would go away. So I moved it.

Then Trish said, The Neue Nationalgalerie is also nice.

I'd like to hear the Philharmonic, said my father.

Me too, I said.

I can help you get some tickets, said Trish.

My father rapped the table with his knuckle—he was showing his approval. He asked Trish if Germany was a US foreign policy priority or a backwater. Something in between, she said. It was her first posting. She'd started late in the State Department because of her army career, but generally people in the Department thought Berlin was a solid posting, because it was a nice place to live and the embassy was busy and moderately important. Still, she would have rather gone to China or the Middle East. Her husband had hoped for London or Sydney, so he could find work. It must be difficult, said my father vaguely. Then he looked at me, and I wasn't sure if he wanted confirmation, or if he wanted to accuse me of mishandling something far less difficult—a comfortable life in a nice apartment in London with a smart, pretty wife who had a good job and wanted kids—because he did not know anything about my wife or my marriage. So I said, Yes, must be difficult. Trish said, He found a job a few months ago, but it's in Munich.

Without realizing it, I had begun to pick at my father's potato—just the toppings. Lots of sliced, pickled jalapeños, which were not spicy, and which were not crisp. Chunks of unmelted cheese. Too much sour cream. An overdressed salad on the side. I only realized I was eating when I grabbed his fork and stuck it into the potato. I was half-alarmed. I said, I can't believe it. What's that? said my father. I thought about not saying anything, but then I said, Well, what else, that Miriam starved to death. My father's eyes got very soft, and we waited to see if he had anything to say. He didn't. But I had ruined lunch.

That first week, I rented a bicycle and returned twice on my own to Miriam's apartment. My father met Trish for lunches and dinners, and even had an unexpected drink with the American deputy chief of mission—the second-in-command behind the ambassador—a history buff who seemed to think my father was a famous historian, and who wanted to express his sorrow about Miriam and assure my father that her case was special. My father told me the deputy ambassador also asked him what the *Indo* in *Indo-European* meant. He had always assumed it meant *collective* or *entire*. Then he laughed at himself for a while. It would have been a funny thing to say, admitted my father, on a different type of trip. Another thing the deputy ambassador kept saying was *hot dog*, with a swift emphasis on *hot*, then a long pause, then a slow and exhaling *dog*, without any excitement, whenever my father said anything interesting.

The first time I went back to Miriam's apartment, I met a neighbor and old friend of Miriam's. It was the day after I had been there with Trish and my father, another of those cold and perfectly clear mornings. I parked my bike outside Miriam's place. I got a coffee in the square, and a squashed, tasteless croissant. I had two large canvas tote bags with me, in case I felt like rescuing some things. I didn't plan on staying long. But as soon as I arrived, I realized I hadn't any excuse to rush. And I was starting to adapt, already, to the pace of life in Berlin, which was much slower than that of London. I checked Miriam's mailbox. There was a newspaper in it, some advertising leaflets, and a letter that looked official. I threw everything in a bin that was beside the mailboxes and was already overstuffed with newspapers and advertising. I had to cram them in, push them down hard and hold them down. A woman came down the steps, saw me, and appeared disgusted, but I wasn't sure what had disgusted her. Three weeks later, I have come to realize that the look of disgust is just the way Germans look at each other.

I entered Miriam's apartment, and for the first ten or fifteen minutes I sat at the dining table and did nothing. I drank my coffee, that was all. The room was bright. I didn't really know where to begin. I left the front door open. I was sort of hoping somebody might walk by and stick a head in. When my coffee was finished, I turned on a small silver radio and tuned it to a classical station. They were playing movie soundtracks. I kept searching. I found NPR in English and listened for a while—the conversation was insipid. So I found some pop trash that could not be accused of being good or bad, it was just fundamentally catchy, then I found a station in Russian. They were playing very strange stuff, so I left it on that. Then I went into the kitchen and checked under the sink. There were trash bags and cleaning supplies and yellow rubber gloves. I put the gloves on. I opened the window in the kitchen, then I opened the windows in the sitting room. The front door promptly slammed shut. I went into the bedroom and grabbed a few large, heavy books. I used them to keep the front door open. Then I divided the apartment into cells and gave each cell a category—books, kitchen stuff, papers, electrical applian-ces, furniture, and so on. Slowly, I moved everything into these cells. Slowly, I emptied the wardrobe of clothes, a sideboard of DVDs and tablecloths and place mats and glasses, and a drinks cabinet of mostly full bottles of spirits. This is when I first started to pay close attention to Miriam's possessions. I was so focused on the small things that I did not even notice how nice the large pieces were. They were not heavy, and when they were empty, I moved them easily. Only the couch was heavy. I did not want to scrape the floor, so I had to move it inch by inch, now this end, now that, then I stood it on its end to maximize the space. Then I got some trash bags from the kitchen and put stuff that was obvi-ously trash into them. Then I beat all the dust out of the cushions. Then I swept the dust around the floor. Then I wiped clean all the surfaces. Then I cleaned the windows. Even though the day was cold, and even though a steady frigid breeze was moving through the apartment, and even though I worked slowly and took a lot of breaks, by the time I was done I felt overheated, sweaty, and covered in dust. I wanted a long hot shower. But then I went into the bathroom and realized I couldn't use it until I cleaned it. At the level of close inspection, it was extremely unclean, and the tiles needed to be scrubbed. I decided, because I did not want to get my clothes dirty, and I did not want to sweat or stink in them anymore, to close the front door and get undressed, completely, except for the yellow gloves, and clean the bathroom thoroughly. It took a while, and I threw up several times, but finally it was sparkling and smelled like lemon and bleach. Then I took the long hot shower. Miriam's shower was a lot better than the hotel shower. It was better than my electric shower in London. It had one of those tropical-rain showerheads, and it had great pressure. She also had a lot of shower gels. When I was finished, I dried myself off with one of her towels, then threw the towel and everything else from the bathroom into trash bags. Then I got dressed, back into my dusty and slightly damp-from-sweat clothes, and realized it was already past lunchtime. I took the croissant out of its bag and decided it wasn't going to be enough. I closed the windows, turned off the radio, and put my coat on. I would go through the piles of things after lunch, I decided.

When I opened the door, I found a man standing in the hallway, and we gave each other a fright. Then he stiffened up and rolled his shoulders back, as though he had not been frightened at all. He was slight and thin and had black hair. He wore a black leather motorcycle jacket over a T-shirt, jeans, and boots. He looked past me, he didn't seem at all happy.

Hello, I said.

Can I help you? he asked.

I don't know, I said.

Who are you?

I'm the brother.

What are you doing?

I'm going for lunch, I said.

I mean, he said, what are you doing with Miriam's stuff?

I turned around and looked at the apartment, now compartmentalized like a storehouse, and I wasn't sure I knew what I was doing.

Who are you? I asked.

I live upstairs, he said.

You knew Miriam? I asked.

Yes, she was a friend.

59

I closed the door behind me and locked it and said, You have thirty minutes for some lunch?

The man's name was Otis. He was from New York, but his accent was as corrupted and neutralized from living in Berlin as mine was from living in London.

You're cleaning, he said.

No, not really.

You're throwing stuff out.

No, not that, either.

Those books, he said. They...

I could see he felt we ought to be standing in each other's places. He wanted something, and he didn't feel he needed to weigh my pleasure or displeasure with the manner in which he expressed himself. He was the friend, and I was the intruder. Let's talk about the books at lunch, I said. He wasn't hungry, he said, but he would come along and watch me eat. We walked out of the building and turned toward the square. Otis walked with his hands in his pockets, even when he smoked he walked with his hands in his pockets. He didn't say much. I spoke, and he mumbled. I tried to be friendly, because I wanted him to warm up, relax, and tell me something about Miriam, even something he might think I wouldn't want to hear. I told him I lived in London, had lived there for twenty-five years. I told him my father and I were in Berlin to take Miriam's body home and bury her. I told him where we were staying, and about the close quarters, and my green bathroom, I may have mentioned the botched phone call home from Bedford Square, or the lunch I had afterward, and what the Frenchman had said about the English. Nothing interested him enough to cause him to respond. So I asked Otis if Miriam had said anything about either of us, my father or me.

Just the usual, he said. I said, I saw her twice in the last decade, have you known her that long? He said, I have. The day was going gray, and the sunlight was thinning, and the air took on the scent of ice, and I was certain I could see snow.

Are you in contact with anyone who knew Miriam?

Not regular contact, no.

Could you make contact with them, if you had to?

Why?

I wasn't sure what I was proposing. I think I had in mind a small gathering, something that my father could attend. I didn't want to make a speech, nor did I want to hear my father make a speech, but I would have liked to see the faces of the people who knew Miriam once. I didn't think it would remedy my grief, in fact I was sure those faces would populate my nightmares for the rest of my life. Nevertheless I wanted to see them, and I wanted my father to see them. Trish wasn't getting any information from the coroner's office, which suggested we'd be in Berlin for another few days at least. If it had to be canceled, so be it, but in the meantime it would give me something to anticipate.

I said, I'd like to just invite anybody who knew her to a casual drink.

He had stopped abruptly on the road. What do you want to eat? he asked. I don't know, I said, something nice. He said, I'm not sure anything around here would suit you. He was being sincere, and he looked at me an extra half second after he spoke. We were, at that moment, surrounded on all sides by restaurants, cafés, takeouts. I'm not fussy, I said, really. I could see that Otis had no real interest in my fussiness or unfussiness. What was really going on, possibly, with this strange and severe taciturnity, was that he was treating me in the way that he felt Miriam would want him to treat me. If that was the case, then whatever she had said about me, or however she'd behaved whenever she mentioned me, had caused Otis's behavior. I think I grew teary-eyed. But I didn't quite accept it. I turned around, this way and that, to look for a place where I might like to eat. It was such an ugly street. It was such a cold, miserable day.

You like soup? he said.

Soup?

Asian soup.

Sure, I said, though I did not want Asian soup. The moment he proposed it, I realized that what I wanted was a salad—I had been in Berlin for a few days and hadn't had a single fresh vegetable. I was beginning to have constant indigestion during the daytime, which I suppressed with just enough alcohol in the evenings to forget that I felt a little sick. Otis took me to a busy and loud place that seemed deliberately half-refurbished, in a manicured state of collapse, and Led Zeppelin was playing, and it was full of people who were also named Otis. I ordered some soup and Otis got himself something to drink, a kind of lemonade with some mint and a thin layer of froth at the top, and we crammed into an overcrowded picnic table, opposite each other. I asked, When was the last time you talked to Miriam? He said, A long time, if you mean the last time we really talked. Me too, I said. My soup came. It was full of tofu and bok choy and chilies. I took a spoonful and Otis said, Is it good? I said, Yeah, it's really good. Some people Otis knew came by and briefly spoke with him, in English. I was completely ignored, which was fine with me, because the only things I had to talk about were Miriam and the fact that I did something professionally that they probably all thought was evil. I ate my soup and did not even bother eavesdropping. When they left, I asked him if those people knew Miriam. No, he said. I felt like saying, If you want some books, Otis, you had better tell me something about Miriam, but instead I asked, Did you and Miriam ever date?

Date?

Or whatever.

He paused, and then he said, Not really.

I said, I saw her five years ago in Cologne, I knew then, I knew she was in trouble, she was so thin, but I didn't do anything, I didn't say anything.

I finished the last few spoonfuls of soup. He checked his watch a few times and dug in his pocket and jingled his keys, as though he was about to get up and go back to Miriam's apartment. But I wasn't ready. I said, What did she do for money? He said, She did a little bit of everything, taught English, movement therapy, life coaching, artist, translator, waited tables, got unemployment. He said this very casually and sleepily. But he awoke from the torpor of his list to lean forward and say—and as he spoke he hit the table hard once or twice with an outstretched index finger, and he revealed an aggression or rage that threatened to overflow from him—At no time in history have human beings had less freedom, less happiness.

I didn't understand how this connected to Miriam's work or to her death, unless he was suggesting that a lack of freedom and happiness had caused her to want to kill herself by starvation, or, alternatively, that her death was some form of courageous social protest. Possibly he was accusing me personally of taking Miriam's freedom and happiness from her, or accusing both of us of doing that. I thought it was a preposterous thing to say, no matter what it meant, but I responded anyway. I said, At *no* time?

That's right.

I bet that's not true.

It's true, he said.

I looked down. The empty bowl of soup was in front of me. I pushed it to the side. I stood up and Otis stood up, too. I said, I think I'm going to head back to my hotel, get some rest, come back to Miriam's another day to finish sorting everything. He said, The books. Yes, I said, what about them? Some of them belong to me, he said, and some other stuff. I said, I don't give a shit about the books, Otis, or anything else. Before we leave, you can come over and take whatever you like. He thanked me and we exchanged numbers. He said he'd see me tomorrow, or whenever I returned to Miriam's, and I sensed that he was telling me I would never get to spend time in Miriam's apartment without him finding out and joining me. I reminded him about getting Miriam's friends together, something modest but sincere, to mark the occasion. We parted in front of the soup place, but we were both heading in the same direction. I waited until he was out of sight, then I followed. I went back to my bike. The ride back across town, in the snow or freezing drizzle, whichever it was, was slippery and frigid. I got back to the hotel and took another shower and a short nap. I heard my father come in. I went to his room and told him that a neighbor of Miriam's had explained to me that human beings have never had less freedom and happiness than now. He sat on the edge of his bed and undid his tie and started taking off his shoes. What on earth is that supposed to mean? he said. I don't know, I said. I suspect he's forgotten the tenth century, said my father. I suspect you're right, I said. I sat on the little yellow tulip chair in his room and started flipping through a complimentary tourism magazine.

The lodge, in Scotland, where my mother and father honey-mooned, is way up in the Highlands, pretty remote, and luxu-rious. It stands on a tiny little island near the shore of a lake, and long ago they built a land bridge out to it, wide enough for a narrow road. It's at the bottom of a valley. When you arrive, by car—though some arrive by helicopter—and come down into the valley, you can usually see smoke coming out of the chim-neys, or at night you can see the distant lights that make it seem as though a ship is in the water. Inside, there are numerous little rooms where fires burn, where you find soft chairs and isola-tion, and where you can sit and read a paper or a book for a long time and get a pot of tea served to you. The restaurant is very good. The view is nice. Most of the people who go there are older, and they have been coming for years and years and years. I don't know how my mother and father found it. They went three times together—the honeymoon, again when Miriam and I were young, and again when I was a teenager—though we never came with them. I know they had plans to return, and after my mother got sick they contemplated going again. But she was too tired to travel. So they waited and put their faith in her recovery. A few years after she died, my father decided we ought to have regu-lar reunions there. I knew that he would have preferred to have regular reunions at home—home was where he wanted us—but he also knew it was easier on me if he came to Scotland, and a little more likely that Miriam might come. He paid for me and my wife to come meet him one year. He invited my wife's par-ents, but they couldn't make it. He invited Miriam, but Miriam was too busy. He accepted it. The three of us had a nice time to-gether. My father asked for the wine he and my mother drank the last time they were there—a Bordeaux that cost about seventy pounds a bottle—and we got quite drunk on that wine. We sat in one of the booths, under the red lampshades, listening to somebody play a piano, and we talked about our flat in Fulham Broadway, how we were slowly modernizing it, first the bathrooms, then the kitchen, about when we might next visit him in the States—my wife never did come with me—and if we were thinking about having children. My wife said she wanted children. I said I wanted children. I even think we decided to start trying to have children after that trip to the lodge. The dinner lasted forever. It was summer, so the evening had some light in it all the way to midnight. We were the last people in the restaurant, and afterward my father and I went for a little stroll down the land bridge and around the lakeshore. My wife went to bed. The stars came out. My father said to me, Why do you think Miriam hasn't come? I said, You said she told you she was too busy, I guess that's the reason. He said, Yes, still, it's a pity. Maybe next time, I said. Yes, he said, maybe next time. Eventually we went to bed.

Leaving the airport bathroom, I am a little less tired. I must have slept, for a moment, standing up. Or else it is the effect of the spaciousness of the terminal, after fifteen minutes in a cubicle. The hunger and the nausea have passed completely. I feel almost as though I have exercised, that I have not walked out of a busy airport bathroom but from the men's dressing room of a gym. I half expect to see Richard standing here to say hello, standing with that lean of his, which masks his sloped shoulder. Perhaps he waited for a few minutes. Perhaps he got tired of standing in a busy spot.

The terminal seems twice, or ten times, as crowded now as it did when we were sitting in front of our breakfasts. All you have to do is look around to see that there is not enough capacity and there are not enough hours in the rest of the day to get everybody out of here. We are no longer all in it together, this paralysis. The haze that was the fog is bronze now. It is the moment, now, just before it burns up, a spectacular moment. The horizon, in virtually every direction, now, is visible. Airplanes are landing, taxiing. I walk around a bit, up toward the gates near the bathrooms. There are gates on both sides. The gate areas are enormous. The names of destinations are listed on the displays by the gate numbers—Cairo, Bucharest, Madrid, Manchester, Warsaw, Moscow, Athens, London Heathrow, London Gatwick. When we land in Atlanta, the displays will show place names like Memphis, Charlotte, Jacksonville, Indianapolis, San Antonio, Des Moines, Chicago. I stop at the London Heathrow gate. I stand around. I watch a television with some other people, then I move, and stand around some people checking their phones, and I check my phone. I see Richard sitting with a magazine, no more than twenty feet away. He is sitting beside a woman, and the woman looks very like the woman he was married to when I knew him, but is not that woman. She has red hair and pretty brown eyes, and next to her is a child, a boy of about six or seven, who looks like Richard. I move closer and closer. The woman is reading her own magazine, and from time to time Richard stops reading his to look at hers. The woman is beautiful. Richard is handsome, more handsome than when I knew him, having acquired an extra ten pounds or so. The magazine he is pretending to read is about cycling and the magazine she is reading, and which Richard appears to prefer, is a celebrity magazine. I decide to stop watching them and say hello. And just as I move forward with intent, Richard looks up, as though he has known the whole

time that I have been there. The look on his face is one of the
strangest looks I have ever received. It says, This is not for you,
what you see here, go away. We have not seen each other in many,
many years, and I am making a face that stupidly says, Good to
see you after all this time, Richard. The woman looks up. It is no
longer possible to turn around and walk away, so I stick my hand
out for Richard to shake. I say, Funny to meet you here. He stays
sitting. The woman smiles at me. I introduce myself. She says her
name is Catherine. It's very nice to meet you, Catherine, I say.
Richard says, You are looking good. I say, As are you. Catherine
says, Are you flying to London? I am, I say, though it doesn't seem
like we're going anywhere for a while. Catherine says, It's clearing, not long now.

What has you in Germany? I ask them.

Richard says, Catherine is from Germany.

You're German? I ask.

Yes, she says.

You have no accent, I say.

Catherine smiles. Richard yawns. I almost say, Well, sorry for
bothering you, but instead I say, Well, it was nice seeing you
again. You too, says Richard, then he adds, Are you here for
work? No, I say, my sister lived here, and she died a few weeks
ago. Your sister? he asks. That's right, I say, her name was Miriam,
she lived in Berlin for twenty years.

I'm sorry to hear that, says Richard.

Catherine says, Yes, me too.

The child looks up from the screen he is watching, but not for
long.

Richard looks at Catherine and says, Mind if we go have a
quick drink?

Listen for the announcements, she says, and he says, I have my phone, text me if something happens. He gives her a dry, swift kiss on the temple, then he waves at the boy by sticking his hand between the boy's face and the screen, though the boy just moves the screen. As we walk away, Richard says, Do you have any kids? No, I say, nope, no kids.

The first bar, seven or eight gates away, does not have the atmosphere Richard desires, or else he wants to put a bit more distance between himself and Catherine and his son. We go another hundred yards and find another just like it. It is grossly overpacked, and it feels humid, tropical, like it has been raining warm beer. There is an English stag party heading home, more than a dozen men, some of them in oversized Union Jack hats, others in oversized Irish tricolor hats, and some in no hats. Frankenstein! they yell at Richard. They are flying to Manchester, not London. I can see exactly how their day has passed. At seven or eight, just hours or minutes after most of them passed out, they crawled out of their hotel beds, showered, had a greasy breakfast. They gathered quietly in the lobby, all of them pale, stinking, and ill. Some of them had to throw up. They slept in chairs and on couches in the lobby, they wore sunglasses even though it was dark, even though it was foggy. Arriving at the airport, they must have felt like dying. Security took a year off all their lives. After that, they wandered around like a lost flock, encountered a mostly empty bar and entered because somebody realized that a drink was the only way to avoid the pain of this hangover. There are two staff behind the bar, a pale blonde girl who is serving drinks and a pale blond boy who is furiously cleaning everything. They are both wearing black button-down long-sleeve shirts. The girl's is too tight and the boy's is too loose.

The boy looks exhausted. The girl looks traumatized. Richard starts to speak to her in English. She refuses to speak English, or she can no longer speak English, so I order. Richard gets a scotch and I take a sparkling water. The only table that is free has a puddle of beer on it, so we find a ledge along a wall and place our glasses there. Richard leans against the wall. I try not to touch anything. The smell is potent. A man from the stag grabs me around the neck and says, Oi! And his breath slithers into my breath. I think he will kiss me, on the lips, until his friend pulls him away from me.

Richard says, What are you up to these days?

I'm on my own now, started a consultancy. Twelve years now. You?

He says he left the bank and got rehired back at four times the salary as a consultant. Now he runs a consultancy with six employees. I tell him what I've been doing, the supermarket and various other clients, but that I'm starting up full-time work with a French aerospace firm as soon as I return to London.

Just over Richard's sloped shoulder, I see a man from the stag—no, the stag himself—trying to kiss a woman at the bar. She will not kiss him back. This is an airport, she is telling him, and I have a husband. We cannot, of course, hear them, but this is what I imagine she has told him. This is how she gazes at him. Richard looks behind him to see what I am looking at. He turns back and says, referring to the stag party, Fucking trolls, fucking scumbags.

You've got a new wife, I say.

Yes, he says. But we're not married.

She's very pretty, I say, and the kid is good-looking.

Thanks, he says.

What happened with your ex?

Nothing, he says, we're still together. We've got two kids.

For a moment I think he is joking, and I laugh, but then I see he is not joking so I grab my glass of water and pretend to drink.

Richard seems to grow very large suddenly with thoughtfulness. He says, I asked for a divorce, and she said I was insane. We see each other once or twice a month, the rest of the time I'm in Germany or the States, we have a house, let's keep the house, let's keep the kids in school, I do what I want, she does what she wants, I come home once or twice a month to see the kids. After Richard says this, he smiles and cheers up, and comes down to his normal size.

This works out okay?

Yes and no, he says. I mean, I don't know how the alternatives are going. He takes a drink and says, Have you remarried?

No, no, I haven't.

He looks into my thoughts, sees that he doesn't want to press that question any further. Behind him, I see that the stag has stopped trying to kiss the woman, now he is just handling her, placing his hands on her stomach and back, and she seems okay with this, this seems proper. They seem to be having an ordinary, lighthearted chat now. She is pretty, with big eyes. She has a couple of kids, they are young, one is well behaved and the other is not. The husband does something creative, but it doesn't pay the bills—he supplements this work with a regular job, but it demeans him. She stands by him, however, and believes in him, and though he has attempted to give up the creative thing many times, she demands that he stick with it. Even now, she is thinking that the man talking to her, handling her, touching her beneath the bar, where nobody can see, is a worm compared to her husband.

I never knew you had a sister, he says. What was her name

again?

Miriam, I say.

I had a sister, she died when I was very young. What happened to Miriam?

She starved to death.

Richard asks me to repeat myself, so I say, It's true.

How is that possible? Was she ill? Was she trapped in a snow-storm?

She died in her apartment in Berlin. She just stopped eating. Anorexia.

I shrug. I don't have another word for it.

That's awful, he says, truly awful, I'm sorry to hear it. When was it, when did she die?

A little over three weeks ago.

It's madness, he says, it's unbelievable. Was it…he searched for a way to phrase it…something that surprised you?

I nod my head, because I cannot really bring myself to say it did not totally surprise me. I saw her five years ago. She was sickly thin, obviously not well, physically or otherwise, and I never bothered to check up on her after that. I said, The last time I saw her was in London, about nine years ago, and she was fine.

Nine years?

Nine years goes quick.

Richard downs his drink and says, It sure does. Then he says, One more, and he goes to the bar again. He doesn't have to speak German or English, he just points to his glass. The woman in the corner with the stag has entered a sort of trance. It seems she is on the verge of succumbing, not out of a desire for the stag but out of indifference to the act of betrayal. When Richard comes back, I say, That's very strange, those two. He looks. We both stare for a while. She sees us staring but she doesn't care. The man looks over and we look away.

Richard tells me I really should think about meeting him for a chat.

About what?

Just a chat.

I say, I'm happy where I am, I really am.

Of course you are, it's just a chat. He hands me his card.

I'm actually serious, I say.

Me too, just a chat.

We shake hands, and he walks away. I remain. I look at his card. I see that he is based in Munich as well as London. This gives me pause. But no, I don't want to live in Munich. I put his card in my wallet. I hold my glass of water but don't drink, and I watch the woman at the bar. She and the man are kissing softly and discreetly, looking around after each kiss, as though they have convinced themselves that they are going unnoticed. I put my glass on a ledge. I check my phone. There's a message from Trish on it. She and my father are wondering if I'm all right. They're at some sort of historical exhibit down the other end of the terminal.

On the last night of our journey outside Berlin—which took us up the Rhine valley, then down from Koblenz into the Ardennes and into Luxembourg—we decided to treat ourselves to a five-star hotel in Brussels. From the road, from my phone, we booked two rooms in the Radisson Blu Royal. We had a nice dinner, and after dessert my father had a cognac and went to bed. I went out. A funny thing happened to the weather during our trip. After that first cold week, the temperature shot up, the clouds disappeared, and it seemed that an early summer had arrived. When

I went out, I did not even need a jacket. I met a woman. She was nice and funny. She was about fifty. She showed me a few places. She took me to her studio. We ended up back at my hotel room. When she left, she wished me a pleasant journey back to Berlin. When I was alone again, I stood naked in front of the huge closet mirrors. I do not have a full-length mirror in London, so it isn't often I get to examine what has happened to my body. At first I tried to stand erect, tighten up, suck my stomach in. But then I relaxed. I breathed out. The days of gluttony hadn't helped, but there was no denying that I had grown soft. I sucked in my gut. I squeezed the flesh in my chest and arms, then I flexed my muscles to see if flexing made that flesh taut. I bent over, and my gut balled up. It was made of three folds, folds that I poked and squeezed together. A wound I'd given myself the previous night opened up—it was excruciating—and started bleeding. It had been bleeding all day, actually, but only when I squeezed my gut together did the wound completely reopen. I told myself, Well, that was dumb. I had bought, at a pharmacy in Brussels, some dressings for it. I showed it to the pharmacist and he said I might need to see a doctor, and gave me some instructions for cleaning and re-dressing it. So I re-dressed it and sat on the edge of the bed, and waited. I looked at myself in the mirror while I waited, and I felt that I would never be able to exercise enough or eat well enough to reverse the deterioration that had taken place, a deterioration that was more than physical, that was fueled not by time and biology but by memory—my body was made of everything I could remember.

It started to rain, and when the bleeding stopped at last I decided to stop feeling sorry for myself. I got my notebook out, sat on the bed, propped myself up on all the pillows, filled a few pages. I didn't quite understand why the woman had to leave, but it would have been nice to have her stay the night, stay until breakfast, have her meet my father, surprise him. The bar where we met was full of young people. I don't remember how we started talking, but once we did, we admitted that the place made us feel old, so we went somewhere else, had a drink, then somewhere else, and so on, until we arrived at a place that made us feel young, which was not busy, neither too dark nor too loud, and played nice music that disappeared when you spoke. Finally I got her to talk about what she did, and why she was in Brussels. She said she was a musician. She had a residency, it was EU-funded. There was so much money, she said, for artists in Brussels, but nobody wanted to come and stay here, because it was so dull and full of diplomats. I asked her if I could buy a recording of her music somewhere. She said, It's not the kind of music you buy in a store. I used the word experimental. Oh, she said, please don't call it that. I asked her to describe it, and she said it was not the kind of music you describe. Well, I said, I like music that is hard to describe, now I have to hear it. She said, with a tone that suggested she was trying to call my bluff, My studio is not far. But I wasn't bluffing, so we finished our drinks, paid up, and left.

Her studio was in a vast, multistory steel box that had very few windows. I have been to the studios of visual artists, but this was something different. There were three rooms. The first was an office, the second was a place where she kept clutter, and the third was the size of a ballroom, except with a very low ceiling—it must have been a false ceiling. That room was white with glossy white walls, ceiling, floor. The surfaces were so glossy they looked wet. At the far end, a black trapezoidal box hung from the ceiling by fine, invisible wires. She gave me a soft white hooded gown and white paper boots. She put on a gown and boots as well. Then she gave me some large white headphones. I put them on, over the hood. There was a deep noise in them, something like the sound you get when you submerge yourself in a bath and try to be absolutely still and listen. I lifted them off my ears and asked, Now what? Walk around very slowly, she said. So I walked, very slowly. I would have walked slowly anyway, because the appearance of wetness made me think the floor was slippery, even though it was not. There were, as I walked, tiny fluctuations in the low, underwater sound. These fluctuations at first sounded like pure static, but every once in a while I could hear something distinct, I thought. Music, possibly. A slow disorientation began to come over me, and it seemed the slower I walked, the more thrilling the disorientation became. The glossiness of the room started to blur my sense of depth, and after a while I could not tell where the floor stopped and where the wall began. The black trapezoidal box seemed to absorb the room's sense of definition, and remarkably, as I slowly made my way around the room, following what felt like a path made by these fluctuations, the box—which evidently housed the transmitter that was sending out the signal that produced the fluctuations—changed shape. At first these changes were very slight. It bulged a little, or shrank, and sometimes it seemed to rise or fall slightly. But then it started to change orientation, so that it seemed upside down, and abruptly right-side-up again. Then it became a square, a circle, a triangle. These shape-changes were confounding. But also obviously not real, because it remained—all I had to do was stop believing the hallucination—trapezoidal. It changed color, too—from black to green to blue, by shades. Meanwhile, the aural fluctuations continued, and the more I tried to make sense of them, the more I could hear the static-y echoes of music. Whatever piece I thought of, I could hear. Anything I thought, I could apply to the noise, and momentarily this thought could grip the noise and make sense of it. I walked all the way to the box and stood under it. The low noise was strongest right underneath it. So were the fluctuations. I could hear high-pitched drilling, but the harmony I faintly recognized—and which became anything I wanted it to be—remained out of reach. Then I took the headphones off, and I pulled the hood down. The woman noticed, and she took her headphones off, too. What do you think? she asked. You're right, I said, it's not music you can easily describe. We met in the center of the room and I gave her back her headphones. What is it playing? I asked. What is *it*? she asked. I was about to turn around and point to the black trapezoidal box with the transmitter inside, but the tone of her question suggested I'd completely misunderstood what was happening, and I felt so self-conscious for not realizing what was obvious, and maybe even a little irritated, that I just said, If this is in your studio, what will it look like in public? She said, It will be vast. It will be ten times this size, and the trapezoid will be the size of a commercial airliner.

Ten times? I said.

Well, maybe just the same size, maybe twice the size.

Where will you exhibit it?

She named a large, important-sounding gallery in Barcelona, but not in a way that made her sound pompous. She said it with a shy grin, as though she herself could barely believe it. If I exhibit at Tate Modern, I will make it ten times this size, she said.

It was really late when we left the studio. We hadn't been flirting in an obvious way, or touching, but there was something between us, and I think we both had the sense that if anything was going to happen, it would have to happen soon. I felt completely disarmed by the experience I'd just had, and not quite deserving of her, so I did not try to kiss her, even though it seemed like kissing would have been appropriate. She said, Please tell me you are not a diplomat. I'm not a diplomat, I said. Please tell me you do something completely insipid, you're a lawyer or an accountant, or a graphic designer. I gave her a funny look. Well, she said, then tell me you're something evil, like a journalist or a politician. I said, I'm in marketing. Marketing! she exclaimed. That's marvelous, that's a hundred times worse. I said, You don't hear the word marvelous much anymore.

We walked along a lot of empty, dark streets—I mean the windows were dark, and the place seemed very sleepy. She said Brussels was so dull that, after midnight, you could walk down the middle of any street you liked, and she liked to do that. While we were in her studio, a cold front had arrived, just like that, and now the skies were gray, and there was a chill. That chill felt nice after the week of weird, swampy heat, though the chill would transform, in a day, into the return of winter in central Europe, and my father would feel quite proud of himself for splurging on a warm coat. The clouds, which were low, and which absorbed the lights of the city, were bright and fluorescent, and they moved swiftly.

What did you want to become? she asked.

When I was younger?

When you dreamed of your future, I suppose.

Oh, I said, I don't buy in to that stuff.

What do you mean?

I tried to think of a way to formulate a response that did not sound depressing or dismissive. She meant the question honestly. I think she even meant it kindly, as in, I seemed like the kind of person who could be more, or achieve more, than what I had become and achieved in my life. And she based this on the fact that she thought I liked her music, or her installation, or whatever the best word to describe it was, and because, like all artists, she based her belief on the potential of others to be more or achieve more by their capacity to appreciate her music, even though—and perhaps it isn't true in her case—what often happens is that artists base their faith in others on their incapacity to recognize bullshit, or their unwillingness to declare bullshit when they see it. But I did like what she had done. I liked it because she was a nice person and because it was entertaining, and certainly thrilling at times, and I liked the fact that it had offered a respite from the ordinary. And, yes, there was a beauty to it. I could not help thinking, however, that all the thoughts a human being could have about the experience of being in that room were predictable, that the only way to connect to her piece—or to art in general—was intellectually, because to connect emotionally to art was naive and quasi-religious, or because emotion no longer belonged to art, it was simply a currency of pre-existing phrases—musical or visual or grammatical—to describe categories of human conditions. Nevertheless, I thought about her question, and though I said nothing, I decided that if I could have been anything, I would have liked to be a doctor.

It's a mean question, she said, I take it back.

What do you think I would like to be?

She stopped and looked up at the sky. Then she looked at me, measuring my width and height. An archaeologist, she said.

We were less than five minutes away from my hotel. She knew

79

where I was staying, so, without discussion, we simply walked in that direction, and when we arrived she came inside the lobby. I asked if she would like a drink at the hotel bar and she gave it some thought. Not really, she said. So we got in the elevator and went up to my room. In the elevator she said, It's funny, I've been here almost a year, I've got a few months left, and I have no idea what's happening in the world, I don't read papers, I don't watch television, I don't read any letters I receive, not even ones that look official, I don't meet other people in the building where my studio is, or have coffee with my neighbors, I don't have any friends here, I don't want to make friends, I don't have a telephone or e-mail, my parents have died, I have no children. Every few months I just meet a stranger and talk nonsense for a few hours.

In bed, she lay there with her arms crossed, like she was having very deep thoughts that did not at all concern me or this night. I said, Do you have nightmares? She stopped thinking about whatever she was thinking and said, Yes, of course.

What are your nightmares about? I asked.

Let me think, she said. I dream that I am being chased but can't run. I dream that I am being stabbed. I dream that I am being raped. I dream that I burn to death. I dream that my womb is full of centipedes. I dream that I drown. The usual.

Hmm, I said.

And you?

I said, I dream that I am trapped in an underground cell, no bigger than a small sitting room. It is bricked up. There's a door, but it goes nowhere. And sometimes the door disappears. Then it goes very dark.

She thought about this for a little while. How do you know you're underground? she asked.

I don't know. Don't you always know if you're underground?

She smiled and said, That is a strange dream to have more than once.

Yes, I said. It's not the only one, just the one I tell people about. What do you think it means?

I tell people about it in the hopes that they'll know. But then of course I don't really believe that dreams mean things.

Will you have it when I leave?

I don't know, I said. Tonight I might just open up the minibar and drink everything. Then I won't have any dreams.

She didn't seem entirely interested in my nightmares—she started to touch her bare wrist, where a watch might have been—but I finished my thoughts anyway. I said, Every year or so I convince my doctor to prescribe me some Xanax for a month, and I sleep great for that month. But I am groggy. If it weren't for the grogginess, I'd never sleep without Xanax.

She said, I would like to visit America next, maybe work in Los Angeles. Everywhere is over, you know, except for Los Angeles.

Well, obviously.

Do you ever see yourself living in America again?

No, I said. I'm very happy in London. It's hard to find a flat you really like in London.

But I was already thinking about how attractive Los Angeles suddenly sounded, driving around in a convertible Porsche, eating a burrito and smoking cigarettes, and possibly working as a private detective or being a screenwriter.

The next morning, I met my father for breakfast and told him about the woman and her music installation. He listened, dumbfounded. He was eating a couple of giant sausages, covered in ham and ketchup and scrambled egg. I made myself a bowl of soft-boiled eggs, which I mixed with bacon and some diced red pepper and ate with a spoon. I think it was that morning, in Brussels, when I started to lose my appetite—or else I had, looking at myself in the mirror, already lost my appetite, and that bowl of soft-boiled eggs was the first meal I ate after I had lost my appetite. Every time I consider anything more than a bite of a piece of bread, I think of those eggs in that bowl. My father and I would be, after breakfast, heading back to Berlin, but not before we stopped in Aachen, because my father wanted to visit the tomb of Charlemagne. At first he didn't understand—in my story of the woman's installation—where the fluctuations were coming from, or what the music was, but it dawned on him in much the same way it dawned on me. Ha, he said, *horseshit*. Well, I said, I don't know. I knew I had explained it all in a way that had biased him against her, which made no sense, because I think I had intended to brag about spending the evening with a fascinating woman.

We should look this woman up, what was her name?

I have no idea. I never asked.

He said, Too bad.

I finished my bowl of eggs. We still had Charlemagne ahead of us, so we left the table, went upstairs for our things, checked out, and hit the road. We headed eastward, into a gray, cold rainfall. We entered the Netherlands—a narrow, southerly appendage that took just minutes to traverse—and my father suddenly interrupted a story about the first time he saw Charlemagne's tomb with a look of distant alarm. He stopped talking for a little while. Then he said, Do you think Miriam had a happy childhood? It was, I suppose, his way of raising the idea that had been in his mind, as it had in mine, since we first heard the news that Miriam had died—that we had missed something obvious, that her death stretched back to a time when we knew her and saw her every day. I said, I don't know. He said, But now that I ask, what do you think? I changed the radio station. I pretended to concentrate on the driving. We had been together, in the hyper-close proximity of a road trip, for five days, and we were on each other's nerves. I presumed that our frustration with each other had something to do with the fact that we both had searched our memories of Miriam's childhood so thoroughly and found nothing, or at least nothing so spectacularly out of the ordinary as to explain her suicide. I looked at him, sideways, and saw that he was being truthful in his alarm, and that until that moment he'd been utterly convinced that something in Germany had caused it, or her brain had changed shape, or a madness encoded in her DNA reached its activation age. Since receiving the news of Miriam's death, I had, at the very back of my thoughts, entertained the possibility that my father had done something awful to Miriam, something that drove her away from home, and which settled in her body like a latent and incurable plague, and finally drove her to suicide, but the look on his face that day in the car pointed to his innocence. I was both relieved and disappointed that he hadn't asked whether Miriam and I, the two of us, had happy childhoods, disappointed because it would have been easy to answer—the answer, when he put it like that, was yes, relative to other people's childhoods—but relieved because to include me in the question would have been an insincere gesture, and because it would have been the very thing a guilty man would have done, a man who wanted to know just how much other people knew. I said, To be honest, I never was very much concerned with her happiness or unhappiness, when we were children. He said,

I don't believe that, you were a caring older brother, you looked
after her and beat up kids who picked on her. I said, I don't remember that, either. The rain was getting heavier and heavier, but
I kept us moving fast. A Mercedes passed us, going a hundred
and sixty kilometers an hour, which was reckless for the conditions, and I sped up and followed his lights in the rain for as long
as I could. My father said, Well, you may remember, maybe you
don't, I don't know, but Charlemagne starved himself to death.
I said, That wasn't in your book, I don't think. He said, No, it
wasn't in my book, but it was in Einhard. I said, I didn't read
Einhard, Dad. But he wasn't listening to me. He said, It's true,
he was struck by a fever, and he treated fevers with abstinence
from food, thinking the disease could be driven off, or at least
mitigated, by fasting. I let the Mercedes go and slowed to a hundred and forty, a hundred and thirty, a hundred and twenty, but I
was still shrieking past the cars in the slow lane, which were doing eighty or seventy or less. I said, It's preposterous, what you're
about to suggest. He said, I wouldn't quite know what to suggest.
I said, You're better off forgetting it. You're right, he said. Then he
tried to change the subject, he started going through the various
aches and pains he had, in his knees, his wrists, his shoulders—all
of which he blamed on stiff, small beds, and too much walking,
and too much sitting in the car. I said, Dad, I need to tell you
something, but I don't want you to get upset.

Okay.

On the day I arrived, I identified Miriam's body.

You saw her?

That's right.

Why didn't you tell me?

I thought I might spare you from the discomfort of it.

Discomfort?

I figured you would have done the same for me.

Then we crossed the border into Germany, and the Nether-lands disappeared behind us in the rain and spray.

Our mornings, during our travels, started early. My father woke at five or six, usually went for a walk, and I woke up around seven, stumbled into the restaurant for breakfast, and drank four or five cups of coffee. Our hotel rooms were always next to each other. We sat side by side in the car. I did all the driving, ex-cept for one stretch between Kaub and Koblenz, because I got drunk on some wine we'd bought at Kloster Eberbach—the clois-ter where they filmed *The Name of the Rose*. I was glad it was coming to an end. I was glad to be heading back to Berlin, where we could go back to waiting, and I could have some time to myself. I was sure my father had wanted to spend the night in Aachen, get a hotel overlooking the cathedral, walk around, think about how many hours he'd spent studying the life of Charle-magne in order to understand the Middle Ages and the history of Europe. But now, in the final minutes before our arrival, he was quiet, severe, strange, and the way he was breathing suggested he had decided that his own preoccupation with visiting Aachen Cathedral was tiresome. When I saw a sign for the exit to Aachen, I said, We'll park, see the cathedral, have a bite to eat, and get back on the road. If we leave Aachen by eight, we can make Berlin by one or two.

He said, Forget Aachen, let's just keep going.

I took the exit anyway, and he didn't protest. The stop in Aachen felt necessary to me now, not only because, without it, the previous five days would not have any meaning, but also be-cause it would give my father, or force upon him, depending on his mood, an opportunity to fill the space I'd created by my confession, a chance to imagine what it might have been like to be in the morgue with me. I saw her corpse in my mind a hundred times a day, I still do, and when the memory arrives it is like a blinding light, I go hot all over, it obliterates all other thoughts.

My father's book begins with the fall of Rome. It portrays a continent with an uncertain future, in peril, disorganized, fragmented, heterogeneous. In what is now eastern France, and what is now the Rhineland, the Merovingian dynasty emerges. The first major king of the new era, an era with a troubled but unbroken link to European modernity, to the present day, is Clovis I. The Merovingians are supplanted by the Carolingians. Charlemagne becomes king. He rules from Aachen. From here the ambitions of Rome will be realized by Germans—the Germanic tribes who would become the various nationalities of power and wealth in Europe—a dream of Latin Christendom, but more than that, something new, not conceived in Rome. And this new thing is the embryo of what came to be called Europe. Charlemagne becomes emperor. His principal motivation is a zeal for unity and harmony—*unitas* and *consonantia*—and his principal despair is variety, in particular the differences, among the many provinces of his kingdom, in church music and chant. His successors will inherit and advance the drive for cultural, legal, military, and political uniformity—and Europe, as the story of the rise of, and resistance to, this uniformity, will be born. The push outward from the Rhineland is unlike colonialism of the eighteenth and nineteenth centuries, when colonial powers get entangled in countries that supply raw materials. In the Middle Ages, colonialism is about reproduction. Rather than extract economic value from the colonized place, settlers replicate their own social and religious practices. I was remembering my father's book—I had filled the pages of a notebook with quotes from it, and as we drove along the main road from the motorway to the city center, a road full of warehouse stores and car dealerships, I had the wondrous feeling that we were going to see Charlemagne to tell him that his mission was accomplished, but that it had brought upon the earth a barbarism and slavery as constricting and ignoble as anything he had ever witnessed—though at that moment I could not tell if I had started to sound like my father, like Otis, or like myself, ten days removed from work. My father and I arrived in Aachen just before six, and we thought the cathedral would close at six. So I drove that main road like a maniac, and when we got into the center I ran a lot of red lights. I cut across pedestrians. I went the wrong way down two one-way streets. Be careful, be careful, my father kept saying. Finally he said, I think I'm going to close my eyes. And he really did close his eyes.

Outside the airport, the day is clear, at last. The fog has evaporated. The sun is near its apex, but it is still low in the sky, and through the tinted glass of the terminal its light makes blue dusk. The temperature inside the terminal has gone up, or the temperature inside me has gone up. I have to take off my heavy coat. I simply leave it on the floor and make a mental note of where it is, so I can retrieve it later, though I have no intention of retrieving it. It's a coat I've owned for several years. I wore it the last time I saw Miriam. But I cannot wear it any longer. I cannot even carry it. I take off my suit jacket and sweater, too. My shirt is wet from perspiration. There is nowhere to sit or relax, so I kneel. I just kneel down in the middle of a crowd of people. Then I put on my sunglasses. I don't even stop to worry that people will think I look stupid with sunglasses on. The funny thing is that nobody notices, or nobody cares. I bought this pair of sunglasses the day I arrived in Berlin, or the day after. I also started growing a beard the day I arrived in Berlin. It got pretty long. It had some gray in it, which surprised me. I thought about keeping it, growing it for a few months. But I shaved the beard two days ago. The sunglasses are a pair of tortoiseshell Ray-Ban Wayfarers. I have not owned a pair of sunglasses that cost more than ten pounds since I moved to London. If it was sunny, I either squinted or went and got a cheap pair at a gas station or the checkout aisle at a supermarket. The Wayfarers cost me two hundred euro. When I saw my father later that day he said, Are those new? I said, I think these are the best sunglasses I've ever owned. He said—with a little amusement, because I suppose there's nothing quite so ordinary as ordinary Wayfarers—I'm glad I was here to see them. I said, I think they make me look like Huey Lewis. Who? he said. During our trip around the Rhineland, I wore them every day. It seems to me, sometimes, that I wore them to sleep, wore them at breakfast, wore them in the shower.

Right beside me—I am kneeling down, it turns out, at the Copenhagen gate—are a handsome couple, and they are wearing sunglasses. The woman is pretty and has long arms and legs, and I smile at her. But she is not looking at me. She is looking at her phone. The man is large and muscular, though he wears very dainty, white, woven-leather shoes, and shiny white pants. He is shaved bald, probably a little younger than me, and he has a strong chin. He is, or seems to be, checking his fingernails. Admiring his fingernails, or the perfection of his fingers. My, my, he thinks, in whatever language he thinks, what fingers I have, women love these fingers. The woman is tanned and also muscular, fortyish. I have never seen listlessness like her listlessness. She is sending somebody a message. She is not the kind of person who uses her phone for anything other than text messages, or sending photographs—she does not even use it for telephone calls. She has an expensive smartphone, but if somebody ever said, Please check your phone for the weather, or asked how to spell something, she would have to text the question to somebody who would look it up for her. She wears tight, dark-blue jeans and a black top that reveals one shoulder and hangs loosely from the other shoulder, and little black shoes. Her hair is in a ponytail. Her sunglasses are large and green-black, and momentarily she seems to notice that I am observing her. The green-black lenses of her glasses fix upon me for a moment, then release. The man says something to her, perhaps he has finally grown tired of silently admiring his hands and has decided to tell her how much women adore his hands. She looks at him when he speaks, or almost at him, but she makes no expression. And when he is finished speaking, she returns to her phone. On the other end of these texts, I imagine an equally listless woman chronicling an equally unbearable lull in some other place. But this conversation started years ago and will never end, and it has nothing to do with airports or delays. One could be at the Met, listening to *The Magic Flute*, while the other might be sitting in the Musée de l'Orangerie, surrounded by Monet's *Water Lilies*, and they would be writing to each other of the unbearable quality of these scenes, the noises and these images, and these people. They never encountered a plate of food, no matter how ingenious or expensive or tasty, that they smiled at. They never drank a glass of wine that tasted nice. They never saw a landscape worth a photograph. They take photographs of things like fat people, or handbags, and send them to each other. Instinctively they know that personalities are signs of weakness, or symptoms of self-deceit. A man with a personality is a coward. A woman with a personality is insane. Nobody has more personality than a fat, stupid, cowardly man, or a fat, stupid, insane woman. I would like to get a week with a woman like this woman, not to love or be loved, or for conversation, but to be near her in restaurants, to return her plates of food for being imperfect, to return her drinks for being insults. And to lie beside her in hotel beds while she watches television.

I get a text from Trish that asks if I am on my way. I send one back—I am, but it will be a few more minutes. The terminal, because the weather has finally improved, and because flights are starting to depart, has reached the edge of apoplexy. I stand. I put my suit jacket back on. My teeth ache. My head aches. My eyes ache. And all these aches seem distantly related to the problem of what to do with my sweater, and the consequences of leaving it behind and the burden of taking it with me. Will someone notice that I'm leaving coats and sweaters behind, and will this cause a security problem? Will I get the chills and want my sweater back? Will I regret leaving my nice coat, or have I begun to regret it already? I am sinking and my heart starts to palpitate. I throw the sweater partially underneath the seat of the man in the white, woven-leather shoes, and this makes me feel better. Ahead of me, between where I am and the airport plaza, and beyond, presumably where Trish and my father are, are thousands of people. It has the feel of a great, collective departure, the kind you might imagine at a train station, just before the war. I start to move. I stop at a café and ask for a bread roll, no butter, no jam, just some bread, and this causes some confusion until I tell them the bread is for my son, that he won't eat anything but bread. They give it to me in a napkin. I take a bite immediately. Then I walk to a high table by the counter where some people are already sitting and put my elbows on it, lean over, and eat some more, taking tiny bites. The first few bites make me nauseous, but as they settle in my stomach I feel a little improvement. I put the rest of the bread down beside the people I've annoyed by claiming a space in their privacy, and I place a euro on the counter by the cash register, since I can see that the staff are disgusted with me for lying about my son. Lines have formed at the mouth of every gate, and each line stretches for fifty yards or more, and you cannot pass through them, or you can, but you must first explain that your gate is elsewhere, that you are merely passing through. Even then, they give you looks that say, I'm stuck, I can't move, why have you picked me to irritate? You take the inch they give you, and you try to make sure your rolling case knocks their case over, or runs over their toes, or knocks their child over, so that you can give them a look that says, See what you made me do by pretending you could not move? They close the space while you are still in it, you get squeezed out. It is all completely automatic and emotionless. You never look back. Gate after gate, this repeats. It is as though the people who have rushed into position—who will refuse, once boarding begins, to accept that the passengers behind them in the line, who are in rows fifteen through thirty, for instance, have priority—believe that Copenhagen, Budapest, Vienna, Madrid, Kiev, Amman, Helsinki, and Tel Aviv are not hundreds or thousands of miles away but just on the other side of the gates, just down the jetway.

On the departures board, beside our flight, it reads Please Wait.

When I flew home for my mother's funeral, my father picked

me up from the airport. I had hoped Miriam would come along, but it was just my father. He was standing at arrivals in a white polo shirt and tan shorts, and sockless in a pair of dark-brown penny loafers. He looked like a man who had spent a day grieving on his own, privately, variously doing things around the house, suddenly weeping into his hands, then continuing, looking out the window, thinking he had better mow the lawn, then sitting on the couch for a long time holding something that reminded him of her, then getting up and going through the mail, and so on. When I saw Miriam, we hugged. I asked her how she was and she said, I'm good, how are you? I admitted I was a bit shocked. I had been home just a few days before. My mother's condition had gotten very bad, and I'd come home with the expectation that she would be dead within days. I sat beside her in the hospice. I watched the television in her room. I read books beside her. I held her hand. Miriam was there as well. My mother was mostly unconscious or, when conscious, very groggy, so we couldn't really converse with her. She was very pale and drawn, pink around the eyes and nostrils. If Miriam's starvation had been an attempt to re-create my mother's death—which was improbable, but was at least more plausible than recreating, for my father's sake, the death of Charlemagne—then she had failed, because my mother, though drawn and sickly, did not look horrifying, as Miriam had looked in the morgue. While we sat around her bed, we told her she looked well. She'd received many cards, and we read them aloud to her. Miriam told her that she planned to skip her final year of college and leave home, go traveling, and my mother, who didn't seem alert enough to hear her—and to the astonishment of her doctors—made a recovery. A day later, we were all in her room, speaking with her, she was smiling and her eyes were clear. I offered to quit my job and come home to be with her, but my mother refused to let me. She said, For God's sake don't come back here, you live in London now. So I returned to London, went back to work, and that very day, the Monday I walked back into the office, she died. I got a call from my father. He was calm but obviously very tired. I asked if she had died peacefully. He said, Well, she died. I walked into my boss's office, sat down in the chair across from his desk and said, without any sadness but also without levity, You're not going to believe this. This was back in the days when airlines gave real hardship discounts for deaths in the immediate family, and they put me on a plane for almost nothing.

My mother's funeral was very large. Hundreds of people came. Mostly women whom my mother knew through her charity, or who were connected to the charity, or had benefited from her charity. The women my mother knew had arranged the house as a giant funeral hall, and Miriam and I sat on chairs against the wall. I don't think we were trying to look pitiful, but we probably looked pitiful. Miriam was talking about moving to Berlin. She wore her hair very short. A lot of people stood over us and counseled us. A lot of people put their hands on us. We looked up and smiled at them. I suspect the house will be arranged, for Miriam's funeral, in a similar fashion—arranged by the same women who arranged the house for my mother's funeral—and I will sit down as I sat then, and be counseled, but now I am probably too unfamiliar for anyone to touch, or people will refuse to touch me because I look like bad luck.

After my mother's funeral, in the evening, our father went for a swim and we watched him from the poolside, sitting in white plastic chairs. It was warm and muggy. Everyone had gone. The last people who left had cleaned everything, arranged the house back the way it was, and promised to return the next day to clean it some more. My father told them there wasn't any way to make the place cleaner, so it wasn't necessary. Everything had been returned to its place with a spooky exactitude, and I went around the house wishing they had left it as a funeral parlor, or a mess, because the house needed to be changed, and we needed to be the ones who changed it. But there was nothing to do, nothing at all, so my father went swimming. He'd been struggling with his big book, the book for which his publisher had already waited years, and he'd abandoned it, he said, because on top of all his other duties he was tending to my mother, and now he felt the book was pointless. The day of my mother's funeral had been a strange one for my father, because all day my mother's friends and colleagues had been forgiving him. Not explicitly, but by their affection and kindness they forgave all of his sins—his self-deceit, his tyranny, his absence, his selfishness, his mediocrity. He was cleansed, and he swam around the pool that night, in front of me and Miriam, with a pacific look on his face, and a pacific way of speaking to us, that you often associate with people who have found a religion. The water was lit by a blue-white light in the deep end. As my father moved and swam around in it, the waves he made contained tiny lines of light along their apexes, and, underneath him, refracted light moved in large white tectonic plates along the white bottom of the pool. We watched him swim for an hour. He did almost all the talking, which was strange, because he was never very talkative with us. Our mother had been the talker, but from this moment onward he would accept the role in her absence. We let him talk and talk and talk, and we couldn't leave, I think, until we witnessed him talk his way out of the reassurances he'd received that our mother had been happy, that she had accepted his absences because it was part and parcel of his eminence, the eminence they assured him was real, and that even though things had not gone as he'd planned, he had two fine children who had what he had never had, a community, a home, a place, belonging, and so on. We had to be certain he'd rejected their forgiveness, we had to wait until he felt replenished with shame and truth. My father once wrote, in a review of a book about the Holocaust, that shame, not curiosity, is what drives the historian. The historian of tragic events, especially, he wrote, must cultivate guilt, must find infinite ways to implicate himself in every injustice and atrocity that has ever transpired, and be unworthy of all the heroism and courage that has resisted injustice. And then he must strap his shame down, paralyze it, let it speak but not let it gesticulate. He stated, in his review, that the author of the book had cultivated guilt, felt unworthy of heroism, and was on his way to an illuminating and important history book, but he forgot to strap his shame down, and he had therefore produced a book of gesticulations, a rather *stylish* book. The result was arrogance—sentimentality, flourish, lyricism, hyperbole, opinion—all symptoms of arrogance. In histories of suffering, style is unconscionable. The review was published in the *New York Review of Books*, and I thought it was a good piece—I called and told him so, and I was so proud to see him being so tough and high-minded—and I have, in ways that I have yet to fully unravel or even begin to articulate, tried to translate that way of thinking into my own work. Our house was dark. The clouds had soft light in them, a reflection of the town and some refineries. After an hour, Miriam mentioned that she'd felt a little sickened by the way some of mother's friends kept going on about Christ, about her salvation, about her eternal peace, and about what a strong faith she had. I know, I said, it was hard to take. Miriam said, Mom would have found it sickening, too. My father said, Your mother would not have wanted her friends to say those things to you, and so far as I know, none of them had any idea about the nature of her faith, because she was so private about it, but you should know something, something that will surprise you. He stopped talking for a moment and made little splashes with his cupped hands. We waited and he decided to tell us. He said, Your mother found Christ before she died. I said, That can't be true. He said, It is true, it's the truth. Miriam said, She probably just told you that. I said, She was weakened and afraid. My father said, No, not because she was afraid—and here he sank down, half-reclined upon the water's buoyancy, so that his face was looking upward, up at the clouds, and his head was submerged so that the waterline covered his ears, so that his voice, to him, would be slightly disembodied by the weight of the water—but because Christ appeared to her in a vision and He spoke. My father stood up slightly. He seemed not to believe he had said what he said. His head and shoulders were out of the water. What did He say? I asked. My father said, You know, just the typical religious stuff, I guess, she actually never told me, she just said that He was suffering, and He took her pain away. My father looked up, saw our puzzled disappointment, and lowered his head, and we knew for sure that he didn't feel forgiven anymore.

When he got out of the pool, dried himself off, and went to bed, Miriam and I went for a drive to my mother's family's camp, a big cabin about an hour north of the house, on a river that everybody calls a lake, because it is so wide. We took my father's truck and arrived around midnight. We went inside and got a bottle of something from the drinks cabinet and went out to the boat that was floating in the dock and drank so much that neither of us could drive back, so we stayed out all night. I felt jetlagged and very drunk. The night was full of mosquitoes, the air smelled of rotten fish and creosote, and I thought it was a shame my sister wasn't beautiful. I wanted a beautiful sister. The water was a little choppy, even behind the break. And the boat made thumping sounds as it rocked from side to side. I was wearing a black suit and Miriam was in a long-sleeve black dress. The seats on the boat made our clothes dusty. I put my arm around Miriam, in an attempt to be brotherly, but I stood up ten seconds later and went inside the house for something else to drink, and to go to the bathroom. I stumbled up the jetty. I went inside and found some warm beers and opened a drawer to get a bottle opener and saw a bunch of half-rusted knives. I brought one knife outside with me, a knife for gutting fish. Miriam was half-asleep when I returned, but the sight of the knife woke her up. I could see she was frightened. I sat down across from her and held the knife to my own throat. I kept it there a long time, and pressed it hard into my skin, just under my jaw at the ear. She waited. I don't remember if, at any time while I held the knife there, I truly examined the possibility of cutting my own throat, but I said something like, I am this close to knowing what awaits us, I am so close to actual proof, can you imagine it? She stopped being frightened and said that if the world were ending in an hour, if everybody knew the end was coming, there wouldn't be a context to place my sincerity. For a moment, I thought it would be interesting to see what she would say about sincerity if I held the knife to her throat, but I threw it in the water instead, drank from my beer, lay back, and said, Yes, it would be strange, all right. Miriam climbed beside me on the cushion and said that she would give me a tearful good-bye anyway, even if the end was coming. We slept. I awoke to something strange and wonderful—I can still hardly believe it. We were moving. We were moving across the lake, the engine was whizzing and the boat was rising and falling. I couldn't understand how I hadn't woken up sooner. There was a bright orange morning light all over the sky, and a solid, warm, humid breeze. I was lying on my back at the front of the boat, looking aft, and Miriam, now only in her underwear, was driving the boat, sitting at the wheel and motoring upstream. There was a great stench of water. The sun was just above the horizon, above the trees that lined the shore in every direction. It was already hot. It was already semi-unbearable. I took my suit off, then my shirt and socks, then my watch. I undressed down to my boxer shorts. Then it felt fine. Miriam stopped the boat and dropped the anchor, and we swam for a little while in the brown and opaque water, water that could have been seven or fifty feet deep. When we climbed back in and sat down to dry ourselves in the sunlight, Miriam said, I dislike everything about this place. I dislike the heat. I dislike the smell. I dislike the food. I dislike the mosquitoes. I dislike the people. I dislike the way people talk. I dislike the way I talk. I dislike what people think. I dislike what they buy. I dislike the way they drive. I dislike what they believe. A few minutes later, I said, Do you think I'd like Berlin? She was lying down with her eyes closed, yawning a lot. I poked her. She said, Don't you like London? I do, I said, but I only want to stay there for a few more years, I don't want to be in London all my life, plus if I lived in Berlin, and you moved there, we'd be in the same city. She yawned and said, That might be nice, yes. Then she dozed off. I got behind the wheel and drove back to the camp. Miriam lay still the whole way, with her eyes closed. I do not know if I stared at her that morning, but now, in my memory, I stare at her. She was slender and a little bit muscular, with a muscular stomach. She was pale. She had small breasts and a slightly protruding breastbone. She had long fingers, bony elbows, and arched feet. She needed to gain weight. Her sleeping body trembled on the cushion while the boat surfed the choppy water, and convulsed when we hit a big wave—the river was starting to fill with other boats, water-skiers, jet skis, pontoon boats, and so on. And in the airport, now, I look up and down the columns of cities, trying to figure out a pattern for the cancellations, and the unintended side effect of this is that I keep imagining myself asking Miriam if I'd like these cities, too. Do you think I'd like Warsaw? Do you think I'd like Bucharest? Do you think I'd like Oslo? Do you think I'd like Prague? Do you think I'd like Abu Dhabi? Do you think I'd like Kiev? Do you think I'd like Paris? Do you think I'd like Barcelona? Do you think I'd like Rome? Do you think I'd like Cairo? Do you think I'd like Athens? Do you think I'd like Lilongwe? Do you think I'd like Moscow? Do you think I'd like Riga? Do you think I'd like Istanbul? Do you think I'd like Dar es Salaam? Do you think I'd like Amsterdam? And the territory of my disappointment grows, like the outer boundaries of an empire on a map.

I docked the boat, we put away our empty bottles, and we drove my father's truck slowly back home, in heat that was abominable, and which I sometimes think I can actually feel in my memory. When we got home, Miriam slept a little more, then spent the afternoon and evening putting all her keepsakes from childhood in boxes and carrying her boxes to the street. My father and I observed this and said nothing. She left the next day. She went to visit a friend in Arizona. I think she lived in Arizona for six months. I don't know where she went after Arizona. Maybe straight to Berlin. Maybe somewhere else first. It would be several years before I saw her again. We let the garbagemen load her stuff into a truck and haul it away. Right up until the moment they did so, I believed that I, or my father and I, would run out to the street and rescue everything. But as soon as they left with the boxes, I immediately started packing my own things in boxes, and eventually I took them out to the street. I stayed there for two more weeks. My father left after three or four days, back to California to catch up on a year's worth of falling behind, or simply to be busy with small, achievable tasks. The grieving I'd planned for never took place. And I was in the house on my own. None of my friends from childhood remained, except those I didn't want to see ever again. The people I might have liked to meet had moved to New York, Chicago, Los Angeles, for work. So I went to bars on my own, said nothing to anybody, had a single drink and departed. I jogged. I drove around, aimlessly. I watched a lot of television. Most of those people who left for bigger cities eventually started coming back to raise children, and on subsequent trips home I ran into them and caught up. They had changed. They had become people I didn't have anything to say to. They often asked about Miriam, and though I never said it, I often felt like telling them that Miriam was the only one who had the courage not to come back, not to wonder what life would have been like if she'd stayed. Some of these people have children in high school now, children who drive cars. They returned from New York, from Chicago and Los Angeles, for quality of life, for values—Southern values, values of the suburbs and small towns—big lawns, big houses, interstates, a slower pace, parking lots, large dogs, family, mellifluous accents, polite neighbors, a refuge from variety and risk, and a shared contempt for impiety, for which the great cities were citadels.

My father had decided that cycling in cold or wet weather at my age was proof that I was breaking down, and the way he dealt with this was to say to me, over and over again, Are you crazy? Take the underground! They come every three minutes! But I didn't want to take the underground. I did not want to take any public transportation. I did, at times, watch people go in and out of underground stations. I stood at the top and watched foot traffic. It wasn't that I thought it was especially compelling to watch Berliners, it was how few of them there always were. Even at its most frenetic, Berlin always struck me as quiet, slow, and unmotivated. It seemed half-vaporized. Unless there was construction, I never saw a traffic jam. I never once witnessed a wave of people on their way to, or on their way home from, work. My father said he always got a free seat, or at least a healthy bit of space to stand, in the underground. I asked Trish why this was so. I knew Berlin had high unemployment, but even a city with high unemployment ought to have human congestion at nine a.m. and five p.m., if it has four or five million inhabitants. We were sitting in a café near our hotel when I asked this, coincidentally it was about nine in the morning and the streets were empty, except for a few fathers taking children to kindergarten on bicycles, heavily bundled up, skidding around the corner of a slippery and cold street. Maybe, now and again, someone rode by with a satchel that suggested a day of work lay ahead of them. The question made Trish unhappy. She hadn't spoken much about her husband. I suppose I had begun to think that she didn't much care for him, or that

GREG BAXTER

she didn't mind that he had gone. Her husband hated Berlin, she
said. He really hated it. He hadn't ever been unemployed, she
said, and for two years here he couldn't find work. He'd quit his
career to come with her. There was no other way to stay together.
And there simply were no jobs for him in Berlin. He took German
lessons, but they were expensive, and after a while he refused
to spend money if he was not making any, even though Trish
got a spousal allowance and money wasn't a problem, and even
though the State Department contributed to the costs of lessons
for spouses. He never met anybody and didn't go out, and slowly
he started going a little crazy. We would, later that day, or perhaps it was the next day, go visit Trish's place. It was up on a hill,
on the top floor of a renovated old building—a converted and
completely modernized attic that was large and airy—and it had
a glass wall on the south side, so you could see all of the city. It
felt vast. It had sloped white ceilings, full of skylights. The place
was full of light. And it was mostly empty. It had three bedrooms,
so the husband had an office. My father and Trish went to the
kitchen, where she showed him her small wine collection. I went
inside the husband's office. Beside his desk was a large window
looking west, over a small street and another tall building, though
the building across the street didn't have a penthouse conver-
sion, nor did any of the others I could see from that window. This
must have added, I felt, to his sense of disconnection—his palace
overlooking the exotic-ordinary. Mostly, I could tell, he spent his
time in the office to teach himself German and apply for jobs,
or grow tired of the fact that no jobs existed for him in Berlin,
or simply sorrow over the decision to move there with her. For
two whole years, she said—back at the café, before we visited her
apartment—he was unemployed, and this made him really de-

pressed. She was about to say something else, but she stopped herself. She looked up and saw, presumably, the two of us listening very intently to her and realized that telling my father all this was one thing but telling me was something else entirely. Trish had a big sitting room, a dining room, plus a room that was about the size of the sitting room and dining room combined, and in it was a rented piano. When I saw that piano, I immediately beheld the husband's madness, and I sat there, upon the bench, as he must have sat, and I played one low note over and over and over until Trish and my father came into the room with glasses of wine and my father asked, What are you doing? The room was big enough for a nicely sized cocktail party. I suspected that if there had been any, Trish's husband spent them all either on the terrace, smoking cigarettes, if he smoked, or down the street at a bar, reading a book or a magazine. I like to think I'd be the kind of person who, in a situation like that of Trish's husband, would learn how to play the piano, go for walks in snowy parks, or, in summer, swim in outdoor pools, put a towel down in the grass, and read *The Iliad*. But who knows. Anyway, the husband has found work in Munich. He now lives in a small apartment, and Trish has been spending most weekends there. In Munich, I assume, everyone goes to work at nine, the streets are filled with commuters, there is a common purpose.

I've never met anybody more knowledgeable about the world right now, politically, culturally, and economically, than Trish. It's not because she has to know it all for her job. It's because she wants to know it, because she wants a better job. Right now her work life is mostly administrative, office management, mundane consular work, visas, lost passports—drudgery, for someone of her intellect. There are also criminal cases, deaths, asylum seekers, receiving American VIPs at the airport, and sometimes they can be interesting. But she wants to be doing the very difficult work of diplomacy, she wants to be involved in crises, and take phone calls in the night, possibly work with spies, or become one. So, in addition to her administrative duties, she makes sure she is up to date and knowledgeable about everything presently happening in the world. Every morning she either writes up or reads a summary of all US-related news in the German papers, then she reads a summary of all US-related news in French papers, British papers, Chinese media, Russian media, then a summary of all news relating to the US internationally, in every jurisdiction, then a summary of all the major news stories around the globe—these are all internal reports that are available to State Department staff and other foreign services. At lunch, she watches news online. Now that her husband is in Munich, she volunteers her free weekday evenings to work cultural and diplomatic events—dinners, meetings, briefings—in order to make contacts. And she meets and talks to people who are up to date and knowledgeable about the world. She knows everything about everything, so long as it has just happened, is happening, or will happen within a month or two. There is not a single timely topic of discussion that she cannot speak of thoroughly. It is truly intimidating. The only way to surprise her, or tell her something she doesn't already know, is to talk about something trivial or useless, like a story about billionaires who want to travel to the moon. She is not all that interested in the history of places that are not important to her, but if she can be convinced that information will deepen her understanding of current events, she will learn. She knew hardly anything about pre-twentieth-century European history, but when she and my father talked, she listened attentively, and while we were away, she got my father's history of the Middle Ages overnighted to her from the US and read it in a few days. I overheard them discussing it at times during that last week. I could tell my father was grateful.

Two days after I rearranged and cleaned Miriam's apartment, I returned. I went, again, by bicycle. It was a wet day, so the ride was sloshy and slow, I got sprayed by a few cars, crashed through countless deep puddles, and my pants, by the time I arrived, were not only soaking wet but spotted with oily, superblack gunk. I hitched my bike to a lamppost. My hands were numb, inside the gloves. My legs felt numb, because my pants were wet. But I also felt that pleasant energy you get after steady physical exertion. I looked up at Miriam's windows. The apartment wasn't her first apartment in Berlin, but she had lived there almost fifteen years.

I went inside, checked for mail—there was none—walked up the steps, walked along the corridor. The building was quiet. It was clean. It smelled a little like bleach and a little like wet cement. From the outside, it looked like a dump without heat or water or electricity, and where at night you might have to light candles to read or write. But on the inside it was like anywhere else.

When I put the key in the lock of Miriam's door and turned it, I heard some heavy steps, then Otis appeared, first just his head, then he stepped down and out and put his hands in his pockets.

Hi, Otis, I said.

Hey, he said.

I knew, or thought I knew, what he wanted, but I didn't understand his impatience, unless he simply didn't trust me.

I've just arrived, I said.

I saw you on the street. You're still riding your bike.

It's getting warmer, I said. You want to come in?

I opened the door and he squeezed his shoulders together and walked in with his head down and arms pressed into his sides. I followed him. It still smelled strongly of the cleaning agents I had used in the bathroom. And I had forgotten just how drastically I had altered her apartment. The piles of her things were vaguely equidistant from each other. I took my coat off and threw it on the floor in the corner, then I took off my hat and threw it on the dining table, then I threw the keys on the dining table. I had stacked the chairs up against the wall, so I had to unstack one to sit on. Otis was rolling up a cigarette, and when he was finished he asked, Is it okay to smoke? I said, No. But I don't think he was consciously conversing with me, because he lit his cigarette any-way and said, Thanks. He walked to the pile of books and knelt down. He squinted down into it, then he turned his head side-ways so he could read the spines. Miriam had a couple hundred books. Otis asked me if I'd gone through them. I said I hadn't, I'd just thrown them into the pile. That was the truth. Otis dug his hand in deep, grasped a book, and tried to pull it out without dis-turbing the pile, but the pile toppled and the books scattered on the floor, and Otis said, Sorry.

Is that one of yours? I asked.

Yep, he said.

How did your books end up here in the first place?

Like I said, it's not just books, he said. A lot of the stuff here belongs to me.

Well, I said, how did your stuff end up here?

I regretted asking it, because it was obvious. And if I had ever come to visit Miriam, I would not have had to ask. So I said, Never mind. Otis grabbed another book. He seemed delighted to see it. Then another. A little stack began beside him. I started to feel irritated, so I said, My father wants to ship all this stuff back to the States.

Oh yeah? asked Otis.

Yep, I said.

My father, of course, didn't care. He hadn't cared enough to save her things twenty years ago, and he had no connection to the woman Miriam had become, or the things she possessed. My father had needed to see her apartment, but only once, and not for any reason that he or I could define. Nor could I define the cause of my compulsion to be around Miriam's things, or to organize them into stacks, or to fret over their destinies. I said, Did you give any more thought to getting Miriam's friends together for a drink? He got up and moved to another stack, and another, and another, until he saw a lamp, a really nice antique lamp, and he pulled out the lamp, again, quite delighted with himself. Then he said, It'll cost a lot to ship all this stuff, and the appliances won't work in the States. I repeated my question about the drinks and Otis looked at me, realizing I had changed the subject, and that the new subject and the old subject were connected. Not yet, he said.

I was about to stand up and start going through a stack or two when my phone rang. It was the senior marketing manager from the aerospace firm. Her name was Chris. She first expressed her condolences, saying that she had heard the news about a death in my family. I sat down on the chair. I thanked her, and I said what I guessed she would expect me to say, which was that it was a difficult time but we were coping. Very good, she said, you should take as long as you need. Thank you, I said, I really appreciate that.

I looked up at the ceiling. It was badly stained from cigarette smoke. It was brown-gray and the stains were in streaks, as though she always sat, when she smoked, in the same three or four places, and the path her smoke made on its way upward from the ends of her cigarettes and from her nose and mouth was always the same. She would have come home, placed her keys on the table, grabbed a drink—possibly some tea, coffee, or a glass of water—and sat at the dining-room table to smoke. And after a while she would move to the couch to smoke. She read her books there and also in bed. She didn't have much else for entertainment, just the radio. Though she never did anything for very long, or anything with much determination—so that from month to month her life outside the apartment was full of inconstancy—I imagined that her rituals at home were unwavering without ever being deliberate.

I said, I won't be able to start on Monday. I'm not even in the country.

No, of course not, said Chris. Where are you?

In Berlin, I say.

Oh, she said, with some excitement, though she stopped herself from saying anything nice about Berlin.

It could be a couple of weeks, possibly a little longer.

There was a pause, which I had expected.

My sister died, I said. My father and I are in Berlin, waiting for her body to be released, then we'll fly her home and bury her. We don't know when her body will be released.

Oh, she said, this time utterly without excitement.

I'm sorry about the timing, I said.

Please don't be sorry, how horrible for you.

At that moment Otis dug a small copper ashtray from a mound

of small household items and stamped his cigarette out in it. Then he grabbed something else from that mound—a red-glass candleholder—and placed it behind him. Then he seemed to go about searching for the other candleholder in the set.

When I started my business, I often contrived to take important telephone calls at inconvenient times. I liked the idea of being interrupted, and I liked to be seen to be interrupted, so I made sure a lot of calls came when I knew I'd be at the gym. My phone would ring, I'd slow my treadmill down and talk into the microphone of my headphones. I'd stop doing sit-ups, wipe my face off with a towel, and speak. I'd put the weights back on the rack and sit hunched on a bench, trying to catch my breath. I'd also schedule calls during chamber of commerce events, or business lunches. I was constantly looking for new clients. The search for clients was always my priority. I hoped I would finally get too much work and have to hire somebody. Sometimes potential clients offered me a full-time, salaried job. Sometimes the pay was very good, and I would spend a couple of days trying to decide whether to go for the job, sometimes agonizingly. I'd lie in bed and visualize my work routine the next day—at my supposed consultancy gig, the firm I'd left as an employee, only to return as a consultant—and all the days I could foresee, and of course I knew that the difference between what I did as a consultant and what I would be doing as a salaried employee was slight. But I was more comfortable as an outsider. I valued the degree of distance I could maintain from a client that I could not insist on from an employer, a distance that enforced cordiality and respect and also a fear of confrontation—so if I wanted to go out and stand on a bridge on a sunny day and watch ducks, I could say, I'm going out for a bit, without somebody saying, Where are you going? I also didn't want people to thank me for working. I didn't care if they were personally happy with me. I didn't want a boss to knock on the door of my office, or the desk at my cubicle, and say, Good work on the such and such, or, Thanks for working late these last couple of months. I didn't want to go for drinks with colleagues and celebrate anything. And as I'd lie in bed, thinking these things, I would tell myself, Your freedom only exists so long as you operate entirely within the parameters of what's expected of you, you take shit from people anyway, you can't go stand on bridges and watch ducks, people have called you in to tell you that they must have miscommunicated their wishes because your work was way off, and you hated them, then they came by later and said, Great work on the such and such, and you cherished the reinforcement, and you found yourself out with people from the office having a drink and it wasn't so bad. So I'd think, Take the job, work for five years, then try your own business again. And I'd meet them. I'd make an effort. We'd sit down together in a room with them on one side of a table and me on the other. There'd be water, coffee, some cookies. They'd introduce themselves, they'd explain what they did, I'd tell them about the work that I'd done. The following exchange always took place—

You left your old firm.

That's right. To start my own business.

But you're back with them now.

As a consultant.

Are you willing to work here as a full-time employee?

Yes, I think this is a unique opportunity.

Why?

And I'd tell them, but during my explanation of what it was that I liked so much about the opportunity, a certain gloom always came upon me. I'd run out of energy to make eye contact. I'd look at my hands. I'd yawn. I'd start with ebullience and expansiveness, with wit and a sense of purpose, and with each sentence I seemed to tire myself out, as though I were trying to climb the circular steps of an inconceivably tall tower. The fatigue began before I noticed it, and when I did notice it, I always tried to wrap up my speech as soon as possible. After that, we'd go through other questions and scenarios. But I'd already talked myself out of it. I loved that moment—the moment I knew I was going to say no. It was like stopping, turning around, and coming down the stairway of the tower. I felt revived, and generally the interviews went exceedingly well after that, and though I'd get some questions that annoyed me or felt insulting, or outdated, I'd stay engaged, stay polite, because I knew that when I called them to tell them that I couldn't take the position because my heart was still in my business, I would add, Please keep me in mind for the future.

I finally stopped interviewing for full-time positions.

We can set you up to work remotely, said Chris. You can start when you feel ready, from anywhere, and join us here when it's appropriate.

Absolutely, I said, that's perfect, let's do that as soon as possible.

Perfect, she said, and I was glad to have made her happy, except that I had no energy to work, I had no ideas and I had no enthusiasm. Otis, at that moment, lit another cigarette as he found something else that was either his or that reminded him of Miriam, warmly, or that he figured was worth some money.

Let us know if we can do anything else for you, said Chris.

I sure will.

I could have ended the conversation there. There was nothing else to say. In a week they'd have me set up remotely and I'd be sitting in a café somewhere in Berlin, or in the living room of my father's house, working on a computer. But I also knew that I could not possibly begin work in a week. I felt then, standing in Miriam's apartment, that I might never work again, or I might at least leave marketing. So I said, She starved to death. And I said that I was standing in her apartment, sifting through the debris of her life with some guy named Otis, who probably, at one time, was her boyfriend, and didn't even have the fucking decency to move out of her building after they split up. Chris was silent. I imagined her going immediately to the director and suggesting they find a way to cancel the contract. So I apologized and hurriedly got off the phone.

I went back to wander among the stacks of Miriam's possessions. Not everything was in an orderly stack, or separated into uncontaminated categories, though my mind keeps trying to remember it that way. There was the couch, which I had turned on its end and surrounded with rolled-up rugs. There were tall standing lamps I had gathered and stood in a crowded circle, and they looked a little bit like brass and chrome flamingos. There was the wardrobe and the sideboard and the squat drinks cabinet, and I had pushed them close together. Close together, it was easy to see how fine these pieces of furniture really were. I thought it was telling that Otis wasn't saying anything about them, or going near them. I assumed it was because he wanted them the most. It was fifties furniture, what was called Contemporary in the fifties. And they were original. And as I saw how conspicuously Otis ignored them, how transparently little attention he was paying them, the three pieces assumed a great weight in my thoughts, and I felt that I had better protect or destroy them, or whatever it took to make sure Otis could not get his hands on them. Miriam's wardrobe and sideboard and cabinet were not in perfect condition, but all the brass knobs and handles were original, the keys were original, the glass was original, and the panels were original. They needed some oil, but they weren't chipped anywhere. They were just the things a young family might spend a month's salary on in an antiques store. I knelt down by the pile of books. She had a huge variety of books, a variety that, all by itself, dispelled any fear that she had lived a life of imaginative surrender. I opened one of them and saw that she had made notes throughout the margins, in pencil. I opened another. It was the same. And another. Mostly these notes were one-word or brief responses to passages she'd underlined, but also, in the bottom and top margins, sometimes, the passages themselves, transcribed in her own handwriting. At first I couldn't believe my luck. The first day I arrived, I had gone superficially through drawers and shoeboxes looking for notebooks, diaries, anything that might have contained her everyday thoughts. All I could find were meaningless scribbles on bits of paper, to-do lists, numbers, addresses. I was not looking for an answer to the cause of her death, because I didn't believe such a thing could exist, but I felt as though it would be the closest thing possible to having a conversation with her. I hadn't looked inside the books because I never wrote anything inside books, in fact I was sure I had told her, when we were young, that she was not to write in books. But there it was—the thing I sought, a record—contained within her disordered library. But then the feeling of luck was supplanted by distress, because the notes were self-evidently too multitudinous to achieve shape—either in isolation each note would imply its own incompleteness or in the wholeness of them would be torrential white noise, and anything between was an illusion. I also felt distress because her library, though it appeared disarranged, might actually have had some structure, and in my haste and in my presumptuousness I had mishandled it, and erased it. And I felt distress because I could already see that the discovery was lost. Otis had removed some of the books and whatever he did not take we would leave here. We had the money to ship them, of course, but we had already let her discard her things once, and to act, now, as though we were the kind of people who would unbox them at home and go through them was only going to feed our desire to put off, or possibly delay forever, an appreciation of her death. I knew instantly that I wasn't even going to tell my father I had found them.

Otis had a long dress in his arms, and he was holding it high. He examined it and decided he liked it, and he put it in a pile behind him. The mound of clothes behind him was bigger than the one in front of him. I also saw that he had taken all her jewelry. It was in a small mound by his feet. Hold on with that stuff, I said. He stopped and put his hands on his knees. I said, I just want to make sure there's nothing that belongs to our mother. He reacted in a way I hadn't expected, which was to ignore me and continue, and I reacted to him in a way I didn't expect, which was to do nothing at all, to simply pretend I hadn't spoken. I went back to reading. Otis kept separating out the things he wanted. I was building up the courage to demand that he stop—but that meant preparing for the possibility that I would have to physically stop him, and I hadn't had a physical confrontation since I was a teenager. Then Otis stood. He held another dress up by its hanger. It was a dark spring green. It, too, seemed from the fifties.

Otis said, This is the dress she got married in. Married? I said. He said, It was a fake marriage, he was gay. Oh, I said. But it was a nice day, we had a big party, said Otis, and Miriam was really happy. I felt a little disarmed by the fact he had said something affectionate about Miriam, and I asked, Have you asked him to meet us for drinks? Otis said, I think he moved to Boston about ten years ago, or Portland. I said it would have been nice to have the husband around for a drink, even a fake husband.

I thought he was going to give me the dress. I nearly put my arms out to receive it. But he turned as if to place the dress in the pile of clothes behind him and I said, Hey, wait. He stopped. Do you think we could have that? I asked.

Have what?

Obviously the dress.

He said, If I hadn't told you what it was, you wouldn't care. But you did tell me, I said, why did you tell me? He held it out and up in front of me and said, What are you going to do with it? I was about to say we could bury it with her, then I remembered the wedding wasn't real, and I had no answer, except to say something sentimental, and for many reasons saying something sentimental about wanting to save that dress was unthinkable. I said, Listen, I have to go, I need to lock up.

Right now?

Right this minute, sorry.

Otis was reluctant to go, he moved directly in between me and the things he'd set aside behind him, so I said, Take whatever you can grab now and I'll let you know when I'm coming back so you can get the rest. He didn't believe me so I said, Take the dress now if you want, take anything you can carry out of here. I moved away and gave him a little bit of space. He didn't have a bag with him, so I went and got a bag of my own and handed it to him, and when I handed it to him I looked down at his stack of books, fifty at least, and all of which were nice hardbacks, and saw my father's book. I said, That's my dad's book. He said nothing. Now that I knew that Miriam had made notes in her books, I bent down to reach for it. Otis bent down, too, as though to stop me. I stood up and said, You cannot have that book, Otis, I'm sorry. He said, I was just going to get it for you. He picked it up and opened it and a yellow page of tablet paper came out. He gave me the book but he held on to the piece of paper. Give me the piece of paper, I said. He was reading it. I said, Give me the piece of paper, Otis. I didn't want him to read it, I didn't want him to touch it. So I grabbed it and yanked it from him, and it ripped in half. He immediately gave me back the other half, and gave me a look that said the violence hadn't been necessary. Sorry, I said. He stood and waited for me to look at the piece of paper, but I wouldn't look at it, not while he was in the room. He grabbed some books and some clothes but for some reason he left the jewelry, and I suspected it was because he thought I might confront him over that, too. Anyway, he left. I walked over to the table and placed the two pieces of paper back together again. It was the first page of a letter written by my father to Miriam. I'd never received a letter from him, but that was because, I assumed, we spoke on the telephone, and I visited. I remembered I had seen some Scotch tape around, I went to get it, I came back and taped the letter up. I taped it so thoroughly that it looked laminated. I folded it up and put it in my back pocket. I got the book and went through it, to see if there were any other pages of the letter in it, but there weren't. And there weren't any notes in the margins, either. I closed the book and put it in a bag. It was a big hardback, a thousand pages long, and on the back flap it had a photo of my father that was outdated even at the time. The picture is of a man my age now. It's fuzzy, he's wearing a suit, his hair is brown, and he's standing in front of the sea. It's clearly not a professional photo, he just found a photo of himself he liked and used it. My mother had been alive when the photo was taken.

I didn't take anything with me but the book and the letter. I had a feeling that he'd want to know immediately about this, about the fact that she'd kept the book all these years, and I was excited about being able to hand it to him. I felt as though my time here, from his point of view, would finally be justified. But then I did something that completely contradicted this excitement. I brought the book downstairs and put it in the basket on the front of my bicycle. It was still wet, still chilly. The roads and sidewalks were full of puddles. The roadsides were muddy. When I felt I had got far enough away from Miriam's apartment—I guess I was about halfway between her part of town and ours—I got off my bike, found a spot of wintery, wet muck, and threw the book into it. Then I got back on the bike and rode to our hotel. I walked in and the lady at reception informed me that I'd checked out. I've checked out? I asked. That's right, she said. Am I leaving town? I asked. She didn't have an answer, so I telephoned Trish and she told me the woman was supposed to give me a message saying that my father had had my things moved—later I would learn that it had been done by an embassy intern—to a new place, an apartment he'd rented. So I went straight there. It was the penthouse apartment of a building of luxury, boutique rental apartments. The penthouse had a rooftop terrace that was a hundred yards long and fifty yards wide. You could see everything from it. Every inch of horizon. We had three bedrooms and four flat-screen televisions. Though I didn't know it yet, we were going to rent a car in two days and get away, but we would keep the apartment, we would just leave it empty and return to it.

I don't have the letter anymore. I don't remember when or how I lost it. I folded it up and carried it around with me everywhere, for a few days. If I had a quiet moment, I pulled it out and read it. Then one morning it wasn't there. I checked under the driver's seat of our rental car. I checked the room I slept in. I checked all my pockets. I even checked the trash can on the street, where I had thrown away some fast food the previous night. But it was gone. I thought, for a moment, that my father might have found it, but if he had, I'd have known, he'd have asked me immediately about it.

My father's letter had been written in black fountain-pen ink on yellow lined paper. He'd obviously wanted her to have the book, and he must have felt he ought to send it himself, and if he were going to do so, he'd have to write a letter to go with it. Or, just as plausibly, he'd been wanting to send Miriam a thoughtful letter since she left, and the book just gave him an opportunity to be in touch. I considered the remote possibility that he had finished his book for this reason only. His letter began with a few lines about hoping that she is well and that she'll find enclosed the book he'd been working on for years, which turned out to be a little redundant now that a similar book on the same subject had come out. At the time he wrote the letter, I had just been there to visit him, because even though he'd made nothing of it, I thought it would be nice to visit him around the time of publication, point out the good reviews and shield him from the negative ones. He writes, Your brother was here to see the book off and protect me from depression, I guess, but now he's gone and the house is very quiet again except for the television, which I have no interest in apart from checking the weather and watching a little bit of golf. And I walk around wondering why I'm not back at work. I live in one room of the house, and I sleep in another. I walk through the other rooms to make sure everything is as it was. I took the semester off and used the book as an excuse, but I find that I'm terribly sad to be here without you in some proximity, without seeing you from time to time. I've missed you profoundly these last years and am beginning to wonder if I'll see you again, or if you've simply decided to leave us, in which case it's like a whole new death for me to come to terms with, but it is much more difficult to bear, not only because I know you're alive in some other place, but that I fear that resentment for me has sent you there. I can see that my great failings in life were with my mother, your mother, and you, and I don't know how to account for the expectations of you all that I allowed myself to have. I seem to have sent them to death here and I understand why you might have wanted to escape that. I respect your silence and your distance but I also hope it doesn't last forever. I wonder if you have everything you need in your apartment. I wonder if you could use a washing machine or a new refrigerator. I wonder if you have proper heating, and I'd be happy to get you some heaters. If it adds to your electricity bill, I'm happy to contribute there, too. I wonder if you've found someone there, a companion. I hope you'd contact your brother for help if you wouldn't contact me.

I make my way across the terminal. It takes a long time, but at last I find them, Trish and my father, sitting side by side in soft red chairs, surrounded by the historical exhibit Trish mentioned in her text message. Flights are departing regularly now, but there have also been a lot of cancellations, and people are trying to get

119

on new flights, and this has created a specific kind of mayhem that is equal parts confusion, joy, resentment, rage, incredulity, and Schadenfreude. I'm starting to feel tiny panic attacks. I'm starting to feel that I simply cannot wait any longer. I am starting to feel that waiting is impossible, that it could cause death. I have bought myself and my father a handful of magazines—news and science and so forth—but I am too fatigued, too distracted by fatigue and hunger and nausea, to read. I don't feel up to conversation, either. I have a lot of music on my phone, and somewhere I have headphones, but I can't think of anything I want to listen to. I could not possibly work, or even think about work. My father looks like he could wait awhile longer—he looks like somebody who is starting to not want to leave. There are several red chairs around them. The chairs are situated in pairs, and some pairs are back-to-back, and some are side-to-side. Trish is talking. My father has his arms crossed and his head down, and he nods every now and again, as he does when he is, or when he wants you to think he is, listening. The space they have found is a large oval surrounded by high glass walls and a glass ceiling. At the very center are the chairs, the arrangement of which seems to want to replicate the irregularity of real contemplation—so that travelers, I guess, can properly think about whatever is being exhibited. Around the chairs is the oval arrangement of panels, very much like, or exactly like, the obelisks that contain advertisements throughout the rest of the terminal. From somewhere, classical music is playing. Beyond the space is the tunnel to the gates that many of the US and other long-haul flights depart from. There aren't many facilities beyond the tunnel. Once the gate is announced, I presume we'll go, we'll wait the last hour or two at the gate, we'll never see this part of Munich Airport again.

I stop in front of Trish and my father. They barely look up. Maybe they saw me coming. I've interrupted them, and I cause a prolonged and uncomfortable silence, until my father finally says, My God, you're wearing sunglasses. While he says this, he has to hold his hand above his eyes to shade them from the light, and squint. I ran into an old acquaintance from London, I say.

You feeling better? my father asks.

A bit, I say.

Who was the acquaintance?

A sort of ex-husband of a woman who was friends with my ex, I say.

Complicated, says my father.

My father does not look well, now that I see him close up. He is perspiring, and he has no color at all. Trish looks tired. My father is slightly swallowed by his chair, but Trish commands hers.

You took a long time to get here, my father says.

It's turned crazy, I say. You don't want to go where I came from.

Did you eat? asks Trish.

I had a little something. Am I still green?

A little, she says.

I look at my father and say, You don't look great, either, have you eaten?

I think I have to go to the bathroom, he says.

He tries to get up. My legs, he says. Trish stands and reaches out to him. I say, I've got him.

I've got him, she says. She takes his hand in one hand. He grasps her shoulder, and she steadies his arm. My legs, he says, I can hardly move them. You need to eat something, she says. Maybe, he says. Come on, she says. I can take him, I say. Could you watch my bag? she says. I sit in the seat my father has been occupying. Trish's bag occupies the seat next to me. I can walk now, says my father. Trish lets him go, but when he wobbles a little bit, she gently takes his elbow in her hand and escorts him away. They move at a slow pace, a very slow pace, a shuffle, and my father is unusually stiff. I think I know what the stiffness is about, but I do not want to think about it, I don't have the constitution for it. But trying not to think about it becomes a kind of metaphor for what it actually, most likely, is, and I suddenly grow hot, I am boiling. The light turns sickly. I start to shake. My mouth starts to water. A sickness that feels a little like nostalgia sets in. Then I begin to see the words I am thinking, individual words, and they become repulsive. A word like blue becomes repulsive. A word like airport. Their existence is depressing. I think about listening to music—surely music is the escape, but the sheer amount of new words I would have to think in order to find my headphones is too daunting, and anyway music has its own constraints, and then I realize how many words it has taken to think all that I have just been thinking. I try to count down from five, out loud, like they tell women giving birth to do. But out loud the words are even more repulsive. Then it occurs to me that I am totally contained, that I am right now utterly contained in a medium of symbols with functions or malfunctions, and no amount of rhetorical hyperactivity or adornment will release me, and there is also no language only I can understand—there is no privacy in which to hide. Now I am going to throw up. Once the mouth starts watering, really that's it. It's inevitable. A sense of peace accompanies the surrender. I throw the magazines out of the bag and stick my face in it and vomit. The bread comes up. Then I retch about ten times, but nothing comes out. Then I sip from a bottle of water, gargle, and spit the water into the bag.

Then I tie the bag up. People have turned to stare at me. They wait until they are satisfied I'm finished, and turn back around. I can vomit very quietly, and be still. Poor Dad, I think, because I am past the pain now, and I feel wonderful. I feel like I could float. I feel like I've been swimming outdoors. There is something strange about the pain you go through from not eating, a pain that is everywhere in your body, so that when you pass through it, life feels unreal for a moment. Trish and my father have almost reached the restroom. My father is walking on his own. Trish watches him enter, waits for a moment, and begins to head back to me. She gives me an understated thumbs-up.

My marriage ended thirteen years ago, and I've only had two relationships since then, both of them short-lived—one at the beginning of that time, and one recently. The one in the beginning was my ex-wife's old friend, whom I saw when I lived with the artist in Nunhead. For a little while after my marriage ended, I kept running into my wife's friends, or our old friends, though it was understood that my wife would keep them and I would move on. I guess I was habitually, or automatically, traveling old paths. The conversations I had with these people were always affectionate, and we were sorrowful that there wasn't anything to do in these situations but naturally grow apart and forget each other. It was strange to be feeling such affection for a life that I'd come to regard with such overpowering contempt. But it seemed that, one by one, I met all those old friends out somewhere, typically in places I had seen them before, and had to have a couple of drinks to say farewell. My wife was saying nothing harmful about me to these people, and I was saying nothing harmful about her to them, either. For my part, I simply couldn't speak of her. I think I just wished she had died. So, just as people had mistakenly considered us a happy couple when we were married because they thought we had such a quiet, confident way of communicating, they mistook our reluctance to speak ill of each other as a sign that things had ended amiably. In fact they had ended as unpleasantly as possible. The only person I ever told about the unpleasantness was the old friend of my wife's, a woman I had never, at least while I was married, got along with, partly because I assumed we had nothing in common. Three or four months after the end of my marriage, I saw her out one night. She was drunk. She was a heavy drinker. I said hello and she started accusing me of ruining her friend's life, of stealing her money, of ending the good days we'd all been enjoying. Now everybody would sober up, so to speak. Now everyone would either break up or have kids. There weren't going to be any more parties. Nobody would ever be happy again. She was completely serious. I said, Steal her money? She said, Oh, never mind. So I took the time to explain very carefully just how wrong things had gone. She kept saying, Stop, you're depressing me even more. But I knew I wasn't going to tell anybody else, so I wanted to get it all out. By the end she was just standing there, by the bar, speechless. We had a few more drinks together and we started kissing and she said, sort of pleased with herself, This is the most evil thing I've ever done. The next morning I woke up in her bed and she was sitting on a chair on the other side of the room looking at me. You've got to go, she said, and you've got to promise to say nothing about this, ever. I said, Don't panic, I'm not telling anybody. She said, But you have to go, my flatmates will be awake soon. I asked, What time is it? It's five-thirty, she said. I got my things and left, but not before I said something that completely surprised both her and me, which was, Ever since I first set eyes on you, I've fantasized about this, I have thought of you every day since we first met. She was bleary-eyed and tired, but what I said woke her and made her face astonished, bewildered, and curiously softened. I said, Please don't remember this always as a mistake. When I left her building and found myself walking down the road I thought, What an odd, totally compelling, and seemingly truthful thing to say. Was I in love? I wondered. Although I'd slept very little, and although I was suffering from a headache and a stomachache from the booze, I was in an ecstatic mood. I felt shot through by a kind of divinity. I almost went to the bar of a hotel and asked for a whiskey, which I would drink over the course of an hour while reminding myself all this was real, it had *happened*, that a few down years had been wiped out by a night. But I had to hurry home to shower and change before work. I got a coffee. The city was awakening. It was summer, so it was already bright. Every time I crossed the street, the volume of pedestrians around me, also crossing, seemed to double. It was invigorating. At Victoria Station, where the announcements blared out in the high empty space above the trains, I was going against the grain so I got jostled and looked at. But it felt like the best morning of my life so I didn't care. I got a train to Nunhead. I looked at the time and realized that if everything went as fast as possible, I'd still arrive at work late. So I decided to relax and try not to think about work. The train from Victoria to Nunhead at seven in the morning is of course completely deserted—going the opposite direction at that time it is miserably congested. So I got a seat in an empty car, by the window, and as we started to move I felt a rapturous, sad relief that I was starting over, from that moment, that I had come to Europe for this reason, to feel as though I had been born without a past, that I had come from nowhere and knew nobody, there was nobody to tell good news or bad news, there was no reason to behave one way or another. The view on either side of the tracks seemed to me so beautifully distant from the place where I was born, which seemed to me, at that moment, destroyed, obliterated, by the power of my desire to never see it again. The woman and I began to see each other. We met all over London, in pubs and restaurants. Places we wouldn't otherwise eat or drink in. But we also went away in order to be fearlessly together and anonymous. We flew to Paris, Lisbon, Riga, and Reykjavik. We drove to Bath and the Lake District. We stayed in nice hotels. I didn't care that the ghost of my old relationship was following so closely, that it slept with us and ate breakfast with us. I didn't care that this was happening so soon. Though we never spoke of a future, I assumed the future was safe. Then one day, about seven or eight months after we'd started seeing each other, as we were walking around London after midnight, I said something to her and she started crying. There were people on the street, but not many, and they stopped to watch her. I tried to get her to stop but she fell to her knees. I tried to lift her and she struck me. What's the matter? I said. She asked me how I could treat her so badly, how I could be so cruel. I thought she was joking. Or I thought maybe she was having a psychotic episode from the drink, maybe somebody had drugged her. I asked, Did someone find out about us? But she was sobbing, and every time I tried to reach for her and lift her up, she struck at my hands. Then all at once she stopped crying and I thought she was going to say something like, Sorry about that, I must be drunk. Instead she said, I won't do it. I said, Do what? She said, I won't belong to your wretchedness. I said, My wretchedness—who says that? Just then, two policemen came by and asked her if everything was okay. She was done crying, she was composed, and she was composed because she was finished with me. She said, Everything is fine. Move along, they said, to both of us, and she said, We're not together. I was dumbfounded by her unexpected mettle and a little annoyed that I would now have to get a taxi to Nunhead. The policemen said, You heard her, move along. So I went a different direction and hailed a taxi. She really was finished with me. It was impressive. I telephoned a few times but she never picked up. I wrote to her. I was distraught. After a few weeks, I waited outside her office and waved her down. I walked over and she gave me a dispassionate smile. I asked her to meet me. I wasn't trying to win her back. I stated this from the outset. I said, Honestly, I'd like to ask for your help. She said, I've got an hour right now. I took her to a nice bar with comfortable brown couches. She had an orange juice. I drank a beer. I said, Please don't mind me saying this but you look great. She said, I haven't had a drink in a month. We spoke of nothing important for ten or fifteen minutes, then she said, What is it you want help with? I asked her to explain what it was about my behavior that caused her to call me wretched. She laughed, but then she saw that I was serious and she stopped laughing. She said, I shouldn't have broken down like I did that night, the crying was just the drink, and probably exhaustion. I should have told you like this, soberly, and somewhere like this. She said, It just became completely clear to me, even though I was drunk. The things you always say, the way you passively undermine everything, the way you dislike everything, yourself most of all, women second to yourself. She paused here to look at me, to see if I'd do or say something to undermine the accusation about women, but I did nothing, I stayed still, I had asked her a question, and if I disagreed or argued, she'd leave. She

127

said, Maybe you just hated your wife so much that you decided to hate all women, or maybe you hated women from the day you started to desire them. I don't know. But that night, our last night, I started to realize that I hated you, except I didn't hate you, or I didn't want to hate you, but you had cast this spell over me. I was sitting next to you, and I realized I couldn't stand you, I was going to have a panic attack, but this was precisely what you wanted, this was why you cast the spell, because somehow it was going to vindicate your hatred of me, which you harbored in order to validate your self-hatred. She leaned forward, grabbed a peanut from a bowl on the table between us, then added, And to escape responsibility for it. When she got up to leave, a little while later, after having tried to explain the same thing a few more times, I thanked her. She said, What will you do now? I told her that maybe I ought to just stay away from people for a while, especially women. She said, That's not the answer, that's just as bad, it won't change anything. I said, Anyway, I appreciate your time. Before she left, she said, Can I trust you won't say anything about us to anybody? I barely heard her, but I nodded—Yes, sure, of course, no, I won't say anything. She left the bar and I watched her through the window. She walked away, then turned a corner, and I thought, God, that was a strange and unreal experience. I ordered another drink—this time a double vodka—and I sat back on the comfortable brown couch and observed everybody else interacting. On one level I felt affection for all of them. I was so happy to see everybody there. I felt so relieved to be in that city, sharing that city with them. But in this affection was a curious despondency, a fatigue and hopelessness that, if I turned my mind's eye directly at it, if I stared right at the source of it, came from a realization that I was terrified, that I was trapped in this one life, that I was within time and this body, that there were no other times and no other bodies.

I liked my solitude. It wasn't total. I had plenty of human contact through work, plenty of meetings, plenty of lunches. I did a great many things on my own, in the evenings. I'd always liked classical music, so I got season tickets to the symphony. I went to the library and read, and to bookstores to hear authors talk. I went to hear lectures on just about everything. I went to the opera. I went to gallery openings. I went to the theater. I went to all kinds of festivals. Once in a while, I asked a woman out. I would go out of my way to seek women with whom I was safely incompatible, and over drinks or dinner I'd try to say things that were winning and untrue. I tried to be a little more cheerful without becoming enthusiastic, or dangerous without becoming shadowy, or dark without becoming despondent, or poignant without becoming piteous, or funny without becoming malicious. In many ways this was purely an extension of my everyday work challenges. And the success of these nights was completely measurable, and the relationships were totally disposable. Sometimes, however, the woman and I were not safely incompatible. We actually got along. I found that I liked her or I suspected that she might like me. On these occasions, I didn't try to say winning things, nor did she. We drank our drinks or ate our dinner, then walked around the city, and all the times it went this way, the woman I was with ended up taking me to a bar she used to frequent long ago, in her twenties. We didn't speak too much—our compatibility was not of the all-the-same-things-annoy-us variety, nor of the we-love-all-the-same-books-or-films variety—we drank a little bit more than we normally would, and we watched people try to communicate, express themselves, and seduce each other. In the bar to which she would take me, we often had to stand, and if we wanted to talk, we'd usually have to shout, and often the woman, who did not smoke, borrowed cigarettes off strangers, and we went out to stand in the cold night, away from the noise, while she smoked. Sometimes we separated in time for the last trains home, and other times we stayed out so late we had to get taxis. But we separated, and I wished her well, and she seemed to understand that we would never see each other again. I went home. I listened to music on my headphones—even if I was in a taxi—I stumbled around the sidewalk, I wondered whether or not to urinate in some bushes, and when I walked inside my door I made myself a gigantic pan of scrambled eggs, mixed with everything I had in the fridge. Sauerkraut, goat cheese, jam, barbecue sauce, whatever meat I had, and any vegetable that did not stink and wasn't moldy.

Trish sits down beside me. She stretches her legs out. She yawns. Then she takes out her sunglasses and puts them on, and now we are both wearing sunglasses. I say, What's your dad like?

My dad?

Yeah, your dad.

Why do you ask?

I don't know, I was just asking.

He's all right.

What does he do?

Does it matter?

Is it a secret?

He's a teacher, in high school.

He's not a history teacher, though?

He teaches algebra. And he's the football coach.

He's a disciplinarian?

You could say that.

Do you visit home much?

I go back to the States a lot, I don't go home that often.

She looks down at the bag I have tied up and left beside my feet, and the magazines I've taken out of it. Her sunglasses are extremely black, glossy, and I can see myself in them, and I can see the history exhibit that surrounds us, like Stonehenge. I stand up. It's a history exhibit about women in aviation, and it's in German, English, and French. It begins with Katharine Wright and Baroness Raymonde de Laroche, and it ends with astronauts, test pilots, and corporate leaders in the aviation and aerospace industries. There are two panels devoted entirely to German women aviators. Hanna Reitsch, I read, was a test pilot for the Luftwaffe and a protégée of Hitler. As one of the few women who broke from traditional roles in Nazi Germany, she flew the first helicopter, the piloted version of the V-1 buzz bomb, and the rocket-powered Messerschmitt Me 163. She was the first person to demonstrate a helicopter to the public. After that there is of course a panel about aviation and the Holocaust, because you cannot have an exhibit in Germany, it seems, without mentioning the Holocaust. It feels right, even though it sometimes feels unnecessary. There is also a panel that seems disconnected from the story of the exhibit, a single panel with a brief and uninformative history of Munich Airport. I decide I want to know more, so I sit down and open the Internet on my phone. I read what I find out loud to Trish. Munich Airport is just over twenty years old, I say. It's the second-busiest airport in Germany, the seventh-busiest airport in Europe, and the twenty-seventh-busiest airport in the world. Over forty million passengers pass through it per year. Its full name is Flughafen München Franz

Josef Strauss. Franz Josef Strauss was the youngest-ever German minister for defense, a minister for finance, his party's chairman, and, for his last ten years in public office, the president of Bavaria. Trish gives me a look that says, Are you really going to continue? So I do not. I simply read it silently. The most interesting things about Strauss, it seems, are that he jailed a newspaper editor under false pretenses for more than a hundred days, and was accused of accepting bribes from Lockheed in return for the purchase of nine hundred F-104G Starfighters. Strauss was a pilot himself, and served as the first chairman of the supervisory board of Airbus. Before this airport was built, flights went out of Munich-Riem Airport, an area that now contains a convention center, lots of apartments, and parks, and is called Messestadt Riem, or Convention City Riem. Munich-Riem was home, in 1945, to possibly the greatest-ever collection of German fighter pilots, the Jagdverband 44. The commander was General Adolf Galland, the former General of Fighter Pilots, who had recently been removed from his staff post by Hermann Göring for relentlessly criticizing the operational policies, strategic doctrine, and tactics mandated by the Luftwaffe High Command. It was hoped by Galland's superiors that his return to combat flying in a frontline command would result in his death in action. He was only wounded. Munich-Riem Airport was the site of the Munich Air Disaster, which resulted in the deaths of eight Manchester United soccer players—their plane crashed while trying to take off from a slushy runway. It was also the site of the Munich Massacre of 1972. In 1982, there was a bomb attack on passengers headed to Israel. The closest concentration camp to Munich was Dachau. The new airport—the one through which we are passing—is less than twenty minutes away from Dachau. Himmler called Dachau the first concentration camp for political prisoners. Strangely, not far from our first hotel in Berlin, there was a park with a water tower in it, and a plaque outside it claimed that it was the site of the first concentration camp for political prisoners. Of course, they would have been on entirely different scales. On my phone, I enlarged pictures of bodies in trucks, dead bodies being placed into crematoria. Pictures of children on their way to death. Images of fat and smiling guards on short vacations in the woods nearby. Late in the afternoon of 29 April 1945, the camp at Dachau was surrendered to the US Army. I read the following passage, written by Brigadier General Henning Linden, which describes the surrender—As we moved down along the west side of the concentration camp and approached the southwest corner, three people approached down the road under a flag of truce. We met these people about seventy-five yards north of the southwest entrance to the camp. These three people were a Swiss Red Cross representative and two SS troopers who said they were the camp commander and assistant camp commander and that they had come into the camp on the night of the twenty-eighth to take over from the regular camp personnel for the purpose of turning the camp over to the advancing Americans. The Swiss Red Cross representative acted as interpreter and stated that there were about a hundred SS guards in the camp who had their arms stacked except for the people in the tower. He said he had given instructions that there would be no shots fired and it would take about fifty men to relieve the guards, as there were forty-two thousand half-crazed prisoners of war in the camp, many of them typhus infected. He asked if I were an officer of the American Army, to which I replied, Yes, I am Assistant Division Commander of the 42nd Division and will accept the surrender of the camp in the name of the Rainbow Division for the American Army.

Then another excerpt from a letter to his parents by American Private First Class Harold Porter, who wrote—The trip south from Öttingen was pleasant enough. We passed through Donauworth and Aichach and as we entered Dachau, the country, with the cottages, rivers, country estates and Alps in the distance, was almost like a tourist resort. But as we came to the center of the city, we met a train with a wrecked engine—about fifty cars long. Every car was loaded with bodies. There must have been thousands of them—all obviously starved to death. This was a shock of the first order, and the odor can best be imagined. But neither the sight nor the odor were anything when compared with what we were still to see. A friend reached the camp two days before I did and was a guard so as soon as I got there I looked him up and he took me to the crematory. Dead SS troopers were scattered around the grounds, but when we reached the furnace house we came upon a huge stack of corpses piled up like kindling, all nude so that their clothes wouldn't be wasted by the burning. There were furnaces for burning six bodies at once and on each side of them was a room twenty feet square crammed to the ceiling with more bodies—one big stinking rotten mess. Their faces purple, their eyes popping, and with a hideous grin on each one. They were nothing but bones & skin. There were both women and children in the stack in addition to the men. While we were inspecting the place, freed prisoners drove up with wagon loads of corpses removed from the compound proper. Watching the unloading was horrible. The bodies squooshed and gurgled as they hit the pile and the odor could almost be seen.

These are the types of notes I tend to keep when I read. I read something, and I realize that I must write it for myself, word for word. I write down my thoughts, too, and I write down the names of places I've been, or things I've seen, but mostly it's just sentences and passages like these. It is the way my mind works. I have to pick things up and examine them in order to remember them, and writing is a way of doing that, of examining a passage in greater depth, of ensuring that a memory lasts. In London, I have maybe five hundred notebooks full of notes like this. I suspect that if a forensic team came in looking for evidence of madness, they would say my notebooks were that evidence. I am sure my father has more notes, perhaps a thousand times more—certainly I learned the behavior from him—but he probably had a workmanlike relation to them, whereas mine have no purpose. Unless that purpose is to produce evidence of madness for anyone who might come looking.

I put the phone away and say to Trish, I entered the raffle for the race car.

What race car? she says.

You didn't see the race car?

I didn't, she says.

I don't believe you, I say.

I look over her shoulder. I pick myself up from the seat slightly and point. That way, I say. There's an actual race car.

What would anyone do with a race car?

I used to race cars, I tell Trish.

Did you? she asks.

No, not really, I only drove fast when I was a teenager, I raced my friends. But I did sign up to win the race car.

She says, What will you do with a race car in London?

I say, It turns out you don't win the race car, you just win some money.

She seems to think this is a better idea. But I say, They charge you twenty euro to sign up. It's a scam.

Why'd you do it?

I don't know. The wait is making me crazy.

Trish sends a message from her phone, then she starts to check e-mails, or the Internet, or whatever. She's just killing time and giving herself something to do. It doesn't take long before her personal phone buzzes—a response. She checks it. She reads the message quickly, or it is a short message, then puts the phone away. Her expression doesn't change. She's composed, or she is very cool. Then she turns to me. You're staring, she says.

What do you mean by *all right*?

She takes off her sunglasses, but I don't take mine off.

I say, When you say your father is *all right*, what do you mean?

I don't know, she says.

Are you close?

I guess.

I talk to my dad once a month. Is that more or less than you and your dad?

She says, I talk to my dad much less than that. I talk to my mom. If my dad answers, he tells me about the dogs, then he gives the phone to my mom, or if there's nothing to say about the dogs, he gives the phone to my mom. I don't know how to talk to him. I have brothers and they don't know how to talk to him.

I say, Miriam and my dad never talked.

Trish stops doing everything she is doing. She stops thinking all the thoughts she is thinking, about work and her relationship and her flight and everything else, and she gives me her full attention, because, I guess, I have finally mentioned Miriam by name. Perhaps she thinks I'm going to reminisce. Instead, I say something she is not expecting. I say, Have you and your husband split up?

She stays very still. She crosses her legs. She smooths out her pants legs.

I yawn.

Yes, she says. Did your dad tell you?

I say, Yes, he told me. Sorry to hear it.

It's fine.

In my situation, I say, it was definitely for the best.

Are you in contact with your ex?

Me? No, never. Why do you ask?

Your dad has mentioned her a lot.

He spoke about her?

He just mentions her, said it was a shame you split up.

He tells me the same thing. He once said to me, You will never be fulfilled until you understand that you must live your life for others, not for yourself.

He said you had a really beautiful wedding.

I say, He told you my wedding was beautiful?

He did.

Well, he wasn't there.

I stand up. My back is sore. My joints are sore. My jaw is sore. There is acute pain that jabs, now and again, in my gut somewhere, and also in what feels like my bladder. I feel constriction in my chest. I have a headache in my eyes. The muscles in my arms and legs won't stretch. But all of this strangely amounts to a feeling of vigor and adventure, of—to put it simply, and also probably falsely—getting thinner. I ask Trish if she needs anything, like a bottle of water, or a magazine. I'm fine, she says. I say, Do you think your husband will go back to the States or stay in Munich?

It's a very good question, she says.

Is he black or white?

He's white.

What does he do?

He's an engineer.

Was he in the military?

Yes.

Was that the career he left in order to come with you to Berlin?

Yes.

Do you think he wanted children?

No, she says.

Did you?

No.

I say, If I could go back in time, back to my marriage, I would want to have children.

Trish shrugs, so I say, Don't worry, I'm not trying to give you advice.

She says, Do you mean that kids would have kept you together?

No, I say, definitely not.

I walk over to a trash can and dump my tied-up bag. I come back and say, I changed my mind, I wouldn't have wanted to have children.

The truth about my ex is that people liked her, she was successful, punctual, liked to read, liked to go out, liked vacations, knew a couple of languages, was good with numbers, was pretty, stayed fit, and was a good driver. I don't think there was anybody who saw us together who thought she was the luckier half. Everybody said to me, You have married up! But it wasn't that simple. Nobody knew my wife in the way I would get to know her. For the last twelve months we were together, every week seemed like rock bottom, every week something happened that made me think we'd reached the very lowest point two people could reach. About a month before I moved out, we found ourselves in the office of a marriage counselor. Outwardly there were still signs that we cared for each other, so perhaps we thought a counselor could help us build upon that care and find a way to be content together. We cooked for each other, we washed each other's clothes, we ran errands for each other, we picked each other up after the last trains had stopped, and we even wrote kind and tender notes to each other at times, but we couldn't bear physical proximity, and every phone call turned into an argument. I got out of the house whenever I could. I ran miles and miles on Saturday and Sunday mornings. In the afternoons, I bought a paper, went to a pub, watched sports—sports I'd never watch, such as soccer, or snooker, or cricket—and had a few beers. It wasn't always necessary—she was out, too, usually, at brunch, or shopping. I worked late most weeknights. So did she. We had dinner around nine. We forced ourselves to eat at the dinner table, across from one another, but when she spoke, my eyes closed, and when I spoke, she spoke over me. We slept in separate beds. I snored, so we explained the separate beds to each other as a consequence of my snoring.

The counselor worked from her home, in a little white room with wooden flooring and a rug and coffee table. My wife and I sat on a white couch. The counselor sat on a sleek chrome chair that had legs like a spider's. The door between the room and the hallway that was part of the rest of her house was very thin, and the sounds of domesticity—two children, a dog, a nanny, a television, and toys, and laughter—loudly rattled through it, as I suspect the sounds of our conversations, and the conversations with other clients, quietly gargled back. The counselor was very tanned, good-looking, South American, with very thick dark hair, and she wore high heels and white pants. She was quite made up. She wore a tan, loose top that nearly fell off her shoulder, and a thin gold necklace. I don't know what made her think it was okay to dress like that as a marriage counselor. It wasn't that she looked attractive. She had every right to look attractive. The problem was that she looked like she was going somewhere more important, that our problems made us a nuisance to her, and it made her interest in us seem entirely false.

We never went back to the counselor. We returned to our house, did not speak, did not touch. She went into the bedroom and closed the door. I walked around the place. We had high ceilings. Big bay windows. My ex came from a wealthy family. Her father was a banker. Her mother was a doctor. I went out to the shared garden behind our apartment. It was late spring, and cloudless, and in late spring our shared garden got the sunlight all afternoon. It was obvious to me that my wife and I, finally, could not go on. I tried to think of ways to keep all this from my father, to go on pretending everything was fine until he died. I sat out there for an hour, wondering if it were possible. It felt absolutely necessary to conceal the separation from him. Up in the apartment, behind one of the windows, my wife was sitting, or pacing around the bedroom. I went upstairs eventually and started getting some things together to go out. I knocked on the bedroom door and entered after she said, What? She was sitting on the bed. I got a new shirt and a light tan jacket. She asked, indignantly, You're going out? I said, I think it's probably best right now to be apart. She said, So it's over. I said, Yes, I think so. She climbed off the bed and went to the kitchen and got some vodka out of the freezer and poured herself a shot. I followed her. Do you want one? she asked. Sure, I said. We sat down across from each other and had a couple of shots each, without talking. Finally she said she might go stay with a friend for the night. I said, Okay. She said, I think I should. I said, If you think you should, I'm sure you're right. I got up and left her there. I went out and sat at a bar and smiled for a few hours. I talked to nobody. I didn't really drink all that much. At eleven, when the pub closed, I went home and found her asleep on the couch, with the television on. She'd had a lot of vodka. I sat and looked at her in the light of the television. I took the bottle and finished, slowly, the little bit left at the bottom.

A year passed, more than a year, and I hadn't told my father. It was obvious that something had happened. I was sure he knew. He telephoned the apartment a few times and was icily told by my wife that I wasn't there, and he never telephoned again. He asked me how she was doing for about two months and instead of catching him up on her life, I said, Good. So he stopped asking about her. I guessed that he was waiting for me to confess. But I wasn't going to. I had just decided never to mention it. If he died, I wouldn't have to tell him. If he didn't, maybe I would one day bring a new wife and some kids home and when he picked me up from the airport and gave me an astonished gasp, I'd say, Oh, we broke up years and years ago. After more than a year, my plan began to seem achievable. I had hardly spoken to my father that year. I figured we were falling out of contact. It was a shame, but it was better, somehow, than admitting that my marriage hadn't lasted. Then one day I telephoned him and he said he was going to book a flight to Scotland and get us rooms at the lodge. It seemed he would wait no longer. I agreed to meet him, because my bigger fear was that he would come to London, and I booked my flight to Glasgow. I almost missed the flight. I sat at the gate while everyone else boarded. All I could think about was my father sitting on his own at dinner, at the same table where he had honeymooned with my mother, and the same table where he had met me and my wife a few years before. And I couldn't decide whether I pitied him or wanted him to suffer. The airline woman kept looking at me when she spoke into the microphone, Final call, this is the absolute final call, the gate is closing. I got up. If she had given me the slightest amount of grief, I would have turned around and gone home, but she welcomed me and wished me a pleasant journey. When I arrived at the hotel, I checked in and left a message for my father. I unpacked and showered. I was getting dressed when my father knocked on the door. I was going to wear a suit for drinks in the lounge. I had my pants and shirt on. I put my jacket on. I wore no shoes or socks, though. I answered the door and my father was standing in a suit as well. He looked a bit tipsy and he immediately took my arms, studied me up and down, and embraced me. He came inside and saw that I was alone. He sat on a chair near the bed. I said, Guess what, I've started my own business. Good for you, he said, is it going well? I started it up about six months ago, I'm optimistic. We went down together to the lounge and he ordered a scotch with water and I ordered a beer. We had about two hours before dinner. It was late autumn so the sun was already down. It was already night at five p.m. I said, I suspect you had your suspicions about my marriage for a long time. He said nothing. I said, It just got very bad, it ended, it wasn't too painful.

How long ago?

Oh, about a year and a half ago.

Christ, you didn't tell me for a year and a half?

I had a pretty crazy year after it ended. I'm not sure it was the right time to tell you.

What happened with the apartment?

What do you mean?

The one you bought together?

I moved out. She stayed.

But you used your mother's inheritance, didn't you?

I said, I got bought out, I made all that money back.

That satisfied him, and I've never told him any differently.

We put on our coats and walked outside to get some air. The place was crowded. It was, as it always is, I think, full of retired people. We walked along the lakefront in the darkness. A little light from the restaurant spilled outward on the grass behind us, but the lake itself was darkness, and above were dark-gray, swiftly moving clouds. He said, Miriam was too busy again, said it was too short notice for her. Have you spoken with her?

I haven't, I said.

You should go to Berlin.

To visit her?

Come up with some excuse, go there for a weekend and check in on her, make sure she's okay.

I barely had the time to come here, Dad.

I know, I know, he said. I appreciate it. It's good to see you.

The lake seemed to be pulling us into it, urging us into its oblivion, but by then it was seven and our table was ready. We got the booth? I asked. You bet we did, he said.

When my father and I entered the airport this morning, we wandered around for a while, went up and down a couple of escalators, flipped through some magazines at a newsstand. We went to the information center—who can say why—but it wasn't open yet. Eventually we called Trish and told her we were going to head through security, find a seat, and wait for her. We had a strange energy before we got to security, the kind of energy you have at the beginning of a very long car journey, when you find yourself singing along to the radio, loving the road, loving the sensation of driving. About halfway through security, however, the sense of purpose and avidity dissipated. Suddenly my father became very worried that Miriam's body would not be properly looked after. It was clear—though he didn't say it—that he feared she would be left behind somehow, mishandled and lost, and we would leave without her, which would make our time here totally meaningless. He started to panic and talk to himself, and look all around for somebody who might be able to help. There were two or three hundred people in front of us and two or three hundred behind us, and when my father started to panic about the fact that Miriam was in some vague trouble and he could not help her, I also started to panic, because I realized that no amount of worry or panic would move time any faster, or make Miriam any safer. She would never be safe or unsafe again, in fact. What an absurd trip we had made after all, what had we been thinking, why were we bringing a body home? By the time we got through security—I can't say how long it took—we were on the verge of anxiety attacks. But then we saw how curiously peaceful the terminal was, and we walked into the great bazaar like weary travelers who had at last arrived in the free city.

We decided to take an elevator up to the Skywalk—a long, wide, glass corridor on the roof of the terminal. It was a hundred and fifty feet high, or something like that. It doesn't sound very high, but it feels very high when you are up there, I'd bet. From it, on a clear day, we could have looked out in all directions, to the city, to the mountains, we probably could have killed a lot of time. But there was nothing to see. We stood close to the glass and examined the fog. I enjoyed feeling closely encapsulated by the grayness, it seemed vaguely like being in deep outer space—the outer space you might imagine near the boundaries of the universe. Everyone who was up there stood very close to the window, waiting, presumably, for signs of dissipation, or simply to observe the strange properties of this unusually thick fog. I had never seen anything like it. It seemed to move like a heavy gas, gas you could spoon out of a bowl, gas that would suffocate you if you stepped outside, or freeze you. My flat in London—the one in Spitalfields, though it is actually Hackney—is on the fourth floor. It overlooks Columbia Road and a small park. These were originally social housing, but by the time I moved there it was all architects, like the one I sublet from. I drink coffee by the window and look out over Columbia Road, or eat a sandwich, or have a drink if it is evening. Lots of bicycles go by. I play music quite loud and, on warm evenings, open the windows so that the sound will carry over to Columbia Road, so that people might vaguely hear something as they come closer, and enjoy an unexpected moment of romance in the city. I sometimes even go down myself—I leave the music playing, lock my door, go down the steps, open the outer doors, and walk until I can not hear the music anymore, then turn around and go back.

There is no more evidence of the fog. The mountains to the south, though far away, are clear and sublime. They are completely white. The sun is above them. The city is between us and the mountains, but you can't really see it. There are just the runways, then some grayness, then, miles and miles away, the mountains. It must be very cold, despite how bright it is. I walk to the window and look out. I don't have the energy to go back up to the Skywalk, and I presume it is busy now, I assume there are children running all over, people having picnics on the floor. But I wonder if, if I were to go back up, I could see the city. The tarmac is busy. Food trucks. Baggage transporters. Fuel and de-icing trucks. Bundled-up airport personnel, with puffs of smoke for breath—the bald ones with steaming heads. A plane departs every sixty seconds. The queue of jets taxiing for takeoff is long, and it moves slowly. I imagine it must be a bit dispiriting to find yourself on an airplane after five or six hours of waiting, only to wait two hours on the tarmac, squashed in a seat you can't leave.

When I arrived at the upscale apartment to which my father had moved us from the cramped little hotel with the green bathroom, the receptionist gave me a key and told me to go all the way up to the penthouse. The rooms had names instead of numbers. I went in, felt completely shocked by the size of the place, and read a note my father had left on the kitchen bar instructing me to grab a drink from the fridge and come up to the rooftop. Between two large sitting rooms, and opposite a giant, open-plan kitchen, was a south-facing terrace that was just level with the rooftops of the buildings all around, with a large table on it, some chairs, and a couple of recliners for sunbathing. There was also a spiral staircase leading up. I thought, You gotta be kidding me. I opened the fridge. There were six bottles of wine and several bottles of beer. I got a beer, searched in the cabinets for a glass, and went up to the rooftop. The rooftop terrace was totally bare, except for the chair my father was sitting on, and an empty chair beside him. Apparently the embassy intern had brought the chairs up at my father's request. The weather was funny. It was still a cool, almost cold day, but from time to time a brief puff of warmth enveloped us. The sky was gray and very close. These were the very first intimations of spring. You are filthy, said my father. I looked down at my pants. The spots of superblack gunk went all the way up to my thighs, and had also spotted the front of my windbreaker, and the cuffs of my pants were wet and gritty. I had a pretty good beard already—relative to the fact that I'd never had one in my life. Maybe it had gunk in it, too. My father was in a suit, a black suit, and he was drinking wine. He looked serene. He was up there, on his own, just drinking and looking at the city. It was a spectacular view. We were nearly at the highest point of Prenzlauer Berg, which made it nearly the highest point in Berlin. Berlin doesn't look much like a German city from street level. But from the rooftop terrace, Berlin looked German again, because of all the red rooftops, and vast. We've got the Philharmonic in a few hours, don't forget, said my father. I haven't forgotten, I said.

I drank that beer, got another, drank it, and when we heard thunder, we went downstairs. I said, I don't get to hear thunder very much anymore. My father turned on the television and I went to shower and change. My room was enormous. It had its own flat-screen television. The bed was huge and square, as though I might like to sleep sideways, or bring multiple partners home with me each night. I also had an en suite, which was half the size of the bedroom—and as big as my sitting room in London. I felt a little bit silly sitting on the commode, looking around at all the empty space. I picked up my legs and kicked them, just because I could, and made funny faces in the full-length mirror across from the commode. I missed the old hotel.

I showered for a long time, under a massive tropical shower-head, and I made the water as hot as I could bear. When I came out, I was bright red, and I sat naked on the end of my bed for ten minutes, sweating. Then I put on the only suit I had brought with me—black suit, white shirt, black tie—which I had chosen in case my father decided to bury Miriam in Germany. I came out to find my father and Trish drinking wine and watching downhill ski racing on television. They stood. Trish wore a gray dress. In certain light, it turned black. You look very nice, I said. Thanks, she said, so do you. Four hours later we were back in our neighborhood, at a bar right beside Trish's apartment, and not too far from our apartment, which was dark, crowded, smoky, and which played Jewish folk music until three a.m. We drank a lot. I must have talked to a dozen people, and I think I spoke a lot of German, which is interesting, because my German is very elementary. We walked Trish home, then we got a bit lost trying to find our new apartment, which was pathetic because Trish's apartment was less than five minutes from ours. I helped my father into his room. I put him into bed. I took his shoes off. Then I went up to the roof and sat in the rain—under a complimentary golf umbrella—and drank a final beer, and up there, drunk, in darkness, I looked upon the wet and sparkling vision of the city, and it put me in mind of something I'd have liked to do in my youth. My father slept late. I woke, opened the blackout curtains to a bright blue late morning, and realized that I was not, to my surprise, hungover. And with that realization came the sound of bells, church bells, exaltation. I went outside to go shopping. There was a little café nearby that contained a small organic supermarket. You could get fresh produce, meats, and bread. The change in the weather was extraordinary. It was warm, the rain must have brought it. In the light, it almost felt hot. I took my sweater off and tied it around my neck. I bought food for breakfast. I got a little bit of everything. I went back to the apartment, and my father and I had eggs, bacon, mushrooms, broccoli, hash browns, beans, sausages, bread, and some coffee—all served on the rooftop.

On our second morning in the new apartment, my father woke me to say he had a surprise. He had been up a few hours, but I hadn't heard a thing. He said, I've got a surprise, get dressed, get some clothes for a couple of days, pack them in a bag. So I got dressed. I packed up everything I'd brought to Berlin. I ate some breakfast, then we went downstairs and walked around the corner, and my father pulled a key from his pocket, pressed a button, and the car we were standing beside—a big, black, sleek Toyota Camry—unlocked, and the lights flashed.

Hey hey, I said.

Hey *hey*, he said.

He threw me the key and said, You drive.

We're going now?

Why not?

Well, how do we get out of Berlin?

I got a GPS, he said.

But I'm still drunk from last night.

We're fully insured, he said, crash as often as you like.

But we just got the new apartment.

It'll be here when we get back.

We sat inside. The seats were soft. It had automatic transmission. The steering wheel was thick and soft. There was great leg space. It had cruise control. The dash beamed bright white and red. I pushed my seat back, lowered it, reclined it a bit—all electric—adjusted the mirrors, and turned on the radio. The car was very smooth. Once we got on the autobahn, it pulled a hundred and seventy kilometers an hour without any trouble, without much sound. It just flew, and you barely felt the road. Yes, every once in a while, an S-Class went by us, reminding everybody on the road who the king was, but for the most part we zoomed by everybody without being overly conscious of our speed. We stopped at gas stations for snacks, cheeseburgers, slices of pizza, buns, and so my father could stretch his legs. Our journey took us through the Rhineland, then through the Ardennes, then to Brussels. After Brussels, we went to Aachen. The only part of the trip my father let me know about beforehand was Aachen—because on that first stretch my father talked a lot about Charlemagne. Our trip lasted five days. Five days of warmth and sunshine. But then winter returned, and we arrived back in Berlin in a sleet storm, in a fog that swirled as cars drove through it, in the middle of the night, stinking of all that time in a hot car together, and stinking of the long day's journey.

I'd never experienced anything quite like the traffic in Brussels. It seems to be a city absolutely strangled by stupid, overcrowded intersections. And I think our visit coincided with a couple of days of strikes or protests. Every driver there was deranged and homicidal. We waited at a roundabout for thirty minutes, then again, then again, and finally inched along the motorway for an hour before we got to something resembling normal heavy traffic, with low visibility, rain, and fog. When we arrived in Aachen, I was in desperate need of a shower. I had sweated through my shirt and pullover. My pants were uncomfortably sticky. But we thought we had to hurry. We thought we had five minutes. We hurried from our parking spot to the cathedral. And then, to our embarrassment, we couldn't locate the entrance for a few minutes, until we realized that it was obvious. The entrance was in the West Front, like, said the brochure, a great bulwark intended to protect God's house against the outer darkness, at the foot of the tower, leading to the central core. Then through to the Octagon, under the magnificent and low-hanging chandelier, Barbarossa's chandelier, which was built three centuries after Charlemagne's death. My father sat in a pew under the chandelier to catch his breath. The interior was dark, and in my memory it was green. There was candlelight. Charlemagne's shrine was way past the altar, behind rope. I said, Is that it? That's it, he said. It was golden and unexpectedly small. The shrine was elevated, and it rested inside a very modest beam of light that didn't seem to come from anywhere, so that it gleamed in the same way Christ is gleaming in Piero's *Flagellation*. I felt the need to have my father stand beside it. To look into the color and ornament of the tomb that contained Charlemagne's bones. But he was in no mood to stand and walk around. Every few seconds, he coughed. The coughing caused him intense pain that made him double over. Saliva hung from his lips. His hands were trembling. He wiped his mouth and sat up and looked at me. His eyes were blank. His skin was green. He seemed emaciated. Then he started coughing again, and leaned forward, into his own lap. I knew it was the hurrying that had exhausted him, but another part of me wondered if the place itself did not contain a force capable of destroying him, cell by cell, breaking him apart, scattering him in the air. There were three small groups in the room with us. Each group was guided by its own amateur know-it-all, one of those experts on a thousand unimportant things. The people following these know-it-alls seemed variously intrigued or bored to death. I went around looking at a few things on the walls, waiting for my father to stop coughing. A few minutes later, a new group entered the room, this time led by a younger man—obviously a member of staff. He spoke about the chandelier for a while, with practiced stresses, pauses, and gestures, then the statue of Mary, then about the mosaics of the dome. I followed them at a distance. I didn't understand what he was saying, but he was pointing out important things, so that when I went to the souvenir shop and bought a book in English, I would know which parts were worthy of attention. When the new group was led behind the rope to Charlemagne's shrine, I asked if my father and I could come along. He said it was a private tour, and anyway it was in German. I said we had come a long, long way, and we didn't need to hear him speak, we only needed to get behind the rope, my father was a historian and knew quite a lot about Charlemagne. The man peered over at my father, who was still sitting, but the coughing had subsided. I'm sorry, said the man, but if you want to view the shrine, you will have to return next week. I told him my father's name, not because I thought the man would recognize it, but because I thought saying his name would make the man think he ought to recognize it. The man politely admitted the name meant nothing to him. He looked at his watch. The people on the tour glared at me nastily, so I begged their pardon and returned to my father. No luck, I said. Hmm, he said. He stood and walked to the altar, turned around and looked up, to the upper level, where Charlemagne's throne sat, from which he would have observed services. Opposite the throne, at eye level with the throne, was Christ on the cross, staring back at Charlemagne, like a man and his wife. The private tour ended, and the other groups left, and we were alone. I cannot say now why we didn't simply step over the rope. It was just a little bit of low rope. It was just, I think, a suggestion to stay back.

The drive back to Berlin from Aachen was long, foggy, and, finally, frozen. The motorway interchanges around Aachen, Cologne, Bonn, Düsseldorf, Essen, Dortmund—everywhere you turn, you find a medium-sized city—were too convoluted for our GPS—it kept telling us, for instance, to exit the motorway right, so we would exit, but we had taken the wrong exit, not far enough right, the exit we wanted was two hundred yards back—so we spent what seemed like hours doing circles. You're driving too fast, said my father, that's why the GPS can't keep up. If we go any slower we'll get hit from behind, I said. About halfway to Berlin, without any explanation, our GPS went blank, and nothing we did could get it working again. After that we made a few daring diversions to avoid traffic jams—through fog, racing to stay with big trucks that seemed to be headed in the direction of Berlin. We'd see traffic gathering, or hear the word *Stau* on the radio, which is the German word for traffic jam, and then a truck or two would exit, and I'd say, Those trucks know something! And my father would say, Follow them! Around midnight or one, within a hundred kilometers of Berlin, all the traffic on the road seemed to vanish. You couldn't see the lines on the road. You hoped that all the cars ahead of you were running rear fog lights, or else you might not see them until you crashed into them. It was quite

scary. It was so scary, in fact, that after all the arguing and complaining my father had done until that point, he became utterly
silent and still. The fog and foul weather were so bad we couldn't
see the big blue motorway signs right above us, and we made
a few more wrong turns, which meant we had to exit and find
a turnaround, which wasn't always straightforward. These diversions took us down below the motorways, into woods and nearly
impenetrable fog, fog that slowed us to a crawl, trying to find
the entrance back onto the motorway. We always did. My father
kept quiet. Finally we saw a little statue of a bear, the Berlin bear,
and then it was just a matter of driving toward the center until we reached a part of town I recognized. We got back to the
apartment around two and went straight to bed. All night I slept
fitfully and with horrible dreams, suffering sweats and chills, until it was light, and then I got up and closed the curtains—though
I still could see a crack of light around the curtains, so I put on
my sunglasses, and then I went back to sleep, and I slept dream-
lessly, like a drugged sleep—the kind of sleep you cannot move
your legs after. It was one in the afternoon when I checked the
time. I massaged my thighs. I pointed my toes. My back was stiff.
My neck was sore. I drank the pint of water I had remembered
to pour myself on the way to bed. I got up, made some coffee,
opened up my laptop and started to delete e-mails. The only two
e-mails I read were from the aerospace firm. The first was from
the director. In it, she expressed her sadness over my loss, and re-
iterated the offer to take some time. The other e-mail was from
Chris, with condolences again, but also with some details about
working remotely. She looked forward to getting started whenever I was ready. I must have gained fifteen pounds over the five
days we'd been on the road, but it wasn't remarkable in my face,

because my beard had filled out. I had changed my appearance. I now wore that black suit jacket everywhere, and it was getting dirtier and more wrinkled by the day, and I wore my shirts unbuttoned quite low—like I'd forgotten what I was doing in the middle of buttoning up my shirt. I think I was trying to look like an old rock star who had come to Germany to recuperate following a nervous breakdown, or to die, or whatever the opposite of a moderately successful marketing consultant was.

It was freezing again, in Berlin. It rained ice. For hours there was just an eerie premonition, an absence of color, then suddenly the sky would fill with wind and a darkening, and ice swarmed out of the darkening, and the wind blew dust and trash and metal and glass at you. The ice swarmed down for ten minutes, twenty at the most, then the calm returned—and the color drained out of the sky. I was listening to a lot of music, twelve-tone music, music of dissonance. I used my father's headphones, which he'd bought on the flight out, and which he didn't use for music—they were, in his mind, only for canceling sound. I stopped trying to look like an old rock star who had gone to Berlin to die or recuperate, I simply became that old rock star. I'm sure the headphones made me look ridiculous, but I felt, at the time, that they didn't make the aged rock star I'd become look ridiculous. I thought they made him look slightly more authentic. I listened to Debussy and Berg and Schoenberg and Webern and Scriabin and Stravinsky and Shostakovich and Boulez and Cage, and the city was like a future city the music had imagined, a city at the end of time, or a city after time. Finally, a city that had not dismissed the dream of this music, but had succumbed to it! I found myself thinking in quotes—quotes about music—I had noted over the years. Adorno had said that new music, by which he meant twelve-tone music, has taken upon itself all the darkness and guilt of the world, that all its happiness comes in the perception of misery, all its beauty comes in the rejection of beauty's illusion. Boulez said, We assert for our part that any musician who has not experienced—we do not say understood, but experienced—the necessity of the dodecaphonic language is *USELESS*. Cage said, I am going toward violence rather than tenderness, hell rather than heaven, ugly rather than beautiful, impure rather than pure, because by doing these things they become transformed, and we become transformed. Stravinsky said, with great despondency, It seems that once the *violent* has been accepted, the *amiable*, in turn, is no longer tolerable. Benjamin said that fascist humanity would experience its own annihilation as the supreme aesthetic pleasure. Schoenberg said, I do not compose principles, I compose music.

Our trip around the Rhineland, and around the Ardennes, and up to Brussels, was marked at its beginning by music—the Philharmonic—and marked toward its end by music, or if music isn't the right word, then the empty trapezoidal box in the glossy white room. In between, in the car, we had listened to a lot of radio. There were pop stations, and there was talk radio we couldn't understand—in German, French, Dutch, and Luxembourgish. There were classical stations, but we kept catching the shows that played film scores, such as the theme from *Superman*, or *Star Wars*, or *The Mission*. No matter what country we were in, the pop stations played the same pop songs, the classical stations played the same film scores, and the talk radio, though we couldn't understand most of the words, talked about the same news, or different news but in the same ways. By the end of the trip, I knew all the pop songs. I knew all the words. So did my father. I was beginning to sing the songs in the shower. There were only, at most, ten of them. And when I went out drinking late—sometimes alone and sometimes with my father—we heard the songs, or songs just like them, in the bars or clubs we found. The funny thing is that I liked them then. I wanted to drive as much as possible, so we could hear them. As soon as I started to get sick of one, I seemed to realize that I liked another much more, and I scanned the radio for it, and played it until I got sick of it. I turned them up at my favorite parts. I drove fast when the music was jubilant, I drove slow when the music was thoughtful.

At the Philharmonic, we had seats to the side of the orchestra, overlooking the violinists and the conductor—we sat to the conductor's right. The double basses were just below us, but out of our sight, unless we leaned forward. There were a few empty seats in the hall, but not many. What a strange and wonderful building it is. It has a pentagon-shaped center, from which rows of seats rise in irregular directions and uneven heights, and the outward flow of this design continues through to the exterior, to the outer structures, which are large, gold, asymmetrical, Expressionist, and which release the acoustic qualities of the interior into the sky. I flipped through the program even though I couldn't read it. Trish sat between me and my father. It occurred to me we probably looked like a couple, Trish and I. So I tried to take on the demeanor of a man with a pretty and successful and voluptuous and interesting wife, who attends the Philharmonic regularly, and sometimes brings his father. The man beside me, an older gentleman with his wife, sat perfectly still. I looked at him as if to say, You see, I am reading the program in German, and I am attending this concert with my lovely wife and my dear father, but the man, who had silver hair, wore a blue suit, and had blue, bloodshot eyes, only glared at me. I gave the program back to Trish, and she closed it and put it on her lap. The man beside me—how can I possibly describe it—I could almost feel his blood slow down, his thoughts begin to vanish. I decided to try to imitate this stillness. But there were too many distractions. Too many people coughing, clearing throats. Too many people flipping through the programs. Too many strange or attractive people to observe. Then the orchestra took their seats, and there was light applause. Everybody stopped reading programs. Everybody stopped whispering. Nobody coughed anymore. For a moment, it was so silent that it sounded as though we were all falling. Then the conductor appeared, and the applause was slightly louder, but still light. The man beside me clapped a few times, but not enthusiastically. First we heard Debussy's *La Mer*. Then Sibelius's Violin Concerto Number One. I knew them both pretty well. They are both distinctive composers. Debussy is the more respected, probably because he was so clearly an innovator, his music so self-evidently revolutionary and so intelligently about *itself*. During his lifetime, Sibelius was dismissed and reviled by progressives. You were not to be taken seriously if you listened to Sibelius. But it turned out, as it tends to turn out, historically, that the reason we cannot forget Sibelius is that he was doing something not only new but outrageously radical, it's just that he was very subtle about it, so nobody noticed. So now he is spoken of among the masters. He has been rehabilitated. Listening to him, and to the Debussy—both pieces are raucous and dynamic—I found myself not only transfixed by the sound of the music but also by the sight of the musicians, and by the hall itself, the audience in its terrifying stillness and restraint. Trish, too, was transfixed—I watched her chest as she breathed through it, and I watched her look upon it. Everything in the room trapped upside down in the dark black drop of her eyes. The lights. The musicians. The embattled, old, wild conductor. A thousand people across from her, quietly breathing. Our applause for both pieces was modest. I made sure I did not begin to clap until after the glaring man beside me clapped, and to stop before he stopped. So I clapped my hands three or four times and put my hands back in my lap. During the intermission, my father asked me, What did you think? Terrific, I said. I happen to know that my father's damn-with-faint-praise word is *terrific*. For example—Bob, the book is just terrific, or, Dick, the steaks were absolutely terrific. Completely, one hundred percent, agree, said my father. In the second half, we heard a short Stravinsky piece I thought was woeful, and was of that permanent flaw in the progressive urge, which is infatuation with the clownish, the preposterously bad, merely because it is change, and it happens to be chic—though I admit, absolutely, that the flaw is necessary, and that the same urge is responsible for Stravinsky's greatness. The final piece was Berg's Lyric Suite. Which I happen to think is one of the great human achievements, one of the strangest and most unforgettable pieces of music ever written. The music after the intermission was not raucous, and a cloud settled over us all, a reminder to return to the calm confusion of our despondency, or be mindful of it. When it was all over, the audience clapped for a long time without heat or passion. It was sustained, but it was not enthusiastic. A good audience always honors fine music by being disappointed in itself. The orchestra cleared and we stood, and I looked at the glaring man again and gave a manly smile. I had clapped so little. I had barely moved. I had not coughed once, nor cleared my throat. He gave me a manly smile back.

On the way home, in a taxi, Trish admitted she much preferred the first half to the second. She didn't like the Stravinsky but she especially didn't like the Berg. My father told her I was a big fan of Berg, and asked me to defend him. It was raining, and there were sounds of thunder. The traffic moved slowly. I turned around and said, Do you go to the Philharmonic a lot?

Trish said, We used to get season tickets, but not this year.

Were they expensive?

Not really, said Trish.

Do you know much, technically, about music?

Nothing.

Then I fear you'd find an explanation of why I like Berg a little exasperating.

I just don't find the music pleasurable.

Berg is a genius, said my father.

I'm sure he is, said Trish, but I cannot like what I don't like.

My father said nothing, but he had lured me in—I wasn't sure if he was interested in what I had to say, or if he wanted to see if I could persuade Trish to reconsider Berg, or if he merely wished to have a little fun at my expense.

First I have to talk about Schoenberg, I said, and twelve-tone music.

Briefly, said my father, and without the technical stuff.

I looked through the rearview mirror to find Trish's eyes looking at mine. I said, Schoenberg found a new direction for music at a time that music was in crisis.

Explain the crisis, said my father.

Well, I only have a general sense of the crisis as Schoenberg perceived it, I am not a musical historian.

We have no interest in disclaimers, said my father, we want to know about the crisis.

The taxi driver drove excruciatingly slowly. He was a young man with a thin beard along his chin line, and he had a diamond earring, and a white zip jacket, and a couple of mobile phones. He seemed like the kind of guy who would drive really fast, and this made the slowness doubly excruciating. He looked at me as if to say, What was the crisis?

I said, Well, music had nowhere to go. It was trapped in tonality.

Nothing technical, said my father.

I said, Twelve-tone music was Schoenberg's response to the dead end music had arrived at. Music had become, to him, something like a dumping ground of human emotion, and each new wrinkle was a movement toward the accessible. Trish said, Did you say accessible? I said, Yes, accessible—how do we make harmonious music more harmonious? How do we make heartbreak more heartbreaking? How do we make happiness happier? How do we make ambiguity more ambiguous? How do we make adventure more thrilling? How do we make art more artful? These are the questions you ask yourself when you have nowhere new to go, when there are no new ideas that aren't just upside-down old ideas, or old ideas dressed up like new ideas.

And Berg was Schoenberg's most famous student, said my father.

We drove over the Spree. Now there was distant sheet lightning on the horizon, which made a rumbling several seconds after it appeared. The music on the radio was bland and energetic, and it was one of the songs we would hear a thousand times on our trip to the Rhineland.

I said, Yes, Berg was Schoenberg's most famous student, but a very different composer. Like Schoenberg, Berg made music that shattered emotional expectations. But where Schoenberg's music was full of dramatic highs and lows, sounds and silences, Berg's music was a music of dissolution, profound indistinctness, and of restraint and of melancholy. And Berg makes you wait. He makes you wait until you think you cannot wait any longer, and just when you think the waiting is about to be over, the music vanishes. His music leaves you unfulfilled.

And you like it, said Trish.

We dropped into a short and orange-tiled and dimly lit tunnel, and on the other side of that tunnel was our part of town, and I thought, I can think of nothing less interesting than Berg's likability. What interests me is the calm he inspires in me, a calm that arises from a sense of equilibrium and dread.

The first destination of our road trip was the city of Mainz, where my father's mother was born. She emigrated with my father after her husband, my father's father, was killed in the war. I wish I knew more about her life before she left Germany. I wish I'd asked her more questions. But by the time I was old enough to be curious about her past, which was also my past, she'd had a stroke that paralyzed one side of her body completely and made her suddenly hideous and unapproachable to me. My father moved her to a nursing home. He came home, took one look at her, and decided. My mother tried to convince him that she should be moved into the house and they would get nursing assistance. But he said he didn't want that kind of life around us. He didn't want the house to become sick. Once my grandmother was in the nursing home, I saw her very seldom. Only my mother visited regularly.

Before the stroke, my grandmother was quite fashionable. She wore gigantic sunglasses that people in my town didn't really understand. She was always well dressed. She wore headscarves on windy days. She was quite athletic, and threw baseballs with me, and played soccer. She taught me how to dive in swimming pools. Even though she lived a couple of miles away, in a boxy little apartment in a building full of elderly people, she was at our house constantly. I assume my father chose her apartment building, and that he wanted something so uncomfortable that she would not want to spend any time there, or make any friends. She and my mother shared a lot of the driving, cooking, cleaning. Miriam was her favorite, but she was kind to me, too. In California, she'd played golf, went on vacations to Mexico and South America, played bridge, and went out with her friends to lunches and dinners, concerts, theater, and so on. I don't remember her ever being frustrated with us, or sick of me and Miriam, or visibly disenchanted by the pit in which she'd landed for the rest of her life. Her stroke was very bad, and her left side was completely paralyzed. She couldn't speak, or at least we couldn't understand her. My mother sometimes could. But I was slightly terrified of her new voice, and of her paralysis. I wanted her to recover, of course, but I also understood what permanency was. By the time she died, I hadn't seen her in six months. Neither had Miriam, but Miriam was younger, and she was following my lead. If only, I think now, she would have lost her memory instead, if only she had spent those final years trapped inside an ever-diminishing loop of discontinuous images, if only I could, now, hide behind the irrelevant defense of her not knowing I abandoned her. But those years must have been very dark years for her. My father, when he was in town, went to see her often, but most of the time he was away in California, working, and he wasn't there when she died. I wasn't there, either. We weren't even told about her death until my father came back from California two days later and he and my mother could give the news together. On the way to Mainz, in the Toyota, my father said he regretted not taking the term off and coming home to be with her, and to have Miriam and me around her more often, because he felt, now, all these years later, that he had introduced death as a triviality to us both. I said, Well, you couldn't have known when she was going to die, exactly. He was beside me in the car, looking out the window at the rolling countryside. He said, No, you're wrong, when she started to deteriorate the doctors said she had very little time. I went back to California anyway. I had such a lot of work to do.

I asked him to tell me what happened. I felt it might unburden him a little, and to my surprise he gave me more than just a glancing reply, which suggested he thought it might unburden him a little, as well. He said, It started with a second broken hip. From there, it took just a few weeks. She lost a huge amount of weight. She was very sick and couldn't eat. One morning, I got a call. They told me she'd awoken in very bad shape. She had an extremely high fever and was vomiting, confused, in and out of consciousness. This is probably it, they said. I told them, I'm in California, even if I left now I couldn't get there. They said she might last until the evening, if I could get a flight straightaway. I called your mother, of course, because obviously I could not get a flight straightaway. Your mother was working in a town about two hours away. By the time she arrived, my mother had died. It took me that whole day and the next to get squared away, then I came home and we told you and Miriam.

Then he said, But, you know, I figure I'll go the same way now. You will be away. Miriam is dead. Sometimes I look forward to it. Or at least I feel I deserve it.

He had opened a bottle of beer he'd brought with him from the apartment, and while he talked about his mother he drank. When he finished, he shook the bottle to see that it was empty. Then he placed the bottle in the plastic bag with our snacks. He took another bottle out and asked me if I wanted one. I said, I'm going over a hundred miles an hour. He said, That is a very good point. He opened the beer and had a sip and said, But let's change the subject, let's have a good time.

My grandmother's family home in Mainz, the place where she was born, was destroyed in the war, and a basic, unadorned house was erected in the spot where her house once stood. We arrived there in late afternoon, and it was warm, warm even in the shade. On either side of the house were more houses like it. Across the street were thick woods. We parked directly opposite the door to the house—my grandmother's old address. We'd been off the motorway for a while so I was drinking my first beer. My father walked up to the door and rang the bell. Then he stepped away from it and looked up, at the windows on the second floor. I stayed beside the car. I took some pictures with my phone. I waited. My father tried to ring the bells for both the neighboring houses, then he came back across the street and said, Nobody's home. That's a shame, I said. I might go for a little walk in the woods, he said, you want to come? I don't think so, I said. So my father went alone on the path into the woods in which my grandmother probably played as a girl. I went down the road to a little convenience store—a tabak—and placed a bottle of water on the counter. The man behind the counter asked if that was it, and I said, No, give me a pack of those cigarettes. I quit smoking twenty years ago, when my mother died, but the man in the tabak didn't know that, and I thought it was kind of funny, the way he just gave them to me, as though they meant nothing. I nearly felt I ought to say, I'm only going to smoke this one pack, maybe another. I bought a lighter as well, and as I walked up the street I smoked, and I felt light-headed. I got back to the car and stood there and watched my grandmother's house. From the bottom of the street, from the direction of the tabak, a woman and a child came. The child was on a bike. The child was a girl. She looked four or five, I guess. The mother had dark-brown hair. She was wearing a blue dress. She saw me waiting, and I could see I made her nervous. I lit another cigarette. I tried to look nonchalant. I leaned against the car. I kept looking at her, because I assumed she couldn't see my eyes through the sunglasses. I thought she would walk by. But she didn't. She stopped at my grandmother's house. I was standing right across the street from her front door. When she got to the door, and realized just how exactly, or precisely, I seemed to be standing in relation to her door, I could see that a part of her was panicking. For a moment, I felt slightly empowered by her panic. I could hardly believe it was happening, that I had become the reality of someone else's nightmare. But I stopped short of trying to terrorize her. I smiled and waved and gave a very short and probably incomprehensible explanation of what I—we—were doing there. I did not stop to think that she had no idea who I meant by *we*. As I spoke I wondered if it were in fact possible that we were related, that if we could sit down and prove our identities, she would realize that we were cousins. She might let us in, let us walk through the house and out into the garden, which might be the same as it was when my grandmother lived there. Then I heard some rustling—my father—and the woman heard rustling. She hurriedly unlocked the door, threw her child in, and slammed the door behind her, and locked it. I heard my father's voice from the woods. I threw my cigarette in the street and took the path into the woods and eventually spotted my father. He had wandered slightly off the trodden path, got himself stuck in some bushes, and couldn't get out. I took his arm. You've been smoking? he said. He seemed a little shell-shocked. How long was I gone? he asked. We walked out to the street. I think you need to sit down, I said. He agreed. I opened the car door for him. I helped ease him into his seat. He patted my arm as he landed. Thank you, son, he said. I closed the door, looked back at the house, and saw a pair of eyes watching me. Then the eyes disappeared. When I went around to my side of the car and got in, my father said, Let's get out of Mainz, let's overnight somewhere else. So we drove. We didn't have to go far. The first place we came to was a village called Walluf. How about Walluf? I said. I pronounced it VAHL-uff. It's va-LOOF, said my father.

Really?

Really.

Well, I said, we gotta stop in Walluf.

Someone is calling my name. A man is shouting my name, shouting in various directions. I hear the shouting before I realize it's my name that's being shouted. I turn around. Trish is standing. There's a man—a man I do not know, a young man—standing outside the men's room, shouting my name. I start to walk toward him. As I begin to contemplate why a man would be shouting my name outside that bathroom, I start to jog. When I reach him, the man points inside. I walk around the blue-tiled dividing wall, and I stop. I take my sunglasses off and put them in my inner jacket pocket. I hear Trish behind me. I hear her shoes batter the hard floor as she runs. She does not wait outside. She comes in, right behind me, and asks what's wrong. Could you wait outside, go guard our stuff? I ask. Is he okay? she asks. I've no idea, I say. Trish does not leave, does not go outside. She follows. I say, Is our stuff still by the seats? It's fine, she says. The first room is full of sinks and hand dryers. The second room, past another dividing wall, has urinals on one side and stalls on the other. Everything is blue or gray. Dad? I call out. A few seconds pass. I am just about to call out again. Then I hear some movement. It is labored, or groggy, or both, like the sound of someone turning over in his sleep, in a sleeping bag at a bus station. Over here, he says. I turn to the source, or in its direction, and then I see it, between me and the stalls. He hadn't made it in time, after all. I feel really rotten for him. I feel a huge sentimentalism rise up. It's okay, Dad, I say, we'll sort this out. He says nothing. I ask Trish to wait outside. Her head is down. Her arms are crossed. She does not leave. Then my father asks her to wait outside. She says, Okay, I'll wait outside, I'll watch the bags. She leaves. I wait a few moments. I say, Dad, you all right? He asks, Is Trish still here? She's gone, I say. The stall doors go almost all the way to the floor. I cannot get down on my knees and look for his feet, and I can't really hear where his voice is coming from. I ask him why it took so long for somebody to come get me. He says, I've been asking for help for fifteen minutes, I've asked half a dozen people. I knock on one door and somebody else answers. I knock on another door and nobody answers. I knock on another door and I hear my father say something. This you? I say. It's me, he says.

Can you open the door?

It's not locked.

Can I come in?

No.

Okay, what do you need?

Everything.

Jeans, underwear, socks, shoes?

Everything, he says.

Shirt, sweater?

Everything.

He moves again, and again it sounds like somebody in a bus station, moving on the floor. He sounds like he's in trouble.

You okay otherwise? I ask.

He doesn't answer, so I open the door. He is lying, mostly naked, but surprisingly clean, on the floor beside the toilet. Not completely on the floor, but half-fallen, holding on to the toilet roll dispenser with one arm and the commode with the other. But mostly in vain, since his legs and hips are already touching the ground. A man comes in and spots us. He immediately turns around and leaves. I enter the stall and close the door. My father tries to wave me away by moving his wrist. He makes an angry face. Get out of here, he says, just go get my goddamn clothes. I'm going to lift you up, I say, and then I'll go get your clothes, you can't be lying on the floor. He says, Don't touch me. I say, Don't be so fucking ungrateful. His eyes are bloodshot. He is breathing quick, shallow breaths. He is gathering the courage to speak. What he wants to say is in his mouth, he is trembling all over, he wants to say it so badly, yet he cannot allow himself. If he could say it—what is it, that he hates me, that I am a rat, that I killed Miriam, I am responsible?—he would be free to die with the dishonor he knows he deserves. I feel no sympathy for him. I hate him back. I grab him, lift him, and place him roughly on the commode. I push him back against the wall and raise my hand, and I think that I might, yes, now, strike him, a fist right to the eye, again, again, again, until his skull is so soft that my fist goes right through it, but he won't lift his arms to defend himself, he does not try to escape. I let him away from the wall. I put my hand on his shoulder and pat him there a few times. It's going to be okay, I say. I can't feel my arms or legs, he says. I can't feel anything. I wait. His head drops. I can see that he is exhausted. He spits over the other side of the commode. He is breathing shallow, painful breaths. Hold on, I say. I gather his clothes. I take all his belongings from his jeans pockets, and all his papers, and everything else, and put them in my pockets. I open the door to the stall and throw his soiled underwear and pants in a trash can, and his soiled socks, and his shoes. His shirt and sweater aren't very dirty. I clean them up a little bit with soap and water, wherever they are soiled. There aren't any paper towels, so I take my shoes and socks off, put my shoes back on, and make my socks soapy wet. I go back to the stall, push the door open, and, while he sits still, silently, I wash him. Then I dry him with toilet paper. Then I cover him up in his shirt and sweater. Then I say, Sit tight, Dad, I'll get all new clothes. I'm going to get you something to eat, too. He lifts his head up. He says, I won't eat. I say, You have to get on that plane.

He says, Yes, I have to get on that plane.

Can you lock the door behind me, when I go? I ask. I think so, he says. I tell him not to worry, I won't be long, and I leave him. I close the door behind me, and I wait to hear him lock it. Then I wait to hear that he is sitting safely down again. I say, All good? All good, he says. The door of another stall opens—only two doors down—and a man starts to walk out. Then he sees me and pretends to have left something behind, something that makes him swiftly reverse, with embarrassment, and close and lock the door. The bathroom then goes very quiet. I can see that a handful of stalls are occupied—by the color of the locks on the doors—and I realize that everyone in those stalls is waiting for me to leave so they can dash away. They are in those stalls quietly panicking, not knowing what to touch, everything is contaminated, only their embarrassment keeps them from fleeing.

The morgue, in Berlin, was in the basement of a hospital. The hospital was an old building and it seemed like a dangerous place to be, a place that would make you sick if you stuck around. Beside every door there were hand sanitizers. You placed your hand below a sensor and a fine puff of alcohol spray came out, and you rubbed it into your hands. Even though I touched almost nothing, I sanitized my hands at every opportunity. I went alone. Trish had offered to come along, but I said I'd prefer to be by myself. There was a coroner and a witness, a police officer. The coroner was a man in his fifties with little glasses, a weak chin, a bad complexion, a lazy eye, and he was bald on top with closely cropped hair on the sides. I found him hard to look at, but not because of his appearance—it was that the place itself had infected him with dreariness. I was given some papers to fill out. I looked them over and said, I can't understand any of this. They said the paperwork was essential. I'm here to identify my sister, I said, can I call the embassy and get them to help me with the paperwork afterward? The coroner spoke quietly to the officer for a few moments. The coroner was in charge, but I could see that he didn't want to be. He wanted somebody else to take responsibility for altering the procedure. The officer, who was young, tall, blond-haired, muscular, who wore a stiffly starched uniform, and who wore a sidearm—and who was probably quite inexperienced—refused to accept the responsibility. The coroner finally

agreed to let me see the body. He said it would be an unoffi-
cial identification. I asked him what that meant—would I have to
come again? No, he said, it would be sufficient once the paperwork was completed. I was taken into a room that had a glass
window. Through the window I could see another room, which
was dark. The officer stood just behind me, ready, I guessed, to
catch me if I fainted. The light in the other room came on. It
was a blue-green light. The tiles on the wall were blue-green—I
suspected they were white, and the light gave them color. The
coroner, who wore a face mask and protective glasses, wheeled in
a gurney with a body under a blanket. Suddenly I thought I was
going to lose my nerve, I was going to be sick, I wasn't ready, I'd
never done anything like this. The coroner stepped away from the
gurney and the body and pressed a button on the wall, and his
voice came through. The officer then said to me, in English, Shall
we proceed? Yes, I said, please proceed. The officer pressed a button on our side of the glass and told the coroner to proceed. The
coroner pulled the blanket down to just below Miriam's neck. He
held the blanket and did not step away. I nodded and he immediately pulled the blanket back over her head. I turned around.
The officer, who was averting his gaze, said, Okay? Okay, I said. I
really needed to be alone, but I had to sit in an office and meet the
coroner again, and then I called Trish and she got the paperwork
faxed to her for me to complete later. And then I went outside
and, for no reason I know, hopped on a bus that looked empty
and sat in the back and rubbed my eyes. She had almost no hair.
Miriam's head was almost hairless. Her head seemed shrunken,
and this made her nose seem gigantic. Her ears, too, looked oversized. The light in the room prevented me from seeing the color
of her skin, but the texture was claylike, striated, and stretched.

Her cheeks were pulled back in a way that gave her a ghoulish smile. If I had not seen her five years ago, when she was already painfully thin, I would not have recognized her. Actually, I didn't recognize her right away. But I finally recognized something in her closed eyes, an expression quite at odds with the torment that had expressed itself all over her face and head and neck. I think I saw surprise, surprise without fear. Or else I have been gradually altering the memory ever since, possibly to make the image easier to bear, as I carry it forth forever, or possibly to extend to her a reward for her courage, to decorate her troubled memory with a millionth of a millionth of a second of grace.

Outside the bathroom, Trish is waiting with our carry-ons. She is facing away from the entrance, looking toward the windows behind where we were sitting, past the history exhibit—staring at the tarmac, or the brightness, or the city hidden in the distance, or the mountains far beyond the city. I get her attention. I put my sunglasses back on. I grab my carry-on and my father's carry-on and start to walk. She walks beside me. She knows what we need to do—she saw the floor in the bathroom—but we don't need to speak of it. I go a little faster than my normal pace, and she keeps up. I tell her I can't believe how much farther we have to travel today.

Will your dad be okay? Can he make the trip?

He'll make it. I'm not sure if he'll survive the flight, but he's getting on that plane.

We are moving fast and I tell Trish I need to slow down. I feel sick, my head is spinning. Trish asks me if I'm going to be okay. I ask her if I look green again and she says no, I look translucent. I am sweating but I am ice-cold. I think my glands are swelling up. I have a headache in my teeth and jaw. I feel fine, I say, I feel like a million dollars. We stop at a departures board and check for Atlanta. Our flight is scheduled, at last. There it is—Go to Gate. Trish checks the time on her phone. I check the time as well. Considering all that lies ahead of us, we do not have a lot of time.

Though I cannot speak for my father, it was easy for me, in the beginning, not to eat. For the first forty-eight hours after our return from Aachen, I simply had no appetite. We went out drinking that first night, and I felt nauseous until I had quite a few drinks, and on the way home I thought about getting a kebab or a pizza slice, but I didn't, because I knew I wouldn't keep it down. That was when we met the man sitting on the curb and sang him Happy Birthday. He was English. I've lost me mates, he said. He didn't know what hotel he was staying in. He didn't know where he was. But he wasn't too worried. And after we sang to him, he cheered up and decided to go find a bar he could drink in all night. I think we hugged him. I can't remember how old he was. He was probably twenty-one. I think he tried to convince us to come along with him, but we were absolutely finished. I hadn't been drunk on consecutive nights for many years, and suddenly I found myself hanging on to life at the end of a nine-day binge. When I woke the next day, I felt truly terrible. I felt as though my insides had liquefied. I couldn't get back to sleep. I was wide awake but unbearably tired. I got up, showered, and went to sit on the couch. My father was up, too. Neither of us was in the mood for breakfast, or even coffee, and we didn't have the energy to speak. It was too cold to sit outside on the terrace. It was obvious that a period of pure waiting had begun—and apart from one last trip to Miriam's apartment, and a night out with Otis and Miriam's friends, that was what I did. I waited. I walked around and listened to music. I cycled. I stood outside cafés. I sat on benches. And as my appetite slowly returned, I staved off hunger pangs. Perhaps, if I had been in London, I'd have started eating sandwiches. In London, I might not have made it through that second day, and there never would have been a question of deciding not to eat. But in Berlin, they have no sandwiches. They have these things that are like sandwiches, but they are not sandwiches—the bread is wrong. And the only thing I could have eaten at that point were sandwiches—bland, familiar, pre-pared sandwiches from supermarkets or sandwich shops. I sat on the couch, checked the time, then stared out the window at the sleet, or just the gray, and thought of how far away London seemed to be, how unreachable, as though I would have to travel back in time to get there. Everything in my life would instantly dematerialize if I were dead. All my possessions would vanish. All my notes would be erased. All my debts would drift away. My remains would become nothing more than impediments to others—banks, bosses, an incoming tenant. But I did not have to die. I could just go live at home. I could work with my hands, I thought, renovate houses, lay roof, learn to drive a backhoe, find work shoveling on a horse ranch, buy a tiny fishing boat, meet a woman twice divorced.

When the hunger pangs started, and the sweats and nausea were strong, and I couldn't stop the trembling, I found that exer-cise could take my mind off it. I did push-ups and sit-ups, or laps around the huge rooftop terrace in the freezing wind and rain. I hopped on my bike and rode up and down hills, crossed inter-sections, raced cars, hurried everywhere. And when I stopped, it felt, sometimes, as though I had eaten. I also thought of food, I placed before my mind's eye huge platters of food, delicious food, expensive food, and I let myself dream of eating it, digging flesh out of lobster claws, eating two-inch-thick rare steaks, sucking the last bits of meat and skin off a whole hen. This was effective but it felt dishonest. It made me feel I was discrediting the whole experience, and Miriam's experience along with it. So I started to refuse to let myself think of food. If I found myself thinking of food, I immediately forced myself to think of Miriam's body, lying in the morgue. After that, I found that brushing my teeth averted hunger. I went and bought some German toothpaste that tasted a little like bleach, and for a while I was brushing my teeth every thirty minutes. When I began to realize that I was swallowing and eating the toothpaste, I quit that, too. And all there was left was to see it through, to face the desire to eat and refuse, to reject the body's need for sustenance. I'd go to my en suite and lie on the floor and convulse and pull my ears out and pull my hair and scratch my face and throw myself over the toilet when I couldn't vomit anything up, and during these convulsions I could see clearly and objectively that to save myself from this pain was hedonism, that everything above this pain was extravagance. And the greatest thing about this pain was that while it was happening you could feel yourself disappearing, cell by cell, breaking down and getting thinner. Then the convulsions would end and I would lie there and think of Miriam and how much she must have hated us, or the pity we wanted so badly to proffer her, in order to go through this. Our faith that she would one day need us again, just as we needed her, no doubt belonged to the hedonism and extravagance and stupidity of life above the pain of starving. I started to eat little bits of bread because the convulsions and attacks were getting more severe. Every time I had a piece of bread, even a bite, I would go and look in the mirror, and I saw

I had fattened dramatically, that I was carrying so much useless and unclean weight. And until I was hungry again—until I knew I was suppressing my body's distress—I saw and felt myself fattening. Whenever I thought of returning to London, I felt myself fattening—expanding with habits, ideas, opinions, things—and it seemed to me that my work was not just keeping me in circumstances that allowed for and required this expansion but it was a plague, an incurable and inescapable plague of superabundance and anxiety. I was so preoccupied with my own struggle that it took a couple of days to realize that my father hadn't been eating, either. He looked tired, emotionless. He said he couldn't get warm, even though we had the heat up as high as it would go in our apartment. He would suddenly sit down and complain about blindness, numbness in his hands and feet, and now and then, if the seat were comfortable enough, he'd fall asleep for thirty seconds. I thought our trip had exhausted him, and the reality that Miriam would be released soon, and that our time here, and his time with Trish, would be over, was sinking in. Then he started vomiting, or at least heaving, in the bathroom of our apartment.

Trish and I stop first at a men's casual clothing store. I need socks, I say. I lift up my trouser legs to show her my bare ankles, and I say, Don't ask. What does your dad need? she asks. Everything, I say. She says, You get the pants and whatever else, I'll get a shirt. I say, I've got a better idea, you run across to the shoe store and grab him some shoes. Perfect, she says, and she walks out of the clothing store. I watch her. She gets about twenty feet away, stops, turns around and jogs back. What size would you say? she asks. I say, No idea, I'm a twelve, that's probably a safe size to get. Okay, she says, and she walks out again. Sizing his clothes is much easier. We're the same height, and though he is thinner around the neck and waist, along the arms and legs—he has the frame of a slim, elderly man—we have similar proportions. I get him a white T-shirt with an ocean scene with a surfer and some writing on it. I get him a soft, blue, thick button-down long-sleeve shirt to wear over the T-shirt, and I get him a navy-blue hooded sweatshirt. It has a design on the back, some writing and a cityscape, but it's for warmth and comfort on the flight. I also get him a pair of jeans, thirty-two waist, thirty-four inseam, some boxer shorts, and a pair of socks—I get a pair of socks for myself, too. At the counter, as the woman is ringing everything up, I look down at what I'm wearing—the ragged suit jacket with sweaty armpits, the shirt that is soaked through with sweat almost everywhere, and which stinks of boozy, nicotine-y perspiration. I go back and get myself a gray hooded sweatshirt with a black scorpion on it for the flight as well. The cost of it all is just under five hundred euro. I don't even try to pretend to not be shocked. I tell the woman behind the counter, That is ridiculous, it's mercenary. She doesn't know how to respond. Do I refuse to pay? she wonders. She cannot see my eyes behind the sunglasses, but I am trying to express my sense of futility through them. What can be done about airport prices? I want to ask. I pull my wallet out. How much is the sweatshirt? I ask. She shows me the price tag. It's eighty-nine euro. Then I see that the jeans are a hundred and fifty. I feel outraged, but I shouldn't be. London is more expensive, and it's actually my job to help make affordable things expensive, mostly by redefining, or reverse-defining, unaffordable. I give her my business credit card. I have a twenty-thousand-pound limit on that card, but every month the bank direct-debits the full amount I owe. When I got the card, I said, Not much of a credit card, is it? He said something about responsible business habits—this was a time when people took advice from bankers—and I said it didn't matter anyway, my business didn't require a lot of credit. I never had to go back and ask for an upgrade. I pay myself a decent salary. I try to expense everything I can—even a portion of my rent, and some of my utilities, and any travel. I pay myself a bonus at the end of each year with whatever I have left—in order to avoid corporate tax. I pay my accountant. And I start over. Every couple of years I take any savings I've accumulated and put them into stocks and mutual funds in the US.

I get everything in a big bag and walk out. I don't immediately see a shoe store. The nausea and fatigue I've felt since leaving my father in the bathroom becomes a sudden and unbearable light-headedness. My legs become almost too heavy to move. I am numb. I find a chair—there is finally some emptiness in the airport. I sit down and put the bag between my legs and think that I must take my phone out to text Trish my whereabouts. But I cannot pick up my phone. The exhaustion is like nothing I've experienced. I have a moment of dream thought, a dream I'm conscious of having. My father and I are digging with shovels. The ground is frozen. Then I feel someone poking my shoulder and it's Trish. I open my eyes and realize my head is all the way back, without any support. I nearly give myself whiplash trying to lift my head. I sit up and cough. I try to speak but my throat is dry. Trish asks, anxiously, if we should go. I don't want to admit that I cannot move. I try to speak but I can't make any sense. I make the kind of noises one makes with a jaw full of novocaine. I shake my head. I clear my throat a few times and I can speak again. I say, Just give me one minute. She sits down beside me and I lean forward. I put my elbows on my knees and my eyes on the cups of my palms. Then I scratch my head for a while. I wiggle my toes and fingers.

I realize she has a large bag, even bigger than the bag I have. I say, Did you get my dad cowboy boots or something? She opens the bag and inside are three boxes. She says, I just didn't want to get him the wrong size. I didn't want to think of him walking across the airport in Atlanta with shoes that made his feet hurt. She opens one of the boxes. They are soft-leather penny loafers. My dad wears penny loafers, she says, he swears there is nothing more comfortable.

I look down into the bag and see two other boxes.

I got them in three sizes, she says.

That is pretty thoughtful of you, I say.

Let's go, she says.

I must have watched my father walk around a lot in penny loafers, sockless, watering the grass, gardening, waterproofing the deck, wandering through the maze of our house, washing the car, getting the paper or checking the mailbox, going to the grocery store, grilling steaks, standing on sidelines while I or Miriam played sports. I remember my father falling from a tree he was cutting. He'd been swarmed by bees. He screamed at us all to get inside and somehow picked himself up after the fall and ran around trying to wave the bees away from his face until he finally jumped the fence into the backyard and dove into the pool. I remember my mother swimming in the pool, drinking iced tea, or, if her friends were over, drinking gin and tonics, and either my father was there or he was absent—but the memory is curiously not of my mother but of where my father might have stood or not stood. One day, when a lot of friends were over, my mother broke her leg while running around the pool. The bone came clear out of her skin. My father was in California, so the neighbors gathered around her and waited for the ambulance to come. When my mother came back from the hospital, she wore a cast from her toes to her hips, and a big gurney came with her, which was adjustable, so she could raise her legs or her back. She was in that gurney for a month, and in the cast for longer. My grandmother did all the cooking. Miriam and I did the housework. My grandmother, when she drove us around the quiet streets of our neighborhood, let Miriam and me stand on top of the car and pretend to be surfing. Once, Miriam fell and broke her arm. Our grandmother was terrified and thought she would end up in jail. She was also terrified of how my father would respond. He was in California and he wouldn't be home for weeks, so my mother decided not to tell him. We all decided, together, that my father would never forgive such recklessness. Even if my mother had tried to take the blame, as she first decided she would do, we all knew my father would know she was lying, and then he would not forgive her deceit. About six months later it came out—it was always going to, I guess—when my father was home for the summer, and he laughed and laughed at our decision to keep it from him—had he inspired such fear in all of us? And we all thought we had escaped retribution until, later, my father quietly took our grandmother away for a talk, and she was—though it sounds slightly overtheatrical to say it—never the same with us again. And I do, now, remember beating up some kids over Miriam. I was a big kid. Miriam was quiet. I remember once hearing that two boys had taken Miriam to the woods. I ran after them. I found them trying to lock her in a shed, or some kind of abandoned house, in the middle of the woods. The woods I speak of—dense pine forests near the Gulf—are dark and endless, they are useless for timber, they are overgrown, they are full of snakes, they are not places you go to for nature and reflection. Everywhere, slim pine trunks rise up to the high green needles that darken the sunlight. There is just enough room to walk between these trees, and at dusk, the shadows that move through them as you walk seem like bodies darting from tree trunk to tree trunk. The ground is nothing but fallen needles, reddened, dry on the top, wet and compacted down below. If you happen to come across a little trail, or a dirt track made of two parallel ruts—made by tires—it usually leads to a natural break in the woods, a pond—dried or not—a clearing, a creek bed, and so on, and generally you find a structure there, a shed or a house that nobody lives in. Miriam was nine or ten, I guess, when she was dragged out there by two boys. It was something that was happening in our town. Boys my age were taking girls Miriam's age out to these places and locking them in these sheds or threatening to lock them in. It was like a game. It's hard to believe, now, that anybody would do such a thing, even the redneck boys in our town. Some of the girls were lucky—they weren't locked inside. Others, like Miriam, weren't as lucky. But I think that maybe none of the girls was as scared as Miriam. I remember I found out about what was happening to Miriam from some girls who were laughing about it, and who claimed that they had been taken, it was okay. But Miriam wasn't like these people. So I ran into the woods. I knew the woods very well, and I knew where the boys would take her. I could hear her crying out from a long way off. I couldn't run fast because of the trees, I couldn't run in a straight line. I was also slowed by the ground, because it was, in places, so soft that my feet sank, and the needles were up to my knees. I finally got there. One boy ran off but I grabbed the other one. I let Miriam out. She

couldn't breathe. I have still never seen, in my life, a face as terrified as her face. She thought she was covered in spiders, I never
had the chance to check. She ran away. She didn't go straight
home. She just walked the streets for hours—I had to get on my
bike and go find her. I beat the kid up. I didn't want to hurt him
so much that he'd go looking for revenge, come back and take
that revenge out on Miriam. But I had to do something. I had
to teach him a lesson. Now that I am here in this airport I think
I probably should have killed him. What would have happened
if I hadn't come? How long would they have kept her in there?
Another minute? An hour? And what might they have done to
her when they released her, when they—these two stupid, violent
boys—realized they had the power to so thoroughly torment and
dominate somebody? A few days after that, I went into the woods
by myself, I walked the path those boys would have led Miriam.
I went slowly. I looked up at the canopy above. I tried to think
of everything as Miriam had thought of it—of how different the
light in the treetops might have seemed to her, of how strange
her own senses might have seemed to her—I tried to emulate
her panic in my senses, to smell and hear nothing, to feel nothing, while all her energies were channeled into the strength to
fight or escape, which was not enough strength. They had opened
the door somehow and pushed her in, and when I arrived they
were holding the door and laughing. That first boy saw me and
ran. The second looked at me and his look said, Well, you found
us, no harm done, though. So I gave him a bloody nose and I
choked him and I kicked him in the head and ribs. When I went
back, I saw that nobody had come to repair the lock on the door,
so I opened it. I was sick with fear. I couldn't see much. There
wasn't any furniture. There was some wood, a lot of cut logs.

There weren't any windows. The shed was like every structure you find in places like that—a cheap wooden frame held together by screws, brackets, and sometimes nails, covered with hand-cut, possibly secondhand, siding. The air inside was hot and stale. I went in and turned around and looked out at what Miriam would have seen last, before the door closed, except for the faces of the two boys trying to close the door on her, their eyes and fingers. Then I closed the door on myself and stood in the darkness for as long as possible. I might have lasted thirty seconds or a minute, but I knew I could escape whenever I wanted, I simply had to push the door open. But when I did push, the bottom edge of the door of the shed got slightly stuck in the earth, just a little—but it was enough to fill my thoughts with dread—and instead of lifting the door to make it open easier, I lunged at the door, shoulder first, with all my might, and tumbled out into the woods again. I found two big spiders on me. One on my shirt and one on my jeans. I figured I was covered by hundreds, so I undressed, as fast as I could, throwing my clothes on the little dirt road that led from the shed back to whatever country road you came to a mile or so later and stomped on my clothes and whipped them in the air. I rubbed my head and danced on the little dirt road. Then I went home.

I say, I'll go back to my dad and give him the clothes. Would you mind getting him something to eat? Something light.

Trish agrees and we separate. When I get to the bathroom, I find a man—a janitor—talking aloud to nobody about the mess he's had to clean up. He's angry. Germans talk to themselves more than any other people I've ever observed. I think they must feel really helpless. I knock on my father's stall door and he lets me in. The janitor gives me a threatening look. I stare right at him and say, in English, I swear to God I will make you regret that threatening look. He defiantly sticks out his fat neck. I close the door and my father says, Who the hell is that man outside and what has he been talking about? He is sitting quietly on the commode, wrapped up in his shirt and sweater. Where's Trish? he asks. I say, Gone to get you something light to eat. Ah, he says. Can you feel your arms and legs now? I ask. I think so, he says. Can you get this stuff on or do you need my help? I ask. I'm sure I can do it myself, he says. But before I can walk out the stall door I see that he cannot even lift himself up, he cannot stand. We look at each other. I've got to make this flight, he says. You'll make it, I say. I kneel down and take the socks and boxers out of the bag. I put his socks on first. He can lift his feet, he can point them. They go halfway up his calves. Nice socks, he says, nice and thick. I've got the same ones, I say. Next are the boxers. I put his feet through them. I pull them up around his knees. Then I say, Grab hold of my neck, can you hold on? He puts his arms around my neck, clasps his hands together and says, I think so. One, two, *three*, I say. I lift, and his thighs and buttocks come off the commode, almost like adhesive tape, but his grasp holds, and I slip the boxers up to his waist. Next I put his T-shirt on. Then his shirt. Then his jeans. The jeans take a lot of effort. I have to get behind and under him to lift him. He has to steady himself by putting his hands on the walls, and I pull his jeans up. They are way too big around the waist. They fall right down. I take out the shoes Trish has bought. I open the stall door so I can kneel down. I say, Trish got three different sizes, hopefully one of them fits. He looks at me quizzically. Did she really? he asks. She really did, I say. He starts to cry a little bit. I put the first pair on and he seems to think they fit fine. Then I put the hooded sweatshirt on him. We walk out together. He puts one arm around me. I hold the hand of that arm, and I also hold the loose waist, so his jeans won't fall down.

Trish is waiting outside for us—she's got him a sandwich—and we all go together down the steps to the seats where we were before. The act of walking with me seems to give my father strength, or reminds his muscles how to work, and he makes the last few steps all on his own, though I have to pull his pants up. He sits. His arms move fine. He's steady once again.

I'm going to get you a belt, I say.

And then we better start moving to the gate, says Trish.

I look at the time to calculate how long we have been here—in this airport—already. My thoughts go back to the shuttle-bus driver, the man dreaming of his wife. I won't be long, I say, I'll be ten minutes, twenty at the most.

My father's father died in the Ardennes Offensive—the Battle of the Bulge—either in Malmedy or St. Vith, and after seeing Mainz and driving on into Belgium, he decided to visit both places. We had come down into the Ardennes from Koblenz, after a very late night. That morning we'd had a huge breakfast in our hotel. It was a continental breakfast, but we were the only two people in the restaurant, and the owner was sitting with us, talking about the history of Koblenz, so we ordered some sausages and bacon, some fried potatoes, and a lot of ketchup. And we needed some beer for the hangover. And the owner decided we all needed some schnapps. We asked for recommendations—points of interest in the area. He said there was nothing more interesting than Koblenz. It was a funny thing. All the people we met along the Rhine kept telling us that the only town worth visiting along the Rhine was their own. We asked, for instance, a guest-house owner in Kaub where we should go next, and he said, Kaub is the most interesting, most beautiful, and most historically rich place along the Upper Middle Rhine. The people we met and drank with had said the same thing in Walluf, in Eltville, in Kiedrich, in Bingen, in Sankt Goar. In actual fact, all these towns and villages were beautiful, and the Rhine was beautiful. We—or I—climbed the steps at Lorelei, and looked out across the famous bend in the river, and the dazzling blondness of the day, the mountainous green valley, the blue skies, and I saw the centuries turn back. I saw the migrating German tribes arriving from the Bavarian gap. Here was where they naturally landed, guided by the mountains and the northern borders of the Roman Empire. They simply had nowhere else to go. They would all gather and live here and overcrowd, here at the Rhine. The next day I could barely walk, because my calves were so sore. The steps took almost thirty minutes to climb. I had run for the first five minutes, and by the time I reached the top I was nearly crawling. I met my father at the Lorelei lookout café—he had driven up— for a glass of sparkling wine.

We toured the castles along the Rhine. My father spoke with some of the curators, or, if the curator was not available, the sales assistant in the souvenir shop. I spent a lot of time touching the stone walls, knocking on wooden doors, climbing towers. I spoke German with waiters and waitresses. I spoke German with other tourists who had come to see the Rhineland, though there were not many at this time of year. We took circuitous drives in the river valley hinterlands, twice crossed the river by ferry for no reason but to get the sense of the place from on the water. From time to time I wished that Miriam had died a month or two later, so we could have seen the Rhineland covered in flowers, the hills

GREG BAXTER

bright green, and the bars full of people. In Koblenz, the city at
the end of the Middle Rhine, we took a gondola over the water
where the Rhine and Mosel meet. It was a gigantic gondola that
rose high above the water, and shook gently in the breeze, on its
way up to the big fortress on a high rock, then we had some dinner, then we went to a heavy-metal nightclub, the only place in
town where there seemed to be people. We got a break from the
music on the radio, although, after a couple of hours and a few
beers, the music there sounded all alike, too.

Our first stop after Koblenz was the small village of Kesternich,
where, said my father, a largely unknown but critically important
battle was won by the Americans. The drive from Koblenz to
Kesternich crosses flat plains, farmland, long, narrow roads with
a single line of trees on either side, not unlike Iowa, I would
imagine. I was too tired to drive quickly. I had a headache from
the night before. The motorway out of Koblenz had been pretty
harrowing, full of massive trucks, heavy traffic moving way too
fast, and I decided to settle my nerves afterward by traveling
at the speed limit, or five to ten kilometers an hour below it.
Cars passed us on the road, and honked at me for driving too
slowly, but I just waved and thanked them for their concern. I
kept stopping to smoke cigarettes. You okay to drive, son? my father kept asking. You bet, I kept saying. My father explained the
importance of Kesternich on the way. The Ardennes Offensive
was the last major battle of the war before the battle of Berlin, and victory along the western front was still in the balance.
Had Germany been victorious, the war might have continued for
some time. The Germans wanted Antwerp. The front stretched
a hundred miles, and the northern pivot of the front was supposed to be Kesternich and nearby Simmerath. Seven days of

188

fighting, with many dead and captured, produced a major set-back for the Germans. The battle here meant they had to move the northern pivot southward substantially, and gave the Americans a lethal advantage. By the time my father finished telling me all about it, I found myself wanting to get out of the car and approach the town on foot. I don't know what I expected, but after three days of medieval history—of history that is so grown over, and mostly unrecorded in the first place, that it's invisible—I suppose I was looking forward to a landmark, a memorial to the fallen dead, and a preserved battlefield. But Kesternich is still in Germany, and it is still a defeated town, a very ashamed and quiet place. There was nothing to see. I could sense, on its outskirts, how it might have been—houses separated by large plots of land, sheds scattered about, infantry moving under cover of light snow—but once we got in the middle of it, and there wasn't much to it, my father said, Oh well. Just on the outskirts of town we came to a massive shopping complex. There were several parking lots and several warehouse stores full of hardware, office supplies, cheap groceries, furniture, electronics, appliances, and so on. I couldn't—and never did—figure out what population these places were supposed to serve. The only place to eat in all of Kesternich, it seemed, was in this shopping complex, specifically in a dreary, orange-and-brown cafeteria inside the hardware store. It hadn't been too long since we'd had the huge breakfast, but we decided we should eat again, and though we both had something healthy on our minds, we could find nothing healthy, so we had goulash. Our goulash smelled like cigarette smoke. The boy behind the counter smelled like cigarette smoke, and looked as though he'd been fried in the same grease as the unappetizing, cigarette-smelling French fries. The experience turned my father yellow. I said, You've gone yellow. He looked at me and said, You've gone yellow yourself. I said, I'm going to eat anyway. The road west out of Kesternich dropped steeply and wondrously, first it descended into thick woods, then it plunged into the Ruhr River gorge, down a switchback path on a cliff face that was perilous not just because it was narrow but because it came abruptly at the end of a hundred or so kilometers of open, rolling farmland. It was thick with woods. I cannot remember if the trees were green or if they were brown, but there were many, and it was dark. It was so dark that, for the first time that whole trip, I took my sunglasses off in the daytime. I stopped at a patch of widened shoulder at a bend to stand, breathe, and get used to the fact that the road wasn't straight anymore. My father said, Hell, I'll drive. But he didn't move. And I would not have let him anyway. At the time I was thinking, You know what, we have to take a night off, we have to go to the movies and fall asleep sober. We reached the bottom, where we came upon the town of Monschau, which was such a beautifully isolated and awesomely charming old-fashioned village—surely it was a fake—that we stopped and had a huge lunch in the sunshine. We sat on the terrace by a bridge that ran across the splashing, narrow Ruhr below, across from the church, and my father explained that the village dated back to the eleventh or twelfth century and was where, approximately—just south of our position—the northern shoulder of the Battle of the Bulge had moved, once Kesternich was out of the picture.

Here, in the north, he said, the Germans placed their best fighting force in the west, the 6th Panzer Army. The fighting ranged from here, at the northern shoulder, to Bastogne in the south, and also Luxembourg. The Germans made the biggest inroads through the center, through the town of St. Vith. And, he said, I believe St. Vith was where my father was killed. Or Malmedy.

You never speak about your father, I said.

I didn't know him well enough to form an opinion, he said.

You must have some recollection.

Some, he said.

Was he intelligent?

He was a doctor.

Was he kind?

To me? I don't think he was anything to me. He was violent with my mother.

Violent? Physically violent?

With my mother, yes. Consequently, as a sign of respect to her, I never put much effort into him. I looked him up, but when I thought I was getting close to the answer, I halted, I put away everything and gave it no more thought.

It's hard to believe, I said.

Is it? Why?

I was in no mood to quarrel. My father was obviously having a strange reaction to his proximity to the deathplace of his father, and I found it annoying because it was so predictable. I said, I just meant that it is not easy to think about her getting beat up by her husband. She seemed like a strong woman, a warrior, she got you all the way to the US. I still don't know how she accomplished that. Neither you nor she ever spoke of it.

Well, he said, you never asked.

Bullshit, I said. I'm not supposed to have to ask.

He tried to get the waitress's attention. I wasn't sure if he had or not, because I was staring at him, waiting for an answer. He waited for a moment, looking at his hands in his lap. Then he said, Mother had a wealthy friend in America, in California. A friend from school had moved there after the war to marry an American soldier, and he was wealthy, he sent money to my mother and two other women to come to California. The others never went. I don't know what happened to them. I convinced Mother to go. She was very frail and depressed. She was so hopeless that at times it seemed that she would have preferred if I'd taken the money and gone alone. She also hated the idea of leaving Germany, leaving her own mother, heading into the unknown without a husband, even one as brutal as my father, and there were many times she nearly gave up, she often sat on some steps or the side of a road and wouldn't speak. The journey involved many grueling hours together. There were days I had to shout at her. I struck her once and she struck me back, she beat me severely. So this is probably why we never told you about it.

The waitress came by with the check and he paid, stood, and suggested we get back on the road. He'd put both of us in a gloomy mood. But it was such a nice day that once we got back in the car and found ourselves driving up the high winding roads out of the Ruhr valley, in blazing and redemptive sunshine, we forgot about it all, we forgot about the hardship he and his mother had faced, and we forgot all about the people whose destinies had come through the crucible of that hardship, and my father said, As you may or may not know, St. Vith's liberation is one of the most famous of all of World War Two, in part because of the prayer General Patton had drawn up, in which he asked the Lord for clear skies to bomb the Germans. Then my father spoke a little bit about the place, and about the fighting there. The word liberation called to mind, for me, girls in skirts and scarves throwing tulips at tanks and jeeps, even though I knew, from my father, that the town had been reduced to rubble by Allied bombing, so there had been no girls to wear skirts and scarves, nor a single, solitary tulip. I expected several monuments to the Allied soldiers who had died, as well as tasteless living memorials like a souvenir shop with tanks that shoot sparks, and a bar called Uncle Sam's, where the photographs of all the Americans who had come to visit since were hung on walls, and where every night at closing they played Springsteen. We did find small memorials to those who fought and died in and around St. Vith, and they were tasteful if incongruous with the complete lack of spirituality—lack of ghostliness is perhaps a better way to put it—one felt in St. Vith. But there were no American bars and no souvenir shops. On the way to St. Vith, we had come through Malmedy. Malmedy is set inside the mountains, and the center of the town is full of narrow and winding streets that rise and fall sharply. It is charming, and one can easily imagine the fighting that must have taken place there, building by building, nightmarish, bloody. St. Vith was nothing like Malmedy. St. Vith was unsightly and sterile. It had the character of a satellite suburb, a lot like Kesternich, in fact, or the shopping complex outside Kesternich. My father relished the ordinariness of the place. He was glad it was an anticlimax. The town stretched pointlessly along the artery roads in and out, the way American towns and cities do, for miles and miles. Perhaps it had been more like Malmedy before the war. I never saw any pictures, but a woman working in the tourist office there assured us that the prewar St. Vith looked nothing like the present version. We asked for information about the war, about what the place might have looked like, what it might have been like to fight here, and she said there wasn't any at the tourist office. It was mostly information on beer, wine, food, hiking, wellness, restaurants, and shopping. She told us to go meet a local historian. His name was Klaus Klauser. She gave us a map with some information, and she marked Klauser's museum on it. On top of the map, in four languages, it read, St. Vith is worth a trip! The woman spoke German. Everyone in the area spoke German, even though we were in Belgium, and nobody seemed to speak English particularly well. The Museum of History in St. Vith—where Klauser worked, and where he acted as head of the local historical society—had a library of about ten thousand books and something like fifty thousand documents, records, and reports, the woman said. And the current exhibition, she said, was about life under the Nazi occupation of St. Vith. If there was ever going to be a place and time for my father to confirm his father's place of death, it was that day. The woman told us that Klauser would no doubt love to talk for hours on the subject. He was such a lovely man, such a lovely, lovely man. She became almost watery-eyed, thinking of his loveliness. I said, We'll go, definitely, and we'll say hello from you. My father wasn't sure. Local historians, he said, there's something creepy about them. Something very creepy. And he was right. We walked to the museum. It was down a hill, past the church, through a vast parking lot, and in a big green field. It was in the old railway station. The walk took five minutes, and my father walked the whole way with his hands in his pockets. Bad idea, he kept saying, this is a bad idea.

I wonder if we looked official and menacing, like inspectors out of Kafka, because the woman at the museum's front desk almost hyperventilated when I told her we were there to see Klaus Klauser. She didn't even ask our names. She just turned red, started sweating, and ran to a nearby door and knocked on it. Her reaction was so strange that as she was running from us, I looked at my father and said, That was weird. He shrugged and said, Creepy, creepy places, creepy people. The desk attendant disappeared behind the door. A few seconds later, a team of men appeared. My father sighed. He even rubbed his temples. Herr Klauser? I asked. The man in the middle, wearing wire-rimmed glasses and with clipped-short brown-gray hair, nodded. I told Klauser that the woman at the tourist office had sent us. I apologized for having to speak English, but then I spoke German. I attempted to make a joke about how much the woman there seemed to like him, and either my German made a mess of it, or he, and his entourage, were not amused. If it had just been Klauser, by himself, in an office, my father and I might have sat, relaxed, and simply started talking. But the way we'd been surrounded in this tiny museum, a museum with no visitors, just local historians and administrative staff, created the tense atmosphere of a standoff. They demanded, presumably, to know what it was we wanted, why we had come unannounced, and how it was that we knew to ask for Klauser. Our explanation about the woman at the tourist office, for whatever reason, had been collectively rejected. It was sort of dizzying. The only answer I could give them that was mostly true was that we had come for no reason, we were just passing through, we were just looking for a chat, possibly a coffee or a beer. In my mind, local historians were supposed to be the kind of people who could be relied upon to drop whatever they were doing and go have a beer with visitors. I don't think my father wanted to know about his father. And I didn't feel I had the right to ask on his behalf, nor did I want to say, in front of everybody, that my father lost his father, a Nazi officer, most likely, in the battle for this town, especially at a time when the wounds of occupation had been opened by the exhibition. I had no answer for him, so I said, Well, I'm writing a book about the area, a travel book, nothing serious, and I wondered if you could tell me a bit about the fighting here. The men around Klauser dispersed, mumbling. Klauser seemed to be busy. There wasn't going to be a relaxed chat. My father said, Let's get out of here. But Klauser said, I may have something for you. He walked us through the door to the library, which doubled as the museum office. There was a large rectangular table where the men around Klauser had sat back down. Behind the table were several dozen shelves, going back a long way, full of books. Klauser disappeared in the shelves for a minute, and we stood over the men at the table, who glowered at us. Then Klauser returned with two huge books. This is all we have in English, he said. Each was a foot tall, or more, and a couple thousand pages long, in tiny type, though with lots of pictures. Have a seat, he said. Take as long as you like. I was too embarrassed to admit I didn't want to do any actual work, that even if I were here for important research, I'd have preferred him to boil it down for me, as though I was a general or a CEO who doesn't have time for details. My father sat down because he needed some rest, but then he opened his volume and pretended to look at it. Klauser suggested to everyone else in the room that they get back to the budget meeting they were having. They did. A woman came up to us and said, in perfect English, If you'd like anything copied, please let me know. My father asked, Is there a good place to get pizza around here? The woman started to answer him, but Klauser put his finger to his lips and made the following noise—*shhhhhhhhhhh*. My father leaned back. He was acting like a bold child in school. He started making *drop drop drop* noises by flicking his finger against his cheek. He picked up a pencil and tried to balance it, upright, on the tip of his finger. It kept falling on the table. He was ignored. I flipped through my book, politely. I waited exactly five minutes. Then I asked the woman to copy three pages of the book for me. This turned out to be an ordeal, an ink cartridge had to be replaced, and Klauser had to halt the meeting again to open the supplies cabinet. He was furious with the woman. She was mortified and apologetic to us, and she shouted back at Klauser. As we left, I thanked the men for letting us interrupt their meeting. They smiled and said it was their pleasure, and they hoped we'd found some useful information for the book! Send us all copies! they said. Klauser stood up and shook my hand heartily, as though we had gone for that beer. He had a brochure with him, and he gave it to me. He said, This museum might be more suited to you—the Musée National d'Histoire Militaire, or the National Military History Museum, in Diekirch, Luxembourg. My father walked out of the room. I said, Herr Klauser, my father is also a historian. Or he was.

Yes? Do I know him?

Probably not, I said. I mentioned my father's name, and Klauser said, I'm afraid it isn't familiar to me.

His father may have died here, I said.

He glared at me sharply. I'd antagonized him. Perhaps he thought I would ask him to do some work for me. He said, finally, Many people died here.

My father didn't have the energy to walk back up the steep hill, so he sat on a swing in an empty playground while I retrieved the car. When I picked him up, he said, It's funny, that guy's whole career is this little museum, and the local history of this town and surroundings, which wouldn't even be on the map but for the war, and two people come in and ask him to talk about the one subject he ought to have considerable expertise in—the war—and he has a budget meeting. That's your local historian in a nutshell, he said. Where to now? I asked. Got me, he said.

What about this museum in Diekirch?

What about it?

They've re-created battle scenes in dioramas, look.

I gave the brochure to my father and he said, Oh dear, that looks awful.

And it was. But it wasn't awful in the way we—or at least I—expected it to be, which was like the basement of a crazed old man who believes he is the veteran of many wars in many centuries, and who wears a helmet and a belt full of live grenades to bed. It was a little like a crazed basement—because it was a private collection before it was a museum—but the exhibits were vast, orderly, and exhaustive. It generated sorrow in me, the way that one pathetic, creepy, artificial diorama after another finally, by sheer repetition, attained a grotesque, or inverted, lifelikeness. I started on the ground floor, and I had no idea how colossal it would be. I was standing in front of a diorama—all were on the scale of one to one—that depicted a scene of German soldiers in a bunker. Two soldiers were working on a radio. One was making coffee. From down a stone-walled spiral staircase beside the diorama, a group of people was coming, speaking English. It was a tour. The tour guide was American. The people in the group were English, a family. The guide, who turned out to be one of the founders, was telling them about the history of the museum. He and two other collectors had joined their collections to create the largest collection of Second World War memorabilia in existence. It's fascinating, said the English man, earnestly. All we needed, said the founder, was the space, and the Luxembourg government was very keen to give us this one, we love it. I butted in on their conversation. I said, It's a terrific space. They gave me uncertain looks and moved on. It was my good luck that they came down that staircase, because when I first saw it, I assumed it was for staff only. I hadn't realized the museum was on multiple levels. It was a strange assumption, seeing as the structure, from the outside, was so obviously large, but I guess I felt that nobody could possibly fill up a structure that size with so many of the same uniforms, weapons, and vehicles. But it was on six levels, two below the ground floor and three above it. And each level was a sprawling series of twists and turns, big rooms and small rooms, scenes of daytime and nighttime, indoors and outdoors, in battle and at rest. Except for the ground floor, the rest of the museum was dimly lit, and there were no windows, which gave you the impression that you shouldn't be there, that the place was closed. The brochure stated that the dioramas were meant to illustrate the technical and logistic evolutions within the armed forces of the belligerent parties, which I assumed was a bad translation of French, or Luxembourgish, or perhaps just bad English written by a Luxembourger. Furthermore, it stated, the museum intends to maintain high respect and gratitude on a national level for all the soldiers who died for the liberation of Luxembourg, first of all on the American side. Furthermore, as a place of gathering for Allied and German veterans, the museum conceives itself also as a provider and mediator of the reconciliation by its commitment on the European and world stage. The museum is now offering workshops for children, it is a center of education. At the entrance, on a tall standing display, there was a blown-up version of an official letter, in Luxembourgish, with English, French, and German translations running down a column beside the letter, declaring that the Luxembourg-ish authorities have decreed that this museum serves a public purpose. These words—respect, gratitude, reconciliation, public, education—were exactly what the place was missing. In their place was the superficial thrill of fake engagement, fake learning. In one room there was a sniper on a high telephone pole. Obviously it wasn't the entire telephone pole. Just the top third or so. I ran into my father in that room. We had separated upon entering, as you do in museums. I found him looking up at the sniper. Hey, I said. Hey, he said. What's that? I said. A sniper, he said. I looked up. I could not see anything, just a bunch of metal and leaves. And then I saw him. Oh, wow, he's well hidden, I said. My father said, Do you have the keys, I think I may go for a rest. It's a very strange museum, isn't it? I said. It sure is, he said, and I think I've had enough.

But we were only on the ground level. He left and I stayed. I found a huge room with a diorama of US soldiers marching behind some jeeps in snow. The walls were black, the light was way down, except for a diffuse, artificial moonlight that made the white coats of the soldiers glow. They were up to their knees in snow. They leaned forward, as though marching into a gale. And all around this massive scene in the middle of the room were smaller dioramas along the walls. One of them seemed to re-create the themes of a manger scene. Another was of men trying to get an armored personnel carrier unstuck from some muddy and snowy terrain. There were men cramped inside the APC, and there were men outside the APC, an officer and some enlisted men, trying to figure out a solution. Every soldier wore an expression. An artist had given them faces. Faces that expressed what it might be like to march in heavy snow with cold feet, or to be thirsty, or to need to go to the bathroom, or feel home-sick, or attempt to solve a problem, or be afraid, or feel coura-geous. Except that each expression was slightly off, so that the man cooking himself some beans in a manger needed to go to the bathroom, and the man trying to solve the problem of the stuck tire was afraid. This made every scene—which was otherwise at a level of detail that was staggering—just incoherent enough to be ghoulish. That was on the second level, and I thought that snow scene might have been the centerpiece—it was on the cover of the brochure—but then I found another dozen scenes just as grand. I went all the way up to the top and found a scene of sol-diers firing howitzers and antiaircraft guns. On my way down, I found many rooms I hadn't seen on the way up. When I got back down to the ground level—having not yet explored the two lev-els below—I found a new corridor that took me to a room the size of an aircraft hangar. In it was everything they could not fit into the rest of the museum. It was a little bit like that mo-ment, in science-fiction films, when our hero stumbles through a doorway to discover the scale of the evil alien enterprise, the space where they keep the million or ten million human bodies, et cetera. There were howitzers, tanks, APCs, cargo trucks, jeeps, fire engines, cars, airplanes, bombs, shells, and other ordnance, gas cans, shovels, mortars, helmets, flamethrowers, and more, all crammed together in a space that could have housed a couple of commercial airliners. But there were no dioramas. I left. I was a little embarrassed for having been so enthralled by everything, and when I knocked on the glass of the passenger window to wake my father, a few hours after he had departed, now in the dark-ness of night—the museum had actually closed—he asked me where I'd been, and I lied and told him I'd gone for a walk around

Diekirch. Did you find anything good in that enormity? asked my father, as I got in beside him, started the car, and plugged in the GPS. The evening was warm, and I rolled the windows down to release the smell of stuffiness. I did, actually, I said. There was an interesting letter written by a soldier, they identified a man from a photograph and contacted him, a Roy Lockwood, and he wrote a letter back about his experiences, I said. Roy Lockwood, said my father, slowly, as though he was supposed to know the name. Anyway, I said, it was a good letter. Well, said my father, I'm glad.

The Roy Lockwood diorama was on one of the underground floors. The scene itself wasn't extraordinary, or different from anything else—two soldiers in a foxhole. One was resting, the other manned a machine gun. The resting soldier was Roy Lockwood. In front of the scene was a lectern displaying a typed letter, with handwritten corrections, behind some glass. A white light that shined down on that letter was so dim that it did not upset the blue darkness of the scene. Beside the letter was a photograph. It was the scene the diorama had reproduced. The scene, like a lot of others in the museum, had been re-created from a photograph. That was the last room I visited, and I nearly turned around at that moment, but I read the letter instead. After I read it, I read it again. I read it many times. Then I took a photo of it with my phone, and later on that evening, before dinner, I transcribed the letter into my notebook. Roy Lockwood, on 14 November 1982, responds to a letter he has received asking about the photograph, and about his experiences in the fighting here. Please excuse my delay in answering your 3 August 1982 letter, he writes. In the army unit I served with, please be advised it was Company G 320th Infantry Division, 35th Division, 3rd Army. I was the one sitting to the left of the machine gun.

The letter is only one page long, but he explains that in that picture, his friend Jack McFarland had taken over manning the thirty-caliber gun after a German counterattack. Jack McFarland had passed away in the spring of 1982, which made Lockwood the last remaining member of his machine-gun crew, of which there had been six.

As to the towns we were near at the time, I don't remember, he writes, as for over thirty days we were constantly out in the fierce freezing weather, without the opportunity to even be in a house or a barn and we were also occupied with the constant front-line attacks and counterattacks. As to my memories of the Battle of the Bulge, we were in fierce combat with the Germans and were fighting for our lives. The artillery shellings were unbearable, both the German and our own artillery which landed short. Mostly it was brutal and nerve-wracking going. It was labeled by the men who were there as a White Christmas and New Year's in a White Hell.

Lockwood explains, after that, how on New Year's Eve, men made toasts to their own death. Eat, drink, and be merry, boys, tomorrow maybe we're dead! And many of them were! he writes. They fought in close quarters, and in the bloody hours of slugging it out, men won each other's praise for skill and guts!

He writes, This terrible period in which foxholes were walled with ice, water froze in canteens, and medics carried blood plasma under their arms to keep it warm, was not without its beauty! Shimmering crystalline snow clung delicately on branches and bushes and communication-line wires, as if placed there by the hands of God! On the few brilliantly sunny days the sky was bluer than the oceans. Like invisible needles pulling fussy white threads through the blue skies, fighter escorts trailed vapor at an arctic height. Then came the bombers in wedge formations, glinting in the bright blue firmament like tiny crosses of mother-of-pearl. This gave us some indication the bombing of Germany would soon end the terrible war!

Thirty-eight years had passed between the night in that fox-hole and the composition of Lockwood's letter, and more than thirty years since the composition of that letter and my visit to the museum. In closing, he writes, please extend my many good wishes and regards to the wonderful people of Luxembourg who greeted us so friendly during those trying times. Sincerely yours, Roy W. Lockwood.

We stayed in the city of Luxembourg that evening. It was not far from Diekirch, and we'd sort of been chased out of Diekirch by an SUV I'd cut off. The SUV seemed to be following us, waiting for me to stop in order to have a word with me, so I just never stopped. My father didn't know what had happened. He just kept asking, Why are you driving so erratically? In Luxembourg city, we went out for dinner in a restaurant near our hotel. I asked my father if we ought to go to Aachen the next morning, see Charlemagne, then head back to Berlin. I was starting to feel immensely run down. Although I found myself wanting to eat all the time, I'd stopped tasting my food. He thought about it. Why don't we go to one last nice restaurant, something we'll remember, a place with a couple of Michelin stars? he asked. Paris is probably too far, at least in terms of getting back to Berlin, I said. I was thinking of Brussels, he said. Sure, I said. Good, he said, we'll get a five-star hotel, live like kings for a night. You know, I said, that Brussels is actually a shithole? He said, I hear it's quite dull, but we're in Luxembourg—what could be duller than a night in Luxembourg? We had a few glasses of wine each over dinner, and suddenly I couldn't help myself—I read out Lockwood's letter to my father from my notes. He listened attentively. He asked me to read it a second time. Then he got a little sad halfway through and asked me to stop. We sat in silence for a little while longer. We were in a white restaurant, with white tablecloths and waiters in white aprons and dark-burgundy cravats. It was half-full. I ate pork belly. My father ate vegetarian risotto. And when we were finished with our main courses, we each had some grappa, then we had some dessert—I got the crème brûlée and my father got a dark chocolate cake with strawberry sauce. I could barely move from overeating. My father was winded, he had to take deep breaths between bites. I said, Debussy's *La Mer* isn't realism, and that's why it succeeds. My father had to gulp down a few breaths of air in order to ask, How do you mean? I said, I mean it clearly isn't representational, it is clearly abstract, it's not about the sea. What's it about? he asked. Music, obviously, I said, and other artistic representations of the sea. Surely it's also about the sea, he said. I said, You're missing the point. He said, I think you're overthinking.

We were tired, and the overabundance of food had suppressed the drunkenness I'd enjoyed through the first half of dinner. I hardly ever eat desserts, so when I do, my belly swells up, and my face goes red, and I have to burp a lot. My father's eyes closed. The waitress came by. I ordered us both a second grappa and an espresso. Then I said, Two double espressos.

When the waitress left, my father opened his eyes and said, Do you know that Schoenberg, when he finally got to Hollywood, begged a producer to let him produce a score for a film? I didn't know that, I said. Well, it's true. Schoenberg turned himself into a musical fascist before he left Berlin, and when he got to Hollywood he made himself a tennis player. In the end, all those European exiles—those composers you admire so much—were all making dreck music for shitty films in Hollywood, selling out, one after the other, swimming in money and debasement and feeling famous. It was too much for Schoenberg to bear, being left behind like that, being left out of the future of music. He demanded fifty thousand dollars—which is like a million dollars today—to compose music for a movie. He demanded full control. But really he just wanted to be working in movies. They ignored him. He sent a letter begging them to reconsider. They never answered.

My father looked away, then wiped his face with his thick white cloth napkin. The waitress served our last grappas and our coffees, and my father said, We have officially had way too much to drink. I agreed.

When we went back to the hotel that night, I felt unusually sobered by the conversation. Even though we blamed it on exhaustion and drinking, I was awake and sobered. I turned on the television and ran a bath. I put on my sunglasses. I went down to the hotel reception and asked for a sharp knife. The woman behind the desk said, Big or small? Small, I said, but sharp. She gave me a serrated steak knife from the kitchen. Perfect, I said, thanks very much. I went upstairs and got in the bath. The water was searing. I had to go in slowly. First just the bottoms of my feet, then up to the ankles, then to the knees, and so on. It took ten minutes to get all the way in, and then I couldn't breathe. Not for a while. I picked the knife up from the floor beside the tub and held it in my right hand. I had set my notebook on a little ledge by the bath, and I placed it in my mouth. I bit the spine of the book, I clenched the notebook in my teeth. Then, with my left hand, I took a hunk of flesh in the side of my gut. I squeezed the flesh and started to cut. I started the cut pretty deep, but I couldn't keep it deep. It was more painful than I could have imagined, and I almost bit through my notebook to keep from screaming. I was thinking, If I can get a pound out, just a pound, I will be purified. Or maybe I was thinking that, if I could make a large incision, large enough to stretch back the skin wide on either side, I might, for a moment, before the pain became unbearable, witness the reality of the life of my body, and, by witnessing that reality, eliminate the mystery of who I am and how and what I perceive—because that mystery is such great pain, a pain worth enduring minor pain to eliminate. But of course it had been unbearable from the very beginning. The bath turned bright red. I got out. Bending, twisting, standing—it was all excruciating. I dried off. The wound was gushing blood. I smoked a cigarette. The room filled with foggy smoke, like smoke from a wet campfire—it was totally illogical. Then I called reception and said I needed some first aid. The woman asked me if it was an emergency, and I said, Yes, I would say it is an emergency. A few minutes later there was a knock on the door. I wasn't dressed. I had a little towel around my waist, and it was soaked with blood. I opened the door, and the receptionist cried out something in Luxembourgish, which I assume meant, You are bleeding! I really was bleeding. It was very heavy, and I said, That's why I need the first aid. You need a hospital, she said. There's no need for a hospital, I said. The woman said, There will be a fine for smoking, and you must pay for the towels you have ruined, please give me the knife. I gave her the knife. She gave me the first-aid kit—with bandages and antiseptic. I apologized for the trouble—I made some weird excuse about trying to get a splinter out, and I assured her it looked far worse than it was—and she left.

I had a couple of bottles of hard liquor from the minibar. I smoked some more cigarettes. I was already going to be charged, so I might as well have a few more. I could have opened the window, but I liked the effect of the fog. It took a while, but the wound stopped gushing blood. And I wiped it clean with the antiseptic, or at least around it, and I saw that I'd hardly made a cut at all. The deep part of the cut was tiny, and the rest was just a superficial wound. I got back in the bath—it was still bright red and it was still a little warm. I stuck my hand down into the water to find the rubber plug, attached to a chain, and pull it out. Then I stepped out again. I put the bandage on, then I smoked cigarettes in bed until I fell asleep watching a political thriller that was playing in French with Luxembourgish subtitles. The scar was the shape of a crescent, and I realized that if I were twenty years younger, the scar might have disappeared after months or a year, but now I would probably have it forever.

It still hurts. But only when I think about it. I've got a dressing on it, and I re-dress it every day. I swab it with alcohol, let it dry and scab after showers, then I forget it. Sometimes it will itch, and if I can remember why it's itching, I can stop myself from scratching. But if not, I scratch it, and it usually starts to bleed, and if it gets going, I tend to look like somebody who's been shot, or stabbed. My father hasn't said anything. I think he's noticed, but I also think he thinks it is a nightmare, and he is too afraid of what will happen in the nightmare if he speaks of it. All week he has been screaming through the nights. So have I, I think. I wake up more tired than I was when I went to bed.

I step inside an electronics, photography, and appliance store.

It looks, from the outside, as though it's a place to run in superquick and get some headphones, but once inside you turn a corner, then another, and you realize it is immense. It sells things you wouldn't normally consider—or at least I hadn't considered—buying in an airport, such as flat-screen televisions, desktop computers, and kettles. I stop a member of staff and say, Do you speak English? He blinks at me. He is a bit doughy, with wire-framed glasses and buzzed short hair, and a very thinly clipped goatee that makes his face look like it's held together by the goatee, like it's stitching on a fattened chin. I suspect he's about twenty, and I can see that he finds me, in my sunglasses, preposterous. Of course, he says, how can I help you? I'd like some sound-canceling headphones, I say. And a DSLR, and a big wide-angle lens.

Very well, he says.

And a laptop.

He looks up at the corners of the ceiling, because he thinks this is possibly a trick, and that he's on camera.

A laptop, I repeat. And some headphones, and a DSLR camera.

I turn around. Right in front of me are digital voice recorders. I point toward the most expensive one. And I want this digital voice recorder, as well, I say. It's about three hundred euro. It has 8GB of storage, which means it can hold up to two thousand one hundred and twenty hours of recording at a time, or three months' worth. Plus it has an inbuilt rechargeable battery. The man says, What will you be using this for? I say, Why do you ask? He says, You can get a recorder that is just as good for much less, though it has smaller storage capacity.

Why would I want smaller storage capacity?

Are you a journalist? he asks.

My son is, I say.

The man gestures to a colleague. The colleague moves slowly, and nearly gets into a conversation with another customer, but the man whistles and hurries him. I tell him I want two pairs of headphones. One pair of really big sound-canceling headphones and one pair of in-ear headphones, something to replace the shitty ones that came with my phone. I see myself, I tell him, wearing the big ones on airplanes and at home alone, and the small ones when on the go, or running, and so on. Do you know much about headphones? he asks. Nothing, I say. What kind of music do you like? he asks. Country and western, I say. Hmm, he says. I search the shelves. There are two brands that are the most expensive—they are roughly the same price. These here, I say, which are the best? Those are very good, he says, but they are probably not worth the price, the ones over here offer comparable experiences without the high price. Which one has the most features? I ask. The most features? he says. I pick up the boxes underneath the shelves and begin to compare them myself. I haven't heard of the brand names that produce the most expensive headphones, and somehow that is reassuring. I take the headphones that have something called head tracking. I take a high-priced pair of in-ear headphones, too. We go to the cameras. On the way, I point at a few small things and ask them to include them in my shopping cart. I get a laser pointer and a milk frother. There's another man who helps me with the cameras, while the first man stands by. Another member of staff is also watching. Other customers are waiting. I can recommend, says the man behind the camera counter, a Canon 600D. It is a very good camera with excellent HD video, and it is very fast and lightweight. I want an EOS 1, I say. The man says, We do not offer an EOS 1 here. The first man says something in German to the camera guy, who then says, The highest-priced camera we have is the Canon 5D. Does it have the most features? I ask. The Canon 5D has many, many features, says the man. I'd like a lens to go with it, I say. There are five big lenses in a plastic box beside the camera display. Which would you like? he says. I give him an impatient look, and he responds by pointing to one of the lenses and says, This lens is the most expensive and has the most features.

You said you wanted a laptop as well, the first man says.

Yes. For my son. And I had better get an e-reader, and a tablet computer, as well.

Your son is going to be very happy when he sees you.

My son despises me, I say.

The man lifts his hands, palms up, as if to say, Can't win them all.

I ask the electronics store staff to deliver everything to my gate, except for the large headphones, which I sling around my neck immediately. Good-bye, everybody! I say. They all say, Good-bye! I walk back out of the store. I plug my headphones into my phone. I scroll through the music I have. Nothing seems to suit the mood. I need some rap, some classic rock, even some country. I start going through my online store, buying whatever I come across. The downloads move pretty fast, and within a few seconds my first song appears. I strut around for a while. Then I get a phone call. It's Trish. The headphones have a telephone speaker on them, so I just answer, and talk to the air.

Hey, Trish, I say.

It's been twenty minutes. It's been over twenty minutes. Everything okay?

Everything is fine, I'll be there in two minutes.

We might just go ahead to the gate and meet you there.

Don't go, wait for me, I won't be long.

A woman is staring at me. I look down and see that I'm bleeding. It's not bad, but my shirt is ruined. I lift the shirt up to see how bad it is. It's bad. It's going to need a new bandage. I'm going to need a new shirt. I must have been scratching at the scar while buying all the electronics. The woman staring at me looks a little horrified. I tell Trish I gotta go. She says, Are you on your way? I say, We still have an hour!

A concerned traveler, an American, stops me and asks if I'm okay. He tries to lift up my shirt to see what is bleeding, but I don't want him to touch me. What's going on? Trish asks. I tell the American man that I'm fine. But suddenly I am not fine, I am feeling very weak. Gotta go, Trish, I say, be right with you. I kneel on the floor. I take the headphones off my ears. I tell everybody I'm okay. Bicycle accident, I say. I lift the shirt up and pull the bandage back and show the man my scar, because I fear he will call security if I do not, and I suppose it does look a little like a bicycle accident. He says, You need medical assistance. I say, It's an old scar, it's absolutely fine. They sit me down. I am trembling. I try to imagine some food, but all I can imagine is eating the impurity beneath the scar in me. I think I am in a dream, in clouds, in a gray, turbulent murk, while my body comes apart, it is being ripped apart. I remain like that for a while. The hunger pang is strong and nauseating, and the bleeding makes the nausea doubly swampy. For a moment I think that I am going to die, and just at the moment I pass out of the murk and pain and toil—like coming into the blue clarity of the sky—I realize that I would like to leave a part of myself in that pain permanently, to leave myself permanently inside the idea of dying, but then I am through, completely through, into the blue and serene air above the clouds, and I am filled with regret and unworthiness. I take a few minutes. I recover. I get up. I stand and check my scar, and it doesn't seem to be bleeding now. I have some tissues and I pack them on top of the wound. They stick there. A few people watch me. I buy a bottle of water. I drink some. I put my headphones back on, walk into a men's clothes store, and I buy a nice gray button-down suit shirt. Then I buy a few more shirts. Then I look around and see a bunch of nice suits. They aren't too expensive, a thousand euro each or so, so I buy a bunch of suits. Forty-four longs. Blue suits. Black suits. Gray suits. A tan suit. I'll get them tailored at home. I'll be the guy who drives around in his dad's truck in thousand-dollar suits, which is a lot for people in my hometown. I don't even take my headphones off at the counter. I don't look at the girl behind the counter. I get everything in two big bags. I go to the bathroom and change. I put on a new shirt, and I leave it unbuttoned quite low, and I put on a jacket. I head back toward my father and Trish.

Miriam came to London once, while I was there. She didn't tell me she was coming, but I got a message from her saying she was in the city but probably wouldn't be able to meet. I didn't write back, because I thought her message was pretty cruel—who would write to say they were in town, then add they had no time to see you? But two days later I got another message saying she was feeling very ill, and could I come to her hotel. This was when I was still trying to make my business a success, and doing the MBA at night.

I went across town to see her. It was raining. If she'd let me know in advance that she was coming, I could have set aside a little bit of time and taken her to some museums, lunch, dinner, anything. I spent a lot of time in London wondering about Miriam, and wishing to see her, and I was quite deflated by the idea that she could make a trip to London but not spare the time to see me. But now, because she hadn't given me any warning, I was annoyed that I had to drop what I was doing and come take care of her. I was swamped. I was working to exhaustion, then studying, and I thought I could very easily have a nervous breakdown, if I bothered to stop and observe the pace I was at. But when I got there, I saw that she was really ill, she needed somebody to take care of her. I had to knock several times. She opened the door, but she did not say hello, she merely turned and crawled back into bed. The hotel was musty, cold, cheap, and it didn't have a view. There was a window, but it opened right onto the wall of another building. The distance between the two buildings was the width of a rat. She crawled under her sheets and closed her eyes. I felt her forehead. She was really burning up. Is it bad? she asked. You need to see a doctor, I said. Don't make me move just now, she said. I gave her some soluble acetaminophen. I sat beside her. Within about twenty minutes she was a little more alert. There was some color in her face again. Her eyes were a little brighter. You look good, I said, for somebody so sick. And it was true. She wore a healthy weight, she was probably twenty pounds heavier than she had been when she moved to Berlin, and I thought it suited her. Her hair was long. I checked my watch, it was ten in the morning.

Thanks for coming, she said.

We're going to the doctor, I said.

Let me just rest a little longer.

What are you doing in London?

214

Oh, something really stupid, possibly a job, but it was all a fake, spent all my money getting here, I'm so stupid.

She glanced at my coat, a double-breasted gray mackintosh with large peaked lapel, and underneath it a gray suit, a sweater, and a tie, and she said, This is exactly how I imagine you dressed, you look so sophisticated.

She fell asleep for a while, and I was beside her in the bed, doing some work. Suddenly she started moaning and jerking around. She was trying to get the covers over her head, but she couldn't, because I was sitting on them. She woke, but all she could say was, I'm cold, cold, cold. So I got under the covers and held her very tight. I started to sweat immediately, because she was so hot to touch. But she was shivering. Her teeth were chattering. I'm freezing, she said. I packed all her stuff into her suitcases. You're getting out of this place, I said. I had to help her get dressed. I helped her put on some jeans, and a shirt over her undershirt. Her bag was heavy. She seemed to have packed a lot of stuff. She was also pretty heavy. I checked her out and paid for the hotel, got a taxi, went straight to my GP, got a prescription for some antibiotics—my GP checked the back of Miriam's throat and she said, Oh yeah, that's a bad one—and then we went to my place. She remained very sick the first night, and I let her sleep in my bed while I slept on the rug in my sitting room—my couch wasn't quite long enough to stretch out on. Her temperature kept spiking at 106 degrees, and every time it spiked she would call for me, and I would give her some acetaminophen and lie beside her, hold her very close, try to keep her warm. Then as the acetaminophen took effect and her fever started to break, she would throw all the sheets off and toss around the bed, sweating, trying to find dry spots to sleep on.

The next morning she was a lot better. She was fatigued, could hardly move, and was spaced-out, but her temperature was more stable. She stayed for just over a week. She did not eat, which, at the time, seemed like a normal reaction to such a bad infection. I got lots of takeout and rented lots of movies, which we watched on my computer. I took some time off work. It was probably the best week I'd ever had in London. And one of the reasons I have remained so fond of that apartment, and probably why I like spending so much time there, is because that apartment contains the memory of her visit. I had hoped to show her around, especially Columbia Road on Sunday, when the flower markets were out, but she didn't have the energy for a walk. Then she decided to go home. I bought her a ticket. I took her to Gatwick and put her on a flight back to Berlin.

Four or five years after that, I sent her an e-mail asking if she'd meet me in Cologne. I was heading there for a marketing conference. She said she didn't have time. So I telephoned. I'm going to be there for three days, why don't you come. You can stay in my hotel room. We can go out, I'll skip some talks, I can get tickets to the Philharmonic, I said. I can't get away, I don't have the time, she said. I said, I'll skip all my talks, I won't go to the conference, I'll buy your train tickets. She said, I can't, I'm sorry. I said, Just a day, come in the afternoon, have dinner with me, then get the red-eye home, I'll get you first-class tickets so you can sleep. She said, No, I can't. I was almost going to forget it, I was going to say, Okay, okay, you win, but then I became emotional, and I said something totally unexpected. I said, I'm lonely, Miriam, I am really lonely. When I made this call, I was somewhere in the city, I was traveling across the city to a client's office, and what I was thinking was that four or five years had passed since I'd seen her last, and very little had changed—or rather, much had changed, but nothing had improved.

She came to Cologne for a day and a night. She arrived just before lunchtime. It was snowing. I got a taxi to the station. The conference had been going on for two days and it was a waste of time. The idea was to network, but I could only handle so much of it. The first night there'd been a late dinner, then drinks until it started to get light. The next day I was very tired, muscled through some early talks, had a big lunch, made it halfway through the afternoon, then went home to sleep. I was asleep at four-thirty, before dusk, so naturally I was up very early, still the middle of the night, and anxious to see Miriam. I went down to the lobby at four a.m., got my laptop out and did some work. Some people from the conference came in drunk. I had been among them the previous night, but the lobby was dark, and they didn't recognize me. Then it was quiet again. At around seven I started to get tired, so I went up to my room and drank some instant coffee, watched BBC World News, and when I felt like I was definitely going to fall back asleep, I decided to leave the hotel. I arrived at the train station almost three hours before Miriam's train was due to arrive. So I walked around in the snow for a while, along the Rhine. I watched the snow fall into the Rhine. Then I returned to the station. I met Miriam on the platform. I had a croissant and a coffee waiting for her—something I got at a nice bakery, not at the train station. She stepped off. I waved. She was in a black coat and wore black snow boots, and she had a little rolling suitcase. As she got closer, I saw that she was quite thin in the face. Closer still, I saw that she seemed to have aged a lot since the last time we met, not five years, more like twenty. Then I realized she was emaciated. The train was full—it was just around Carnival, which I hadn't known when I booked the conference—so the platform was trampled by partygoers, many of them dressed in shiny, sequined outfits, or with feathers in their hats. And they had painted faces. They sang songs, and they smelled like beer. Miriam stopped right in front of me. The crowds went all around us, unperturbed. She put her hands on my face and said, My poor big brother. I embraced her for a long time. I thought I wasn't going to be sad, but I found that I was sad. There, there, she said. And after I let go of her, we spoke no more of my loneliness. I offered her the croissant and the coffee. She took the coffee—which was black—but said I could have the croissant. We stepped into a taxi outside the station. We departed. I was really happy to see her, but I didn't have a whole lot, suddenly, to say.

Cologne is nice, she said.

Is this your first time here?

It is.

Would you like to do anything?

Nothing in particular, she said.

What's got you so busy in Berlin?

I'm doing a degree in nutrition, she said.

You like living in Berlin?

It's probably the only place I can afford to live.

Are you still singing?

Still singing?

When you were in London, you said you were taking voice lessons.

Oh, no, that was temporary. Are you still in the same place?

Still in the same place, I said.

The drive from the station to the hotel took a long time. The streets were full of slow, drunk pedestrians, and the traffic was heavy. The snow fell into the city, into the light of the city. When we got to the hotel, some people from the conference were there. It was the last day of the conference, and I guess quite a few of them had decided to abandon the last talks and go out drinking. A man I recognized from our first night out saw me arrive with my sister and gave me a thumbs-up from across the lobby. I thought he was going to come over and invite us out with them, or introduce himself, so I hurried Miriam into the elevator and we went up to my room. She took off her coat. I said, Miriam, you're really thin, are you okay? She didn't want to talk about it. I didn't want to push her, because I didn't want her to leave. But I couldn't conceal my worry. Surely your nutrition course would wake you up to the dangers of being so skinny, I said. I'm fine, she said. You're obviously not, I said. She said that she didn't want to argue, and if I must know, ever since London she'd been losing weight, eating less, and she felt really empowered by denying appetite—the nutrition course was something to discover whether this denial of appetite, which became easier with each missed meal, could be sustained. You like not eating when you're hungry? I asked. But she said she didn't want to have to explain herself, and I could see that if we were to have a nice time together, I would have to change the tone of my voice. She went into the bathroom with some clothes, freshened up, and changed. I dozed off, I think, while watching television. She came out in an olive-and-black sleeveless dress, but wearing a gray polo-neck sweater underneath it, and black tights. You look nice, I said. In fact she looked sick. Her arms and legs were bony, and through the back of her dress, her shoulder blades protruded. She said, Thanks, I really love this dress. I stood up and took her hands in my hands. They were thin, too. Then I gave her another hug and said, Thanks for coming. I felt all the bones in her back.

When I went back to Miriam's apartment for the third and final time, during my last week—it turned out to be the day before her body was released—I looked for, and found, this dress. I propped a tall mirror against the wall and held the dress out in front of me. It was tiny. I really could not believe how small it was, now that I was standing with it. It was not olive and black, and it was not sleeveless, and it was almost nothing like the dress my memory described—but I was certain it was the dress she wore when she walked out of the bathroom in that hotel in Cologne. Later, after we'd been out, I pretended to sleep while I watched her take that dress off. We were both quite drunk. I was lying in the bed near the door to the room, and she was standing by the window, between the second bed and the big window that looked out over the city and the cathedral, clumsily undressing. She took her dress off, and she stood there for a moment in her gray polo-neck sweater. It looked to me like she was dying. Her hips were sharp, the only shapes in her legs were the joints of her knees. Then she fell down. I got out of bed. She'd only had two glasses of wine at dinner and, later, a cocktail, but it was too much. I tried to wake her. Her eyes opened. Come on, I said, trying to lift her. Let me sleep on the floor, she said. I ignored her. I put one arm around her shoulder and neck, another under her hips. She didn't weigh anything. She said, Let me down. I ignored her again. I stood straight up with her in my arms. What are you doing? she said. I said nothing, because it was obvious—I was putting her in the bed. Let me down, she said. I said, You're drunk. So what? she said, and she started to squirm. I turned to put her down on the bed and she started to claw at my face. She clawed at my cheeks and nearly got my eye. I dropped her. There was a big knock. The lamp on her nightstand fell over. I didn't know what had happened. But then I realized she had hit her head on the nightstand. Are you okay? I asked. She was rubbing the back of her head. I was just trying to put you back in bed, I said. She sat up a bit, asked for water. I went to the bathroom to get a glass, filled it with water from the tap, and came back. She was in the bed, asleep. I stood over her for a while, wondering how bad the knock had been, and if I ought to call a doctor. I was also furious. I did not understand why she refused to be lifted into her bed.

In Miriam's Berlin apartment, when I went back that third and last time, I took the dress I recognized from Cologne and sat down on a chair. I laid the dress crosswise on my lap and smoothed the wrinkles out. It was around five in the afternoon. Somehow I had got inside without alerting Otis. Maybe at last he felt that everything in Miriam's apartment was safely his. He had organized drinks with some people who knew Miriam, and I had promised to give him the keys. We were meeting around seven, somewhere nearby. My father said he would drop in later, probably with Trish. My father was completely listless, and kept saying morbid things. I sat in that chair with Miriam's dress across my lap for almost two hours. I didn't move. I guess it was a long time to sit. It started to get dark. Then my phone rang. It was Sedat, from the antiques store right down the street from our apartment. I answered the phone. He was outside. Very good, I said. I told him to ring the bell and I'd buzz him up. I reminded him to be absolutely quiet. I waited. I turned on a light. Sedat came up. He had a friend with him. I shook hands with them. I closed the door. Sedat looked at the furniture. I had already shown him some photos, but now that he was here and saw the furniture in person, he nodded. This is very nice, he said. His friend went around looking at everything else. When he was finished, he and Sedat spoke briefly, then Sedat came to me and said, Everything is in order. I asked him to place the keys in Otis's mailbox on their way out, and reminded him that he shouldn't do anything, shouldn't even leave the apartment, until he got a text from me saying it's okay. I had explained to Sedat about Miriam's death. I offered him all the furniture he wanted for free, so long as he cleared the place completely. When I told him to wait for a text from me, he became suspicious, but now that he was in the apartment and had seen the furniture up close, I was sure he wouldn't refuse it. Sedat's antiques store had very nice furniture in it, and the furniture was hugely, criminally, overpriced. He asked if I was taking anything myself, any books, any clothes—the dress I was holding. Nothing, I said.

I went along to the bar Otis had specified. It was a nice place, small in floor space but with high ceilings, and with gigantic windows overlooking a dark and quiet, dimly lit street. It was in a part of town I hadn't been to, right next to the Schlesisches Tor underground stop—Schlesisches Tor means Silesian Gate. I was on my own for almost an hour and a half. I ordered a whiskey, because I had to order something. But I wasn't drinking anymore and I did not drink the whiskey. The bartender didn't care. The place was virtually empty. There was a man reading a newspaper at the bar, and I didn't see him drink anything, not even a coffee. I think he just came in to read the paper and smoke cigarettes. He read the paper the way people read novels, line by line, page by page, front to back. And when he was finished, he folded it, pushed it to the side, and thought about it for a while. At around half past eight, the man got up, put his coat and hat on, said good-bye to the bartender, and left. When he opened the door to go outside, Otis was there. The man let Otis in, then departed. Otis went straight to the bar. I got my phone out and sent Sedat a message telling him to begin. Otis came over to the table and sat down with a beer. Look at you, he said. I assumed he meant the beard, maybe the suntan. I probably looked quite healthy. But I hadn't eaten in five days—or had eaten very little—and I had a constant headache, and other flulike symptoms. I said, I went by Miriam's apartment today, my last visit.

Oh yeah?

And I found the dress she wore the last time we met.

When was that?

Years ago, in Cologne.

He leaned back and looked up at the ceiling. Then he said, It's funny, I haven't seen some of these people in many years, I don't even know some of them.

Do you think they will come?

I have no idea.

Did they get back to you?

No, nobody.

He sipped his beer, then lit a cigarette. Then he said, I can't stay too long, either.

I think I must have sighed, or rolled my eyes, because he said, Sorry, I couldn't get out of something else.

The door opened and a couple came in, a really handsome guy and a handsome, brown-eyed woman, nicely dressed. I was facing them, but I had to lean to see past Otis's head. Otis, whose back was facing the door, had to twist to look at them. The couple took a look around. Perhaps they saw too many empty seats, or they didn't appreciate the reception Otis and I had given them. They turned around and walked out.

We'll be going back soon, I said.

To the States?

That's right.

Any word on Miriam?

Nothing yet.

Then how do you know?

It's a feeling. I get feelings about things.

Are you looking forward to going home?

I wouldn't say so, no.

Then back to London?

That's the plan. Except...

Otis leaned forward, waiting for me to finish, and I reckon the only reason he didn't speak—to say, for example, Except what?—was that I must have looked like I was going to finish. I was trying to. I was really concentrating. The explanation felt entirely within reach, except that it wasn't, it wasn't even close.

A little while later, a woman named Ulrika arrived. She was an artist, and she was from a little town in Austria. She had round blue eyes, small shoulders, pretty freckles, and brown hair. She had really big thighs and fat hips, but she was skinny from the waist up. She didn't seem to have much interest in Otis. She drank whiskey as well, and smoked long thin cigarettes, and talked about herself and her art quite a bit, which was fine with me, because Otis and I hadn't anything to talk about. She had just been to India and Malaysia. Oh, she said, journalists won't stop calling her, journalists, journalists, journalists. She did not know how Miriam had died. The last time they spoke was years ago. But you came this evening? I said. Yes, well, I never knew anyone who died, she said, except for the very old or the very sick. She was intrigued, said Otis. When we told her that Miriam had starved, she became really intrigued, and requested that she be allowed to view the apartment. It's too late, I said, I've rearranged everything. Yes, she said, but you're the brother, your rearrangement will be very interesting. I doubt it, I said. He's in marketing, said Otis. I finally had a sip of my whiskey. I tried to calculate how much whiskey I could drink before I got sick, and whether that would be sufficient to get drunk. Then another old friend arrived, a nice woman named Anna. She knew that Miriam had died, and she knew how, and she sat very quietly and asked how I was, and she asked how Otis and Ulrika were, and they tried to come up with answers that—it seemed to me—made them sound as though they had been left reasonably broken-hearted by Miriam's death. Anna was German. She had long blonde hair. When she took off her jacket, and then her cardigan, she had bare arms, and there were large scars on both of them, surgery scars, and I suspected—it turned out I was right—she had been in a crash at some point. She worked in a travel agency—Germans still use travel agents heavily, she said—and she knew Miriam from long ago, when they were both doing evening courses in French. She stopped. Maybe the first course was Italian, she said. They did a few courses. Miriam had a gift for languages—her German was flawless, by the way—but she did not travel. Anna asked what we'd been doing, how long we had been here. Before I could answer, Ulrika started a conversation about hunger, and how, with respect, she felt that starving oneself to death was an insult to the many people who were starving involuntarily across the globe. She said, It is also an insult—forgive me for saying so—to starve herself in a country where Jews were put in ghettos and camps and starved. Otis said, A lot of those Jews were gassed before they starved. I said, Miriam was Jewish. I wanted to see what would happen if Ulrika's sense of justice and rectitude were confronted with an inconvenience, but I felt a little strange saying it, even just joking about it. That's absurd, said Ulrika. I said, Whatever, it's the truth. Are you serious? she asked. Ulrika turned to Anna and said, in German, something like, Were you aware of this, did she tell you? Anna said, shyly, or not shyly, more like a person professing ignorance under interrogation, that she was not aware of it, that Miriam had said nothing of it. Then she thought about it, shook her head, and said, But how would it make a difference? Ulrika said, to everyone, My husband is Israeli, we have a Jewish child. I said, Did you convert? Ulrika said, We are atheists. I said, I wish my dad could hear this. Then another woman came in, the last person who would join us that evening. Her name was Dolores, and she was, to our alarm, deathly thin, much thinner, I thought, than Miriam had been in Cologne. And nobody really knew what to say. She took her jacket off, then her scarf, and she wore a V-neck sweater—her breastbone was bulging out, her collarbones were prominent, and her sleeves, which were supposed to be snug, were loose. She had a wrinkled face and neck, and her eyes were tired and sunken. She smiled, introduced herself—the others didn't really know her, either—and said, to me, that she was very sorry to hear about Miriam. She was Spanish, and she had a strong Spanish accent. Then she thanked Otis for e-mailing her. Otis said, I e-mailed everybody I had an e-mail address for. I asked her if she wanted a drink, and she declined. It's terrible news about Miriam, she said. We all quietly agreed. Nobody dared ask if she knew how Miriam had died, because, frankly, it seemed that Dolores would be dead of the same thing in a week. But Ulrika finally thought of a question that was safe to ask that also wasn't empty. She asked, When was the last time you saw Miriam? Dolores thought back. December, she said. I said, How was she, did you speak with her? Dolores said, She mentioned you.

Me?

She was in hospital for most of last year, but she was discharged in December. She was feeling better. She told me she was feeling better. And she said she was going to stay with you in London for a few months.

I said, I didn't know she was in hospital. Then I looked around, and it was clear that everybody there knew it, and that being in hospital was something that had been, for years, a regular part of her life. I said, She didn't get in touch.

Ulrika said, You didn't call your sister in December?

Luckily I caught myself. I almost said, Why would I call my sister in December?

Otis looked at the time on his phone. I asked him if he had to go. I do, he said. Well, the keys are in your mailbox, I said. He got up, put his coat on, put his gloves on, put his hat on, and as he checked his pockets for his wallet and his keys, he said, I'm sorry more people didn't come, this is sort of what I was worried about. Well, I said, our dad didn't even show. Thanks for everything, he said. Likewise, I said. He said good-bye to Ulrika, Anna, and Dolores. Then he said good-bye to the bartender. And he walked out. Anna asked, Where's he going? I said, Something he couldn't get out of, apparently. Ulrika said, He works at the hospital at night, as an orderly. Anna said, I thought he was doing his doctorate. He's still doing that, said Ulrika, plus he sells olives, plus he is a *Hausmeister*, somewhere in Treptow. That's a lot, said

Anna. He's got a daughter, she's eight or nine or something, said Ulrika.

Once Otis had departed, I found myself sitting awkwardly close to Ulrika and awkwardly far away from the others. Ulrika said, How Jewish are you, exactly? I said, I have to go to the bathroom. I did actually have to go. The sip of whiskey I had swallowed was causing indigestion and some nausea. I was shaking. And walking wasn't easy, my legs felt hollow. But the stall was clean. The walls were chipped, and covered in graffiti, but underneath the disrepair I could see how clean the room was, how spotless. And it was a great relief, a relief so great it made me emotional. I closed the door behind me and sat on the commode, which was also clean and dry. Maybe I was the first person in there all day. I put my head in my hands. I didn't think I would get past that night. I thought I would have to eat. I was starving. It didn't seem that I would ever lose my appetite. There was a part of me prepared to eat the toilet paper in that bathroom. My sense of balance was disturbed, and the objects before my eyes were floating like debris in shallow, choppy water. I was looking at the graffiti in front of me, but my sight was swirling—it made me more nauseous to concentrate. Finally I gave in, I threw up, and then I felt a little better. I sat for a while longer. I checked my phone to see if there was any word from Trish and my father. Then I got up and washed my hands. I washed them for a long time, in cold water, because it cooled me off to run the cold water over my wrists. When I went back out, Anna and Ulrika were having a conversation in German, and Dolores seemed left out, so I sat beside Dolores, thanked her for coming, and asked her if Miriam had said anything else in December, anything at all. But before she could answer, I said, So far as I know, Miriam only came to London once, and she didn't come to see me. She looked great. She was sort of plump. But she got really sick, and that's why she called me. The next time I saw her was four or five years later, in Cologne, and she looked...But I couldn't finish the sentence.

Anna and Ulrika were having a conversation that made Ulrika laugh and Anna smile, and that was how I'd hoped the night would go, though on a larger scale. I could see Dolores didn't, or wouldn't, trust me with a single one of Miriam's secrets—assuming she knew any—because I did not comprehend the problem. I said, In Cologne, she told me that denying her appetite empowered her, but it was in London, when she was sick, that she'd had the opportunity to understand, perhaps, the power of that denial. Dolores listened, but she would not agree or disagree. I said, I haven't eaten in five days, well, except for some bread. I think I expected her to be a little proud of me, or maybe I wanted her to know that I did, in fact, understand denying hunger—though of course I did not—but she just smiled and looked a little sad, as though nothing could be done, as though no amount of sympathy or concern or analysis could make the world appetizing.

In Cologne, on the night that Miriam came to visit, we went to a few bars before we decided on a place to eat. It was officially still a few days away from Mardi Gras, but the streets were mayhem. Many were blocked, and those that weren't—at least around our hotel—were being crossed by pedestrians. I saw a lot of people from the conference. They were the soberly dressed ones, with ID badges around their necks. Everyone else was in costume, or at least something sparkly, or a little bit festive. There were several outdoor stages, some were playing folk music, others were playing outdated rock. It was also weirdly nonaggressive.

Instead of people arguing or scuffling, they started dancing, or hugging, or singing. It was snowing. I guess people love the snow. We considered a dozen bars, but we couldn't fit inside any of them. Then we found one that was only mildly overcrowded. The place—I assume everywhere was the same that night—served six beers at a time, little Kölsch beers on a slotted tray. I drank them quickly. Miriam didn't have anything. People kept shouting in our ears. They shouted *Prost!* or *Sláinte!* They wore clown wigs or cowboy hats, and glow-in-the-dark spectacles, or spectacles with hypnotic swirls on them. It wasn't my scene, and it didn't suit Miriam, either, though she always shouted *Prost!* or *Sláinte!* back to them. I just decided to get drunk. Miriam smoked a lot. She had smoked at least a dozen cigarettes by the time we got to the bar, and bought two more packs in a tabak on the way. I tried not to be judgmental, but I must have given her several judging looks, because she snapped and said, Just because you quit doesn't mean I have to. I said, I'm sorry, I know, I don't really care, it's just that it doesn't make sense. Cigarettes cost money and they kill you. Some assholes get rich for making poison, then you get sick, and then some even bigger assholes get overpaid for giving you drugs and operations while you die.

She put her hands on her ears until she could see I'd stopped talking, and I decided not to continue giving her a hard time. I was so happy to see her, and I told her I was happy to see her, and she should smoke as many cigarettes as she liked. We ate dinner in a little Lebanese place down a gray, soggy backstreet. Most of the people there looked like regulars. It wasn't full of shouting. I ordered a big platter of food. Miriam got a glass of wine. To make the evening more comfortable, she ate some bread and hummus. The night finally picked up. This is great food, I said. It's wonderful, she said. After that we went to a cocktail bar, then we drunkenly wound around the streets, taking it in, before returning to the hotel. The next day, she would travel back to Berlin, and I would fly back to London. The conference had been a waste of time, but the trip had been worth it. We had to stop before crossing a street because a yellow streetcar went by, and I put my arms around her, kissed her hat, and thanked her for coming out. I hadn't realized how badly I needed to see you, I said.

Dolores didn't stay too much longer. When she left, Ulrika said, That, too, I find very disconcerting in this country, too much starvation has happened here, I think it makes a wrong statement. Anna went to the bathroom and Ulrika said, I have to go, but perhaps you'd like to come over and have dinner with me and my husband. I said, I have a feeling they're releasing Miriam's body tomorrow, and once that happens, we'll be very busy. She said, My husband is completely open-minded, he's also an artist. I had a feeling he might be, I said. I could call him now, she said. We're only distantly Jewish, very distantly, we're anti-Semitic Jews, I said. She said, Well, that's sometimes as good as you can get around here. I said, No thanks, really. She said, It's a pity, anyway, sorry about Miriam, have a nice journey back to the States. Thank you, I said. She stood, and Anna arrived back. Good-bye, everyone, said Ulrika. Good-bye, I said. Good-bye, said Anna. Anna plopped down in her seat. I'm quite tipsy! she exclaimed. Then she looked at me, frowned, and said, Oh, you're not tipsy at all. She decided to move closer, or I asked her to move closer, because she was far away and she was the only one left. We stuck around for an hour longer. I spoke some German with her, just to get an objective assessment of my language skills. Even though I had done nothing at all to improve my German, except to speak it badly, I felt I was on the verge of fluency. I don't think that's German, she said. In the Rhineland, I said, everyone understood me perfectly. Then I told her all the stories from my trip from Walluf to Koblenz. And then we talked a little bit about Miriam.

Anna lived not far from our apartment, so we decided to accompany each other on the underground. It turned out to be my last time on the underground. I thought it might be. The very next morning, Miriam's body was released, and from that point forward, Trish took care of almost everything, but we had to travel around a lot with her. One of the embassy drivers escorted us—we spent the last two days in Berlin in a black bulletproof Audi. The underground wasn't busy, and Anna and I got seats beside each other. She was smart, witty, and optimistic. Her accident had left her in a coma for almost six months, then she couldn't do much for a year after that. Seven years had passed, and only now was she starting to get her energy back. But I am forty-two, she said, so it's not like there's a lot of energy available. I asked her what had happened. She said, I don't really remember. I saw it on CCTV in the courtroom. I was riding my bike and a truck came from my side and hit me. He was traveling very fast. The court decided it was my fault.

Why?

I have no idea. But I got no money from it. I remember being in the hospital and being told that I'd been in a coma for six months, and I remember thinking, At least I'll get a load of money, I won't have to work anymore, I can travel. But now I still have to work.

Germans are intrepid travelers, I said.

It's true, we love to travel, all day I do nothing but talk to Germans about traveling.

The journey was over very quickly, probably because I hoped it would last a long time. We arrived at Rosenthaler Platz, which was a five-minute walk in one direction from Anna's and a five-minute walk in the other from my apartment. I have a rooftop terrace, I said, would you like to come see it? If I start going up on rooftop terraces, she said, I'll never be able to live in my tiny little flat. I said, Well, it's been nice to meet you. I shook her hand, and she leaned in and kissed me on the cheek. We stayed very close. I put my arms around her back. She put her hands on my shoulders. We looked at each other. I said, Do you want to see something? Okay, she said. I can't show you in the dark, I said. She thought I was joking.

We stepped inside her apartment, first her, then me, pulled our gloves, coats, and hats off, and she turned on a dim lamp with a copper-colored cloth lampshade. Then I closed the door behind me. Her place was very small, half the size of Miriam's. But it was clean. It looked like an oriental-themed railroad car. She said, I could get a bigger place in a different part of town, but this is right beside the travel agency. It's a two-minute cycle. I don't have to take public transportation. You still cycle? I asked. Of course, she said. She offered me a glass of wine. I declined, but she poured me one anyway. I walked to a glass door overlooking a balcony. It was a little bit hazy, white, and there were no cars on the road, even though it was a main artery—the road out to the big loop and the airport. I really wish I had met you at the beginning, I said. She sat down on her couch and I walked around her little flat, looking at the paintings on the wall, and looking at the books on her shelves. You like India? I asked—because there seemed to be a lot of books about India, and the paintings on the wall seemed possibly Indian. I love India, she said, and

Afghanistan, and Pakistan, and Nepal, and China, and Vietnam. I never traveled, I said, I always figure I'll get some incurable disease, or have to sleep with bugs, or be mauled by wild dogs, or get bitten by a snake. That's really strange, said Anna. I'm not finished, I said. I'm also afraid of having to eat insects, or monkey brains, or the heads of birds, or drink filthy water, or be kidnapped. I'm afraid I'll be framed for a crime and end up in jail, I'll be beaten in jail, I'll be executed or raped. I'm afraid it'll be too hot, I hate the heat, I'm afraid I won't be able to take showers, or find clean bathrooms. I will get diarrhea and there won't be toilet paper. I'm afraid of riding in buses. I worry that the buses will be full of mice and chickens. I worry I won't understand how to buy tickets for the bus, and I'll get stuck in the rain in the jungle. I sat down across from Anna and slapped my legs. That's pretty messed up, huh? She said, But you traveled to London. London isn't traveling, I said, at least for Americans it isn't traveling—it involves flying but it isn't traveling. She said, One of the things I love most about traveling is the journey to the airport, by taxi or train, going by all the places you know, the bakeries and markets you visit, the buildings, the streets, the landscape out of town, even the clouds, or the color of grass, or dirt, and the shape of the earth, and I have some music with me, or some books, and I think, This is where I am from, I am only going away for a little while. I said, I could never have that conversation with myself, I could never tell myself such a thing. She said, I suppose I'm just being sentimental, banal. I said, No, not at all, that's not it. My entire life relies on the principle that people really do spontaneously look out the windows of trains.

And have feelings, she said.

If you say so, I said.

You need a vacation, she said.

I leaned back and sank into the low chair. I put my arms out. I was totally at ease there. I was totally at ease with Anna. I said, I *am* on vacation.

She stood. She had finished her glass of wine—I hadn't even noticed her drinking—and was going for more. I picked my own glass up to check it, but I hadn't even had a sip. I put it down. Anna was standing over me. Her hand was dangling right beside my arm. Maybe it was accidental and maybe it wasn't. Maybe she was thinking about patting me on the shoulder, or placing her hand there. Maybe she wanted to say something sweet about Miriam. Or maybe it was something else. I took her hand in my hand. She didn't pull it away. I examined the scar—it went all the way past her wrist, down into her palm. It forked up toward her elbow, and met again above it, then up to her shoulder, where it disappeared inside her clothes. It was a thick scar, with deep indentations where the muscle was gone, depressed lengths of scar tissue. Without another word—and perhaps to avoid further examination—she got down on her knees, so that our eyes were level. We kissed for a while. Then she said that her knees were hurting, so we stood and I followed her into the bedroom. She closed the door and pulled the curtains closed over the white light from the street, over the white haze that had settled over the road, and the room went absolutely dark. I was disoriented and felt for the bed, and sat down on it. She began to undress. I could not see her, but I could hear her. I got undressed, too. She got on the bed and we met at the center of the bed. She put her arms out. I reached out. She held my arms. I think she was trying to avoid being touched while naked. But finally she let go and I touched her. I felt the huge grooves on her body. She was covered in them. The accident must have skinned her alive. I could not get aroused. Finally she stopped, crawled under the covers, and sighed. She pulled the covers up to her eyes. You don't have to explain, she said. I said, It's the darkness, I cannot do this in darkness, I can't see your face. She didn't say anything. I said, Do you know what the darkness makes me think about?

What?

About Dolores.

The woman from tonight?

I said, Yes. Can I crack the curtains just a bit?

A bit, she said, and her reluctance gave me something like a thrill. I got out of bed and walked to the window. I opened the curtains, and I saw that the haze was moving, just a tiny bit, but it was lifting, rising, like a very light but uniform snowfall rising slowly back into the clouds. Check it out, I said. Anna looked but she didn't say anything—I guess it probably wasn't a big deal for her. The room was full of white light now, and Anna pulled the covers up higher. I looked around. So this is your bedroom, I said. She looked around. There wasn't much space. The bed filled most of it. There was a wooden dresser with a mirror on it, but it didn't seem like the bottom drawers had the space to open fully. This is my bedroom, she said.

I said, Bedrooms are strange places.

How do you mean?

I don't know, they're strange. You never know how strange they are until a stranger comes over and gets in your bed. But they are always strange.

What's the bandage for? she said.

This? Nothing.

On her walls there were more paintings, Hindu, spiritual, full of purples and golds and bright reds, and also a big corkboard full of photographs—people in sunny, green places, near beaches, wearing sunglasses and bathing suits. I got back in bed. She said, I thought you were just going to crack the curtains. I said, I didn't expect the view to be so nice. I got under the covers beside her. We began to kiss again. Everything was fine. She gave me head for a long time under the covers, and then I pulled the covers off her, to see her. Then I pulled her away and got on top of her. She looked just as I had expected. She was pretty badly sliced up. Some of the scars were so deep that they seemed like disfigurements. But it didn't look or feel unnatural to me. It was nice. But then I started thinking that it shouldn't be nice, and that I ought to feel disgust or pity for Anna—not the human being but the mutilated shell of her flesh—instead of pleasure. It got heavy and rough. My scar started bleeding. By the time Anna and I had finished, my bandage was soaked through with blood, and the sheets were bloody, and our hands were bloody, and we had bloody fingerprints and handprints all over. Whoops, I said. She got up and immediately put a dressing gown on. What happened to you? she said. I said, I don't dare admit it. She told me to follow her to the bathroom, and sat me down on her toilet and took the bandage off. She looked right at the wound without flinching. It's not so bad, she said, but you need stitches. Forget it, I said. It'll never heal properly, she said. I'm too old for this to heal properly, anyway, I said. She wiped it clean, then put some alcohol on a swab, and applied it. I'd been doing the same thing twice a day. She was about to put a new bandage on it when she looked up at me with sudden alarm.

Is this what you were going to show me?

I couldn't think of anything to say, so I said, Well, um...

She stood and threw the bandage at my face.

Were you trying to be funny?

No, no, not at all, not a bit, no, I'm sorry, I hadn't even thought of that.

I took her hands. I apologized again. Then I said, I did it myself, with a knife. She looked at the wound and said, What kind of knife? A steak knife, I said.

Why?

I have no idea, I said. I was in Luxembourg with my father, we'd been arguing.

Anna's eyes got very wide. Then she put her hand to her mouth. I thought, Now I had better get dressed and get out of here. But she started to laugh, she laughed through the hand that was covering her mouth. I'm sorry, she said, I don't mean to laugh. And then she laughed some more. That's okay, I said. She knelt back down, picked up the bandage, and taped it to my body.

I got home—to the penthouse apartment—at around two a.m., and my father was awake. He had gone to sleep around nine, but, he said, he woke at eleven, and now he couldn't sleep. He was sitting in front of the television, watching a dubbed Hollywood movie. He turned it off. I had a glass of water. I had such a headache. I could taste blood in my mouth. I felt like my teeth were going to fall out. I felt like if I brushed them, they would crumble out like teeth in a dried-up jawbone. How did your drinks go? he asked. I said, They went well. He said, I'm sorry I didn't make it, Trish came over, we didn't have the energy to travel across the city. That's fine, I said. He said, You meet anybody interesting? I said, I met an artist who wanted to sleep with me because I lied and told her we were Jewish. He said, That's a funny way to play a trick on somebody. Then he disappeared into his room.

Trish called the phone in the apartment at nine in the morning, and it rang and rang and rang, because neither my father nor I had the energy to get out of bed. Then I got a matter-of-fact message on my phone. Miriam's body would be released. And that was effectively the end. I woke my dad up, showered, and trimmed and shaved my beard.

My phone starts ringing, but my hands are full of bags, and anyway I can see Trish already, she has her phone out, she's calling me. She is standing and my father is sitting. I shout. I say, Ho there, ahoy! They look over and I raise the bags in the air. They look at me in horror. First I think the horror is a response to the bags and bags of clothes, but then I realize that the wound is bleeding again and my brand-new shirt is ruined. What the hell happened to you? my father asks. Ah, shit, I say, forget it, can we move? We need to get you some help, says Trish. What the hell happened? my father asks. I say, I crashed my bike, got scraped by something metal, weeks ago. My father says, I told you, you're crazy riding that bike. What's in the bags? asks Trish. Suits, I say. You should really get that looked at, she says. I put the bags down and pull up my shirt. It looks worse than it is. I try to explain this. I say, if I go get this looked at, we're going to miss our flight. He's got a point, says my father. My father looks worse than when I left him. I say, I'll get fixed up in a bathroom near the gate.

Maybe we should go, says my father, it will be a long walk. Yes, we should go, says Trish. I'm ready, I say. Then my father says, I like your headphones. I take them from around my neck and let him try them out. He puts them on and says, Nice. Hold on, I say, listen to this. And then I play him some music. What the hell is that? he says. I say, Sorry, and play him something else. I hand him my phone. I gather up our cases and bags. He takes

239

the headphones off, gives everything back to me and says, They sound expensive. He holds them by the headband and says, They *weigh* expensive. How much did you spend? Trish says to my father, Let's get a cart to drive you. My father says, I can make it.

We start to walk. We leave our seats beside the history exhibit. We enter the mouth of the tunnel that leads to our gate. The tunnel is tremendously wide, like the deck of a ship, and it gently descends. The roof of the tunnel is glass and arched. We have a good view of the tarmac and the planes, and the green beyond the airfield, and the mountains. It is easy to see how crisp and cold it must be. We arrive at some escalators. The people all around us hurry down them. But we stand. We wait. We breathe. We go very still and don't speak. It is such a long way down.

In about twenty hours, my father and I will be driving through a swamp, and the night will have heat in it, and there will be mosquitoes. Every time I've been home, I've come home on a hot night. I always fly through either Atlanta or Houston, and in the jetways there I get a sense of the heat and humidity, but then I'm back in the coolness of the airport for a while. I tend to get stuck with long layovers. I plug my laptop in somewhere and write a bunch of e-mails about work I've been doing on the flight. After an hour or so I pack up my computer and find a big window to sit by, and I watch the planes taxi around in the hot afternoon. I always feel as though it's been a lifetime since I last visited—or else I wish it were. I feel old. I feel as though the life I might have had there has become unattainable. Even in my twenties I felt like that. After a while I leave the window and go find a bar that serves food and has a lot of televisions. I forget sometimes that I, too, as an American, love to watch sports and financial news on screens next to each other, or boxing on one screen and baseball on the other, or two football games at the same time. Or all these things on half a dozen screens in a row. I am pretty sure that if I had stayed in the US, even if I had gone somewhere with an intellectual life, such as New York, I'd have never learned anything about music. I'd have stopped reading all books but sports biographies and political or financial nonfiction. I'm quite lucky to have escaped American sports. While I'm eating and drinking, I keep a close eye on the time. I wait until the last call, then I walk to my gate. I traverse another jetway and board the plane, and I look to see if there is anybody I know. There never has been. Then we land, and it's dark. It's a little cooler but no less humid. My father waits for me in the little terminal. We wait for my bag together, then we walk outside to the parking garage. He always lets me drive. We get home quite late and I grab a beer from the fridge. I spray myself with mosquito repellent, I go outside and light some citronella candles in a bucket, I turn on the UV bug lights, and we sit and drink quietly together. He might say it's nice to have me back at home, and I might say how much I've been looking forward to the warm nights. The house has not changed since my mother died. The carpets are the same, the walls the same coat of paint, the same old paintings. The same tableware, silverware, glasses, and coffee mugs. I suspect my mother's clothes are still folded in her dresser, her coats and dresses still hanging in her closet. Nothing has been moved, not the dressers, not the nightstands, not the mirrors, not the paintings. Only the television, so my father can watch it in the room nearest to the swimming pool. Everything is cleaned once a week, but nothing is rearranged. My room, which is exactly as it was when I was twenty, is right next to Miriam's room. My father's room is a long way away. Not because the house is particularly big, though it isn't small, but because it's such a maze, and on so many levels. It's a house that resembles madness, that never comes together, that will go on confusing you forever, and which even has dead ends—you walk around a few corners, find a door, and behind that door is a boiler. It's the only door down that hallway. What in the world is it doing there? There are hallways that connect two entrances to the same room. There are rooms that you must go through rooms to reach. There is a big kitchen and a small kitchen. It is the kind of place two people could inhabit without ever encountering each other, unless they went swimming—there is only one swimming pool.

We reach the bottom of the escalator, and it is clear from the gate numbers that we are facing a very long walk. There are moving walkways, and we take the opportunity to stop on them as well, catch our breath. We go by a Qatar Airways flight to Abu Dhabi. We go by a Lufthansa flight to Johannesburg. We pass by an Air India flight to Hyderabad. We go by an Air Berlin flight to Varadero. There's a flight to Newark. And there's our flight, to Atlanta.

I am disappointed that the crowd at our gate isn't nastier, louder, more like Americans I think I hate, so that I can carry some dread with me on the flight. Everybody seems quite chilled out, quiet, waiting without complaint. We'll make our connection, and our layover won't be as long. There are people at the flight desk. It looks as though things are about to happen. I go to the bathroom to change the dressing on my scar, and to clean it. I have some alcohol wipes in my case. I get them, and a new bandage. The lining of my jacket is bloody, but just the lining.

I find an empty stall and walk in, wipe the toilet seat off, take my shirt off, hang it up on the hook behind me, and slowly pull the tissues back. The tissues have stuck to the skin, so by pulling them, I tear the scar back open. There is a moment of such intense pain that I think I am going to scream, which makes me put my hand to my mouth to prevent the scream from coming out. The pain subsides and I sit on the toilet seat. The wound starts bleeding heavily, so for a few minutes, maybe ten minutes, I have to keep taking wads of toilet paper to sponge it up, and I have to keep getting up so that the sensor will flush the toilet paper down the toilet. This is such a dumb near-catastrophe. Eventually the bleeding slows, and I can start to see the wound properly. Maybe when I get home I'll see a doctor. Maybe I could use stitches.

I go back to the gate and find Trish and my father in an embrace that is a little bit avuncular and a little bit awkward. They have taken my absence as the opportunity to say good-bye. I nearly turn and walk in another direction, but my father sees me, and he does something unexpected. He winks. I go over to them. My father lets Trish go. She turns and sees me. She's been crying. We speak for a little while. My father says, Trish has me thinking about writing another book. That's great news, I say, what about? Well, he says, my memoirs. Oh? I say. Anything else will take too much research, he says. I say, I think it's a great idea, if the book is honest. He waves the comment away. I hope everything will go well on that end, says Trish, without saying, but meaning, with Miriam. I'm sure it will, I say, it's been a real pleasure. It's been my pleasure, she says. There's a pause, and I say, Maybe I'll see you at the launch of my father's memoir. Definitely, she says. There's another pause, so I say, I'm going to look out the window. I leave them. I go to the window.

Once, a long time ago, back when I was still married, my wife struck up a friendship with a very famous old poet—she came from a family who knew families with famous poets in them. He is still mildly famous. Or he is dead. No, he must be dead, otherwise he would be a hundred. The man had a scandalous, rich, wonderful, absurd life. Two of his children were not his children. Other children who belonged to other families were actually his children. My wife thought he was charming, and she truly loved his poetry, which was, in the forties and fifties, scandalous. I met him on a few occasions. He kept telling me that my wife was his last love, but it was neither romantic nor erotic love. What do you love about her? I asked. She's so pretty, he said, she's the last pretty, young girl who'll be my friend. I see, I said. Do you think she loves me, too? he asked. I said, I hope so, otherwise she's after your money. Everything I said disappointed him. The only interest he had in me related to my unworthiness compared to him, but I did not compare myself to him, I did not even care that he existed. Finally, when he realized he could not break me, he could not make me see him as a rival, he stopped inviting my wife over to his country house, stopped telling her about openings he was attending, and wrote her out of his twisted life.

A truck pulls up alongside the airplane. A couple of men get out. They speak for a while with the baggage handlers. Then the baggage handlers step aside. They stand side by side, and they stand in exactly identical ways—heads down, arms down, hands clasped. The back doors of the truck open up and Miriam's coffin is removed. I look back. My father is watching Trish walk away. He is waving at her. Then he stops. Then he waves at her again. And he stops again. And he waves again. I guess she keeps turning around. Finally he stops and sighs, and crosses his arms. He looks at me. He appears peaceful, a little bit heartbroken, but also, unmistakably, determined. He waves me over to him. It's time to come back now, sit down, prepare for boarding. It's over.

The trip is over. I don't move. He waves again. I ignore him and turn back around. In a few moments he is beside me. He says, What are you looking at? I don't need to say anything. He looks down at the men carrying the box with Miriam's coffin in it to the loading vehicle.

He says, Is that . . . ?

I say, I assume so.

My father's face turns red. His breathing quickens.

He says, I don't understand.

What do you mean?

I don't know, he says.

The men—all of them now—carry the box containing Miriam's coffin on the conveyor belt of the baggage loader. My father puts a hand flat on the glass. He says, What is the meaning of this? He looks around him. There are several people nearby who are observing him. He says, a little bit louder, What is the meaning of this? More passengers take note, and some even stand. My father says, What is the meaning of this? His voice is just below a shout. He looks like a man whose army has abandoned the field. I tell him to calm down, but now he says, angrily—and he directs his anger at me—I will not calm down, I will not calm down, what the hell are you so goddamn calm about? An airline official—I think it is a desk attendant, she wears a high-vis vest—comes over, and he says to her, What is the meaning of this? What is the *meaning* of this? Why don't you do something?

He is about to raise his voice, presumably so he may repeat, furiously, Why don't you do something? But he finds himself out of energy. I don't touch him but I stand behind him. The passengers who have gathered—and those watching from all corners of the gate now—want an explanation, but they will not get one from me. The desk attendant does not know what to do. She asks me if she should call somebody. I tell her I have it under control. I stand beside my father. He tries to slow his breathing. He closes his eyes and bows his head. Come on, I say. I've got you, I say. He holds out his arm and we walk back to our seats—all our stuff is still there.

When he is settled in his seat, and the pale red that has flushed him goes blue, I present myself to the same attendant, who is now behind the desk and talking on a walkie-talkie. I give her my name and I hand her our boarding cards. I explain our situation. I ask if we can possibly pre-board, just go ahead of everybody else and skip the mayhem. She consults another attendant and they agree to let us pre-board—by all means, they say. Then they look closely at our boarding cards. They say my name out loud, as though it reminds them of something, then they say, excitedly, There are quite a lot of purchases waiting in the jetway for you. Purchases? I say. A computer, a camera, and more, they say. I say, Oh yeah, terrific! I'd forgotten! We'll have someone help carry the bags to your seats, they say. That would be great, I say. They say, We'll send someone to you with a wheelchair in a few minutes. Perfect, I say. I come very close—because we all seem to be getting along so well—to requesting an upgrade. But I don't want to upset the normalization of relations.

I tell my father he needs to prepare for the wheelchair. I guess you're not going to make it, not quite, on your own two feet, I say. Poor Dad, I say. He momentarily looks up at me, then his head slumps down again.

The man comes by with the wheelchair. He's actually quite young, quite jovial. He's tall and thin, with broad, winglike shoulders, spiky black hair, and dark, slanted eyebrows. He looks to

246

me to have come off a movie set, or a casting call for Draculas. Except he wears a high-vis jacket, is in a good mood, and seems possibly mentally disabled, but not profoundly. Anyway, there is something strange, a malady or malfunction, I think, which is revealed in the symptom of his joviality. He asks my father if he can get up on his own and sit in the chair. My father says, Of course. And he gets up and gets in the chair. The man pushing the wheelchair waits for me to get everything together. He even throws my father's carry-on around his neck. Thank you very much for your help, I say.

It's my pleasure, he says. What is your reason for visiting Germany?

I say, We wanted to see the Rhineland, we went to see Charlemagne.

Charlemagne? he says.

Karl der Grosse, I say.

Wonderful, he says, sorry about the weather.

On the first night of our travels in the Rhineland, in Walluf, I got drunk with the king of Walluf. His name was Hans. My father and I had dinner in his restaurant. We didn't know whose restaurant it was at the time, but we had a large, enjoyable dinner, a dinner without any philosophical controversy. Walluf is a splendid little village right on the Rhine. We parked our car outside a hotel overlooking the river and booked ourselves in. There were only two restaurants open in Walluf that night. I would later discover that Hans owned both of them. I would later discover that Hans owned every piece of real estate in Walluf, practically, except for our little hotel, Zum Neuen Schwan. He was disgusted when I told him where we were staying. My father was drunk, and I was drunk, and we'd had a nice dinner, so we decided to go back to the hotel, get some rest, and start fresh in the morning. We walked back to the hotel in the empty darkness, and instead of going straight to bed, we walked to the river, admired it, and admired the view of Mainz across the river. My father made a growling, happy yawn and said, I'm beat! He went to his room and I went to mine. I got undressed, brushed my teeth, hopped into bed with a book. Immediately I realized I didn't want to go to bed. I wanted to find a smoky bar full of young people, and sit in a corner. I went back to the restaurant and spoke to the bartender. He was young. I asked him if there was anything like a smoky bar where you could drink beer without being sneered at—this was wine country— and he said, Not in Walluf, but there's a place in Eltville with a pool table. You can smoke and drink beer there. How far is Eltville? I asked. Less than five minutes by taxi, he said. I am almost certain this entire conversation took place in German, which means my memory is just an approximation. Can you call me a taxi? I asked. There was a man sitting in the restaurant lounge—right behind me—who interrupted my conversation with the bartender to say, I'll go with you. This was Hans. He was sixtysomething. He wore a red plaid shirt and blue jeans, and had a silver flattop. Before we left, I asked the bartender if Hans could be trusted, and he said, He owns everything in this town, he is the richest man in town. I said, He is the king of Walluf? So to speak, said the bartender.

The place in Eltville turned out to be a kebab shop where the taxi drivers of the region gathered and waited for calls. But you could drink beer there. Hans and I got a table by a jukebox. Mostly it was the kind of music you hear at après-ski. God, this place is awful, I said. Hans shrugged. For about half an hour he said nothing. He said nothing until I said I was traveling with my father, and we were staying at the hotel he didn't own.

I noticed you earlier, he said, because you were with your father. Do you get along with your father?

Reasonably well, I said.

My son despises me, he said.

Are you sure?

I'm sure. He won't speak to me. He never comes by the restaurant. He is always busy with his friends. His *mother*, she poisons him against me. After having sat through half an hour of silence with Hans, I was glad to hear him say something, so we spoke about his relationship with his son, and we spoke about my relationship with my father—and since he had been forthcoming, I was a little more forthcoming. I don't know how much of this conversation I really got, or how much I was able to communicate, because by the end I was absolutely blind drunk, but I know that I definitely, at the end of it all, asked how old his son was. I expected him to say thirty-five. He said, Seven. Then we both laughed loudly for a long time. Then he stopped laughing and became serious, quiet, and dull again.

When we got back to Walluf, I walked around—it was well after midnight—looking for something to eat. Even though I'd had a giant schnitzel for dinner, and a giant potato salad, I was starving. All I could find were some kids standing on a curb who suggested I go to Mainz. So that's what I did. I got back in the rental car and typed McDonald's into the GPS. I was drunk. I was so drunk that I went up to my room and got a bottle of wine so I had something to drink on the road. There was a McDonald's everywhere. Except that it was after one in the morning by then, and they were all, in the immediate vicinity, closed. In order to find one that was open, I drove closer and closer to the center of Mainz, over a magnificent bridge, until I was right in the heart of the city, driving around the streets, enjoying the warm night, having wine and listening to the radio. I found a McDonald's, finally, and I ordered a feast. The restaurant was closed but the drive-thru was open. I got three burgers, a milk shake, an extra-large fries, and some chicken nuggets, and I even got a salad—for the morning. I was going to drive back to the hotel and eat everything in the room, but I thought it might get cold on the way. So I checked the history on the GPS and punched in my grandmother's house as a destination. It wasn't far at all. Three or four kilometers. I parked almost exactly where I had before. I got all the food and the bottle of wine, quietly—though I may have made a lot of noise—then I got out and wandered into the woods across from the house. I sat down somewhere and had my food. I ate it all. I lay back and looked up at the stars.

The woman I used to meet in Bedford Square was married with two children. She worked in the British Museum, she was a professor of archaeology, and she was an expert on the Middle East, Egypt, Turkey, and Greece. She was often flown to these places in a hurry, either to verify something or meet somebody, and she used to send me pictures of her hotel rooms just as she arrived, and then one minute later, to prove how quickly she could annihilate them. She loved bicycles. She loved old bookstores. She was born near Newcastle, but she moved to London at the age of fifteen—she had run away from home. At least this is what she told me. Perhaps it hadn't been quite like that. Her favorite places to visit were Jerusalem, Damascus, Istanbul, Cairo, and Athens. And I think part of her, for a long time, believed she could exist outside London if she could live in one of those places. But that part of her had to face the reality that the life she wanted in those places did not include her family, and she was not ready to leave her family, though she said she expected she would someday. By the time I met her, however, she had already left London. And she was ready to have an affair—but only with a man who lived in London. She was going slowly insane without the pace, without the stress and swarm of life in London. When she lived there, she said, she would wander into the mayhem of rush hour sometimes just to clear her head. She would drift into Underground stations, just to get swept into the madness. Throw herself into crowded trains, trains with no room left for anybody, when she wasn't even in a rush. She would go meet somebody in a pub across the city, just to cross the city. In other words, she said, I was like most people who live in London. The way she talked about London reminded me of my first, warm impressions of the city, and while we were together, I began to feel, once again, proud of myself for living there. She had moved with her family to Wargrave, a forgettable little village not far from Reading, where her husband's parents were, so her husband could focus more time on his career, which was somehow creative. I never really pressed her. I never asked exactly what he did. But I knew she admired him for it, and believed in him, and I knew that deep down she realized I was half the man he was, and that was quite possibly a necessary concession for her, so that if she were ever caught—and she would be caught—she could argue that it hadn't been his deficiencies as a man or human being that gave her permission to betray him, but her own debasement. She was preparing to hate herself with an intensity and purpose few people ever fathom. She was nearing forty, her children were twelve and ten, and it was time—or so it seemed to me—to hate herself in a way that she had been raised, perhaps, to be hated. There had been enough optimism and frivolity. There had been enough of London, enough bookshops, enough pubs, enough taxis, enough harmless flirtation, enough beauty, enough freneticism, enough of everything. If she were just being selfish, if her affair were merely a matter of selfishness, or boredom, she would have picked another version, surely, of her husband, but one who lived in London. Still, while it was ongoing, she professed to accept it without stress, to enjoy it, to not overthink it, and to allow it to last for as long as it lasted. There was no fear of falling in love, she said. But it was still intense. The difficulty in spending time with you, she once said to me, is watching the way you seem so disappointed with everything. I said, jokingly, I *am* disappointed with everything.

When we met, we often met at Bedford Square, around lunchtime, when she could get away from the museum for an hour or so. I would pick up some sandwiches on the way, or some pasta salad. She did all the talking, all the time. Her job was interesting and full of intrigue. It seemed very obvious to me that what qualified for expertise in her field was vastly different from what qualified for expertise in mine. In her field, expertise could be proven in the smallest ways, in the tiniest measures of breathtaking erudition, genius, and skepticism. Whereas the world everywhere else—the one my work inhabited, or held dominion over—strived, with banality and prejudice, to prove expertise in grand ways, in universalities, or the impotent and stereotyped language of political opinion, journalism, corporate branding, critical thought, or art. We first met at a British Museum event. She gave a talk, and I went up afterward to ask her a question. I said I really enjoyed listening to her speak, and then

I mentioned that her talk wasn't the first time I'd heard about the subject matter, but that I'd read about it in a book, and then I named the book. She said, I love that book. I said, My father wrote it. She said, Are you serious? She was about to turn around and tell the whole room, all her colleagues and all the visitors, but I touched her arm and pleaded. I said, Please, please do not repeat that, I should not have mentioned it.

Eight months later, or nine months, just shortly after the affair ended, exactly as she had predicted it would, with pain and humiliation for everyone, I got on a train very early one morning and traveled to Wargrave. I knew where she lived, but I hadn't gone there to find her, or to confront her husband. I think I went there because it seemed like a menacing thing to do, just to be there, and I felt like doing something menacing, I felt like being menacing. I arrived at dawn. It was cold and foggy. It was probably early spring, possibly March or April. I was the only soul who disembarked at Wargrave, but there were a few people waiting on the platform for the train to Paddington, or perhaps to Twyford. The Thames goes by Wargrave, and it is a pleasant stretch of the Thames. I wore a long black coat. I walked around. There isn't much to see there. There are some nice pubs. A couple of housing developments. I got a lot of suspicious looks. I went into a café and had some breakfast. When it started to warm up, I went to the Thames and sat under a tree, like a hobo. Could it be that a new life was within me, a life of menace, of trespassing, of terrorizing small towns by simply visiting them, when I had no reason to visit them? At lunchtime I went to a pub called the St. George and Dragon. I ordered some food and sat outside. I had a couple of beers. It got a little crowded. When I was finished, I told the waitress the name of the woman, and I asked if she ever came around. The waitress said she didn't know anyone by that name, and then a few minutes later the manager came over and asked me who I was looking for, and when I told him the name he told me to wait. I said to him, It was just a question, an old friend, I used to know her. The manager told me to wait anyway, not to go anywhere, stay right there, he knew exactly who I was. I had paid, so I just got up and left, and I hurried toward the station. I ran. I kept looking behind me. I was thinking, Please let a train be waiting when I get there. But there was nothing. I had to wait about thirty minutes for the train. I paced and paced around. I looked for hiding places. I would have taken a train going in either direction. I panicked. I wanted so badly to be the kind of man who would wait for the husband in the pub, or at least the kind of man menacing enough to crawl over a fence and sit and smoke a couple of cigarettes in the woman's back garden. Maybe I should have come at night. I kept watching down the Station Road to see if somebody was coming. My mind produced images of speeding cars, of a gang of Wargravers brandishing lead pipes, cricket bats, possibly oars. Nothing appeared.

What a dull place Wargrave really was. No doubt it is as dull today as it was then. The woman hasn't left. I've looked her up from time to time, and she is still with the British Museum, she still has an office there. She has not run off to Cairo or Jerusalem alone, to live in airy apartments that overlook busy marketplaces, or to walk over hills of sand or dust, wearing a floppy hat and some kind of tan blouse. Nobody in Wargrave is aware of how terrible it is for this woman to be among them, to have quiet English dinner parties, to speak the way they speak, to congregate on sunny days at the pub by the Thames and slowly eat and drink herself to death, alongside her neighbors. My father and I are boarding now. The other passengers are standing, crowding the gate. They watch us. Our jovial friend with vampiric shoulders pushes my father toward the entrance to the jetway, and I follow. I show our boarding passes and passports. My father wants to tell me something, but he is pushed swiftly into the jetway. I am next. I shouldn't be so hard on Wargrave. It's no different from the place I'm going. It's no different, for that matter, from Walluf.

Between the time I met Miriam in Cologne and my affair with the archaeologist, I traveled to the lodge in Scotland alone. It was the hottest summer in England for a hundred years or something. London was miserable. Everything stank. Even Bedford Square stank. So I called up the lodge and said I wanted a room for a night, as soon as possible. They said they had nothing left for the summer, unless I could book for a minimum of three nights. I told them my father's name, I explained he had come regularly, that he had honeymooned there, visited a few times with my mother, then with us. The woman at reception didn't know what I was talking about, but the owner, to whom I finally spoke, remembered, and she offered me a suite, their best room, on the Sunday of the week I telephoned, but they would have to charge full price for it. What's full price? It's four hundred and fifty pounds, she said, plus an extra twenty pounds for breakfast. I flew from London to Edinburgh on the Sunday morning and rented a car. I drove north, in the direction of Perth, but not along the motorway, then east. Actually Glasgow was the more convenient airport, but I'd come through Glasgow on the previous two occasions, and I wanted something different. The air got cooler, but it wasn't quite chilly—people in the towns I drove through wore shorts and flip-flops. I stopped at some places along the way, to get food or stop at fruit stands or ice-cream stands. It was June, so the sun stayed high in the sky all day. I drove with the windows down. As the roads got smaller and the views from the roadsides became more and more magnificent and fearsome, I pulled over and stood. When I finally made it to the lodge, I found the parking lot completely full. I checked in. I was shown to my room. I confirmed my dinner reservation. I'd hoped to get a booth table all to myself—the regular table, which my father always made sure to reserve weeks in advance—but there was no hope. I would get a little table by the window. That'll be fine, I said. I showered and put on a suit and went down to the lounge for a few drinks and to read the papers. The lounge was packed. People had been out on the water all day, or cycling around, or hillwalking, and they were having refreshments and talking about the unbelievably warm conditions. The vast majority of them were retired. The vast majority were English. Many of them must have been there for days, because they spoke to each other like old chums. One of them asked to take a look at a paper I had finished with, and I said, You bet, be my guest. They were overjoyed, it turned out, to have an American there, and they would not believe I was just an ordinary foreigner living in London, trying to get away from the heat. I was wearing a nice blue suit and a white shirt. When they found out—they asked and I told them—what room I was staying in, and that I was alone, they concluded that I must be in entertainment, I looked like I belonged in entertainment. Eventually they rounded themselves up after a few drinks to go upstairs and prepare for dinner. I went outside for some fresh air. It was evening, though still bright, and finally starting to cool. I walked along the jetty where some boats were tied. Little wooden fishing boats with oars. They were very clean and dry.

A man came toward me. He worked for the hotel. He came up beside me and we stood and looked around at the water and the mountains behind them. I said, I don't remember there ever being boats here. He said they'd always been there, but usually it was too cold and the conditions were too dangerous to let people out on them. But that evening it was calm, it was warm and windless, and the lake was flat. I said, I'd like to take a boat out for a few minutes before dinner starts. He checked his watch and asked what time I was eating. Eight o'clock, I said. Then you have time, he said. Does it cost any money? I asked. He said it was free. We stood for a few seconds longer and I said, So I can pick any one I like? Of course, he said—he was putting them away for the night but he didn't mind me being out until eight on such a nice, bright evening. I hopped into one and he untied me, threw me the line, and wished me a pleasant, if brief, boat trip. I rowed out a hundred meters, two hundred meters. The lake wound around a jutting stretch of land in the distance, and I thought I'd row there, take a look at the rest of the lake, then turn around and go back and get dinner. As I rowed, I began to feel a romantic attachment to the view around that corner, even though I had no idea what it would be like, apart from the safe assumption that it would be a lot like the view I had already. I began to visualize the scenery beyond the gap and it seemed to me as though music was beginning to make noises at the mountaintops, in the trees, or as though the music I heard had metamorphosed into trees and mountaintops. I started to feel that I had to see the view around that corner, it was imperative, that I would never know myself unless I set eyes upon the rest of the lake. It did not take very long to realize that the proximity of the gap was an illusion. I kept rowing and rowing, but I never seemed to get closer to it. So I stopped where

I was and floated for a while in the still, black glassiness of the water. The man gathering the boats for the evening was making very little noise. He looked at me when I looked at him, but neither of us waved, and he looked away. I couldn't smell anything except the water and timber of the boat. I leaned over and put my hand in the water. The water was freezing. I leaned a little farther and put both hands in. I picked them out and felt the texture of the water between my fingers, on my palms and on the backs of my hands. I sat like that for a while, slumped over the edge of the boat, looking at my hands, dipping them in the water and watching the water drop off them. When I looked up, I saw that the first dinner guests of the evening had assembled outside the restaurant, on the shore, to see what I was doing. I couldn't imagine what conclusions they had come to. When I sat back up and grabbed the oars and starting rowing again, they waved, and they waved.

ACKNOWLEDGMENTS

The author gratefully acknowledges the assistance of Thomas Lovegrove and Adam Butler, aka Vert.

For material on the Rhineland and Charlemagne, the author is indebted to Robert Bartlett's *The Making of Europe: Conquest, Colonization and Cultural Change 950–1350*. The quotations from composers were encountered in Alex Ross's *The Rest Is Noise*.

ABOUT THE AUTHOR

Greg Baxter is the author of two previous highly acclaimed books, *The Apartment* and *A Preparation for Death*. Originally from Texas, he has lived in Europe for almost two decades. He currently lives in Berlin with his wife and two children.